About the author

Steve Frogley was born in Essex in England. He now lives on the South coast. *The Path of Good Response* is his first novel.

THE PATH OF GOOD RESPONSE

Steve Frogley

THE PATH OF GOOD RESPONSE

Vanguard Press

VANGUARD PAPERBACK

© Copyright 2020
Steve Frogley

A CIP catalogue record for this title is
available from the British Library.

ISBN 978 1 784652 08 1

*Vanguard Press is an imprint of
Pegasus Elliot MacKenzie Publishers Ltd.*
www.pegasuspublishers.com

First Published in 2020

**Vanguard Press
Sheraton House Castle Park
Cambridge England**

Printed & Bound in Great Britain

With thanks to Pegasus and Phil. Also, a big thank you to my test readers for your invaluable input — Maggie, Hannah, Pat, Dawn, John, Al, Paul, Nick, Kev, Mike, Lynne, Andy, Kathy and particularly David.

Chapter One
4th March 2015

There was no sign of Rachel. Should he cross without her?

Joe shielded his eyes from the sun, bright and low in the morning sky, and watched the other candidates milling around the courtyard. Uniformly beautiful, they dazzled in the icy glare, but she definitely wasn't amongst them. The loose arrangements had bothered him from the outset, and he wished that he had persuaded her to travel with him from the flat. There had been little time to discuss anything that morning — all four of them fighting for precious bathroom time. Bleary-eyed and harassed, they had exchanged no more than grunts of recognition as they passed each other through the steam. A vague plan was hatched in the brief interlude between ironing board tag and hunt the keys, but the clock was against them, and he finally ate his cornflakes alone in the car.

Marryfield House loomed in the distance, the two-winged Jacobean building regally unmoved by his predicament. He approached the frozen field again, and pressed the grass with his foot — polished brogue meeting muddy water seeping up from the soil below. It wasn't a tempting proposition. A crow in a nearby tree moaned in agreement.

Where was she? The interviews were due to start in ten minutes, and his fellow applicants were becoming increasingly difficult to tune out. He had wandered away from them all to gather his thoughts, chewing through an entire packet of gum as he circled the courtyard in an aimless loop of procrastination. His conclusion was simple: he could not afford to screw up, today of all days. Their invitations stated that they should arrive at the gatehouse at eight-thirty, with the selection process planned to start at nine o'clock. Many of them, including himself, had arrived much earlier — shivering in the stone outbuilding for at least an hour before. Initially, the mood had been good, but as time progressed their excited conversations lulled into murmurs, accompanied by the anxious clicking of phones. It was obvious something was wrong, but it was less clear what they could do about it.

There was a lot at stake. The Schelldhardt scheme was the ultimate target for every newly qualified graduate that he knew, ostensibly for the unrivalled prospects, but more pertinently, for the instant repayment of any student debt that was promised. Many of his friends had already declined other opportunities to apply for it. Just to be accepted for an interview was success in itself, but the joy of the invite was beginning to feel a distant, foolish memory. Rachel had, of course, been the deciding factor in his application, and once it was clear that she was proceeding, he had barely slept for fear of failure.

He pulled his jacket tighter, shivering. If she didn't arrive soon it would be too late for both of them. A ruddy-faced security guard was still being mobbed by an angry section of the crowd. As the sole figure of authority in sight, he had become the instant focal point of their frustration when he had first arrived. Fellow candidates continued to plead with him — one woman verbally threatening him as he tried to retreat. She stooped into his line of vision, screaming in his face as he turned away from the group. It wasn't pleasant to watch. He felt for the guard, but the choice he offered them was stark: cross the three hundred-foot field that separated the gatehouse from Marryfield House or go home. It had rained incessantly all week, and pools of surface water had gathered into a small lake on the grass. They were all dressed to impress, and the advice was more than a little difficult to accept. The only other route to the house, via the road they had arrived on, was no longer feasible in the time available. He could hear the guard calmly repeating their options, only to be met with yet another barrage of abuse that echoed around the courtyard. Despite their pleas, he insisted that he had no way of contacting the house.

Their anger was contagious. It was clear that many of the attendees were unaccustomed to disappointment. Schelldhardt attracted the cream of all newly qualified graduates, and they arrived with naked expectation and a low tolerance for inconvenience. It was intimidating being around them. Everyone seemed smarter, brighter and more articulate than he was. As he stood amongst the young, immaculately presented throng, it was as if he had gate-crashed the most glamorous wedding party ever assembled. The atmosphere was superficially friendly, but there was no disguising the competitive underbelly. The smiles and laughter were punctuated with stolen glances and loaded questions, weighing and judging the competition. It was impossible to know who actually had the edge; the entry requirements were vague, and the qualities sought equally mysterious. He still had no idea how he had been selected for an interview — awarded only an average degree from a mediocre university.

Crossing the field was not a tempting option for anyone. A few of the candidates ignored the guard, and were heading back the way they had arrived along the road. The remainder hesitated, some still bashing at their phones, despite the feeble mobile signal in the grounds. He had already tried to call Rachel and his other flatmates multiple times, and was now perilously low on battery himself. He moved closer, straining to hear their conversations. A circle had formed around a girl who had managed to reach a friend already inside Marryfield House. She relayed the news in breathless gasps, but he caught the gist of the situation: her friend had been sent different arrival instructions to those at the gatehouse. There was an instant roar of disapproval, and it took him a few seconds to digest the implications of what he had just heard. Rachel could have been sent the same instructions, and might already be inside the house...

He immediately marched back towards the road. Why hadn't he decided to do it before? Having arrived so early, it was ridiculous that he had allowed himself to become late. He muttered apologies as he pushed through the perfumed bodies, head down, gradually accelerating as he moved. A hand grabbed his arm as he reached the extremity of the group, and he wheeled round to find the security guard staring at him, wide-eyed.

'It's too late to go that way,' the guard said, surprising him by the physical contact. Several other candidates were streaming past unhindered towards the road. He was already losing ground.

'I don't fancy the alternative,' he laughed, as casually as he could. The guard was still holding his arm tightly, and he continued to stare at him.

'Your only chance is that way,' the guard said, nodding his white mop of hair towards the field. For a moment neither of them spoke, the guard still clutching his arm and watching him intently. His breath was unpleasant, and a lattice of fine red veins covered his nose and cheeks.

'Okay,' smiled Joe, gently pulling his arm away. He could feel his cheeks flushing, embarrassed that he had acquiesced so easily, and straightened his jacket. Of all the people there, it was just perfect that he was the one to be singled out now. The guard was still watching him as he joined several other worried figures loitering at the periphery of the field. It probably was too late to do anything else anyway. The frozen grass stretched out before them, daring them to cross. The air temperature could only be a few degrees above zero, and they all appeared to be wrestling with the same hopeless thoughts.

'Go now, or you'll miss it,' shouted the guard, who still seemed to be looking directly at him. A friend for life! If the advice was for him, then the words were also the trigger for activity all around him, and a solemn girl — who had introduced herself as Elly "with a Y" — kicked off her shoes and started to roll up her knee-length skirt. Several others were making similar preparations. He squatted to remove his own shoes and socks — rolling his trouser legs as high as he could, caught up in the collective panic. With a final resentful glance around, he stepped out onto the field. The mud was so cold that it felt as though it was burning his feet as it oozed between his toes.

'This is a grand's worth of bespoke suit,' growled a man nearby, as if seeking a witness for an imaginary future court case. Nobody was interested, too focused on their own misery. It seemed that he was going to add something else, but then nearly slipped, cursing under his breath. There was a biting wind whipping across the field, and most of them had sacrificed warmth for style in their wardrobe selection. The frozen mud only magnified the discomfort, and every step was met with a fresh chorus of complaints. They covered the first few yards in unison, like an executive mine-sweeping patrol. Some held briefcases and handbags above their heads, while others used them as a counterbalance at their side. He trudged forward, his eyes fixed doggedly on the field ahead, trying to avoid the mud flicking up in every direction. At certain points the ground was so sticky that the effort of pulling one foot out of the ground endangered his next step, and he was still nowhere near the most treacherous-looking part of the field. Did Rachel think he hadn't shown up for the interview? He tried to walk faster at the thought, but skidded, barely regaining his balance in time.

A pretty girl named Tanya stumbled, just ahead of him. The accident seemed inevitable, firstly because she was so immaculately dressed in an expensive-looking navy suit, and secondly because she had opted to keep on a pair of platform shoes. Heroically, she only slumped to one knee, where she managed to balance like a ninja for several seconds before rising to her feet again. She wriggled out of the shoes and walked on, the discarded footwear dangling sadly at her side in failure. Marryfield House, bleached by the morning light, depressingly looked no closer.

They splashed their way to the wettest part of the field in eerie silence, and the mud became more slippery still. Tiny islands of ice floated on the surface water, glinting in the sunlight, and there was a freezing mist tumbling across the field; the scene was as beautiful as it was uncomfortable. Joe's phone beeped. He was about to check it, but was disturbed by a loud shout a few feet away from him.

'Oh, no!' someone cried. He turned to see that Elly had fallen face forward into the muddy water, and was struggling to get back up. She gasped loudly, and then screamed. A friend was close to her, but he also slipped over as he extended a helping hand, his legs sliding out beneath him at a ludicrous speed.

They were all reverently silent for a moment, only the wind daring to make any sound at all. Joe glanced from the fallen figures to the circle of horrified onlookers around them, immaculate suits and dresses rolled up to their knees, their breath condensing in the air. It was a surreal scene of Armani trench warfare. The man scrambled back up, and they backed away in unison, as if he was about to shake himself dry like a dog.

'This is fucked up!' he shouted. It was hard to argue, but his dramatic exit was ruined by a second slip as he stormed away through their parted ranks. Eventually, Elly clambered to her feet too, covered in thick brown mud. A second friend tried to wipe the worst of it from her face with a tissue, as she stood shivering, ankle-deep in water.

'Is it bad?' she whimpered. Joe couldn't watch her misery, and splashed on towards the house again.

'No time for swimming,' winked a stocky dark-haired guy catching his eye. 'Two less.'

He could no longer feel his toes. Frostbite was beginning to seem like a real possibility. They were now thirty feet from the house, and he could see an open door in the left wing of the building, partly obscured by a holly tree. There was a maze at the front of the building, formed from a series of privet hedges, only a few feet high. He glanced upwards, and caught a glimpse of a figure watching from a second-floor window. It was impossible to determine whether it was a man or a woman, but they continued to stand there for a few more seconds, before turning away. He paid little attention, too focused on ensuring that he didn't falter in the home stretch.

He finally reached solid ground, following a cobbled path that weaved through flower beds towards the entrance. His shoes slipped from his numb fingers straight into a muddy puddle — an irritating final insult. He wiped off what he could and headed towards the open doorway, where the remainder of the party queued in shivering silence.

He hoped more than ever that it wasn't too late.

The security guard back at the gatehouse watched from a chair at the edge of the grass. He opened a plastic lunch-box and pulled out a walkie-talkie from within. Fumbling with the controls, he grunted in approval when it crackled into life.

'They're coming to you now. I counted twenty crossers. Maybe fifteen refused. He's with them,' he said.

Chapter Two

In a fair world, luck would balance itself out over time. A painless adolescence would seem reasonable compensation for an unhappy childhood. By the same token, a fulfilling adult relationship would be fair reward for years of awkward teenage liaisons, but things hadn't panned out that way for Joe. Perhaps he simply hadn't waited long enough; he could only conclude that one day he would be the happiest pensioner in the old folks' home.

When he saw Rachel queuing to complete her registration form, he felt both elated and helpless, as he always did. She was wearing a simple charcoal skirt and jacket that complemented her waspish figure. Her mousy blonde hair was pinned back. Normally, she wore it shoulder length, allowing it to dry naturally after she showered. She was also, unusually, wearing make-up; just enough to accentuate her deep blue eyes and emphasise the perfect shape of her lips.

They were assembled in the Long Gallery of Marryfield House — an elongated rectangular room that stretched nearly two hundred feet along its length. The high ceiling was decorated with gold leaf, and intricately carved wooden panels covered the walls. Many of the regular paintings and pieces of furniture had been removed for the interviews, replaced by canvas folding chairs that sat on the chequered marble flooring like chess pieces.

A Schelldhardt banner was draped across the magnificent central fireplace, flanked by refreshment stands either side — the old sitting uncomfortably with the new. The banner carried the familiar company slogan, "Business for good". There were several desks adjacently positioned to take registration details, and Joe approached the nearest one, passing a girl trying to conceal patches of mud on her dress with a handbag.

To his great relief, the invitation had not been a mistake, and he was given a red badge and a confidentiality agreement to sign upon registering. He wandered away from the desk, looking for Rachel. The noise in the hall was disorientating, and he had lost sight of her. Voices echoed from the high ceiling, and it was difficult to place the source, merging into one muffled wall of sound. It was also cold, despite the hundred or so bodies in the room, and he was shivering slightly. By contrast, his feet still burned angrily inside his shoes, refusing to be forgotten. He wandered towards the leaded glass window — a good vantage point to view the entire room. Dusty shafts of sunlight streamed in, warming his back, and he was reluctant to move again. He jumped when he noticed Rachel standing right next to him.

'Hey,' she said, kissing his cheek.

'Hey, yourself.'

'I didn't think you were going to make it. Looks like you took the scenic route as well,' she said, gesturing towards his trousers.

'I'd recommend it if you have the time.'

'I heard about the confusion. At least you're here now,' she smiled, turning away to drink in her surroundings. 'I love this building.'

'It's a notch up from the Matteron centre,' he laughed. They had spent far too many hours together in that particularly tired old lecture room at university. Rachel loved all things old and quaint, and her enthusiasm for Marryfield House came as no surprise. He was about to point out the features of the fireplace, which he knew she would adore, when he noticed the yellow badge on her lapel. A different group…

'The others are here.'

'That's good,' he said, fixated by the offensive yellow blur at the periphery of his sight. Would they be interviewed for different areas?

'I just know I'm going to say something stupid in the interview,' she said.

'There are no stupid answers, only stupid questions.'

'Are you quoting fortune cookies again?'

'I'm just trying to make you feel better,' he laughed. 'They'll love you. Think positively.'

They were interrupted by the shrill feedback from a microphone, and then a bald-headed man in glasses began to count, testing sound output. The chatter subsided, then rose again immediately after the test, like a wave washing through the hall. The last few people were completing their registration, and there was a sense that everyone was waiting for something to happen. Most were standing in silence, shunning the chairs left for them. Any conversations were now whispered, and the occasional cough was the only interruption.

'Good morning, Schelldhardt sunbeams. Are you ready to change the world?' sang the announcer. The response was enthusiastic, and he milked the moment. 'I'd like to welcome you all to our graduate selection interviews,' he added, adjusting the height of the microphone stand. 'May I begin by apologising for the confusion over the directions some of you were issued with today. This was due to an administrative error.'

There were a few murmurs of disapproval, but no one dared go too far. Joe noticed that the group of people who had taken the alternative route back around the road had arrived just in time. The sacrifice of the field crossers had been in vain, and their muddy-footed stupidity endured for all to see.

'Before we get down to business, there are a few other requirements to cover,' continued the announcer. He proceeded to run through fire regulations and general introductions. Members of staff collected their signed confidentiality agreements while he continued to speak, explaining the schedule for the day in a little too much detail.

People were starting to fidget. Joe noticed that even Rachel was distracted, watching a blackbird wrestling with a worm outside the window.

'Finally, I'd like to leave you all with an exercise before the interviews begin,' he added. The impact of requesting interaction was instant, and the average height of the audience immediately increased by an inch. 'There are eighty-six registered candidates in the room today. We would like you to eliminate twenty-six from the scheme to bring that number down to sixty. All Schelldhardt employees will leave the room during the selection process. Your criteria for selecting these candidates is an entirely personal choice, but you must document your ideas. There are selection sheets on the desks for you to record your name, the names of the candidates you have chosen for elimination, and the reason why. If you do not complete a form or leave it blank, it will count as a vote against your own name. If all of you fail to complete the form, twenty-six names will be drawn at random. You have thirty minutes to complete the task. The candidates attracting the most votes will be asked to leave before the interview process begins. There are no other guidelines. Please circulate,' he finished, switching off the microphone dramatically — somewhat overplaying his part. The Schelldhardt employees began to file out of the room, leaving the audience in stunned silence.

'Is this a joke?' Joe said.

'It's not a funny one if it is,' Rachel replied.

The hall was instantly filled with nervous muttering and laughter. There was much head-shaking and eyebrow raising. Joe noticed his other flatmates, Ryan and Dixon, making their way towards them. Ryan's face lit up in recognition. He had always reminded Joe of a fox somehow: his jaws were filled with small, uniform teeth, and his brown eyes were constantly wide and alert. Dixon trailed behind him, by contrast distracted and pensive.

'Just in time to be eliminated,' grinned Ryan, shaking Joe's hand.

Dixon only nodded towards him in acknowledgement, clearly too horrified by the turn of events for joviality.

'This is outrageous,' Dixon said. 'How can they eliminate anyone without the decency of interviewing them first?'

'Outspoken,' said Ryan, pretending to write on an invisible form.

'It wasn't easy to get here today. If this is big business, you can keep it.'

'Subversive,' grinned Ryan, continuing to write.

'I'm serious, Ryan.' Dixon had a sincere face, and smiled little. He carefully cultivated the appearance of a student intellectual; charity shop chic, challenging spectacle frames, and a haircut that just didn't care. There was always obscure literature tucked under his arm. Interestingly, he had opted for a conventional high street look today, although he would undoubtedly have an alternative take on why. Ryan was grinning behind Dixon's back. He mouthed a third, unrepeatable comment to add to the imaginary form. Joe smiled in return.

'We need to think about why they are doing this,' said Rachel, re-focusing them on the situation in hand. 'What are they looking for?'

'Don't overestimate them. They're probably just covering for another administrative error,' said Ryan.

'Did you see the way that idiot left the stage? They think they're being cute,' Dixon said.

For the first time, Joe noticed a series of cameras mounted at strategic points around the ceiling.

'They're watching us,' he said.

After an initial period of stunned inactivity, people were drifting towards the voting forms on the tables. Dixon had disappeared to fetch some forms for them all.

'Wait!' said a girl, standing on a chair. 'We should walk out together. If we all leave, they won't have a graduate scheme.' It triggered a momentary pause for thought, but then the voting forms started to disappear from the pile even faster.

'She's right,' said Rachel, dismayed at the general reaction. 'It isn't fair to single anyone out. We shouldn't do it.'

Joe nodded in agreement, but Ryan only looked the other way. In truth, solidarity was highly unlikely with this much on offer. Dixon returned with a form for each of them. There were the names of the eighty-six candidates listed down the page, with a column to add their selection reason next to it.

'I suggest we formulate a strategy quickly,' Dixon said. 'In case you hadn't noticed, we are outnumbered.'

He had a point: their conversation was just one of many in small clusters around the room, and some of the groups were already snowballing into larger allegiances. Joe, slightly taller than the others, noticed that several of the candidates were removing their badges so they couldn't be identified.

'Take off your badges,' he said. Even as they fumbled with the clips, they overheard a rumour that there were people trying to identify the names that they *hadn't* seen on a badge, citing "cheat" as their selection criteria. The badges were quickly replaced.

It all made for an uneasy mood in the room. They became increasingly paranoid if anyone looked at them for too long. Joe was horrified to see a girl glance from the mud on his trousers, to his badge. He flashed his most appealing smile, but she still scribbled away at her form as she walked away. He wondered if Elly was sitting in the corner of the room somewhere, losing by a mudslide.

'I feel like this is going badly,' said Dixon, backing away from the crowd. 'How can we improve our chances?'

'Keep your mouth shut,' said Ryan.

The candidates swirled around each other in a macabre dance, sizing each other up and assessing weaknesses. Rachel still refused to vote, and it put Joe in a difficult position. If she was going to fall on her sword, then so was he, but he would have to do it in such a way that wasn't obvious to anyone, particularly her.

'Ten minutes left,' said someone nearby, jolting him back into life. Dixon and Ryan were trying to ingratiate themselves with a group of studious-looking girls at the other side of the hall. Despite their best attempts, it didn't appear to be going well. Rachel had moved away to a chair at the side of the room. She was watching the other candidates with her hands in her lap, refusing to participate any further.

Of all the people in the room, Rachel wanted this more than anyone, and for the best possible reasons. Ever since he had first known her, she had tried to mould the world around her will for the better, but this silent protest was doomed to failure. It was horrible to see her so sad, and it was unfair that she should be eliminated because of a recruitment director's wet dream. He had an idea.

Chapter Three
23rd September 2014

Arnold Shendi sat bolt upright in bed, blinking into the darkness of the room. For a moment, he couldn't place where he was. A myriad of hotel room layouts merged together in his mind, wardrobes and desks dancing together in the darkness, materialising, then dissolving into the gloom. The door was to the right of the bed — a primeval instinct for survival told him that much. He fumbled for a lamp, finally switching it on at full stretch. The monogram of the white bathrobe, hanging from the handle of the wardrobe, was the clue he needed. The Wellington Suite. He had decided to spend a few days in London to gather his thoughts after returning from business. He remembered now. Everything was as it should be. He slumped back into the pillow, his heart pounding.

A toilet flushed in the adjoining bathroom, and a naked woman emerged. Shendi put on his glasses, and watched the lithe figure approach the bed. He momentarily struggled to remember her name.

'Carla,' she smiled, reading his mind.

'Of course, Carla,' he said, pulling back the bed covers. She slipped next to him, running her fingers through the grey hairs on his chest.

'Did you have another nightmare?' she asked.

'Yes, I'm sorry if I disturbed you.'

'It's fine,' she said quickly. A gust of wind blew rain against the window, and they sat for several minutes in silence. 'I'm glad we're in here,' she said at last, pulling the covers closer. Shendi didn't reply, watching the rivulets of water trickling down the glass. His throat was dry and his temples ached. He inevitably caught a cold when he moved between time zones. No technique he had yet discovered fooled his body clock. Carla fondled his chest, slowly moving her hand down towards his stomach. He pushed it back up, abruptly.

'What's wrong?' she said. There was too much to tell, and little he wanted her to know. He hadn't managed to sleep for more than a few hours at a time for the last three weeks. The same problems swirled around and around in his mind without focus or resolution, tormenting him. The injustice made him so angry that his teeth were ground to rough edges with rage. The little sleep he had was haunted by nightmares, forever drawn back to those darkest days of his life. He could not go on like this.

'Do you think I'm a good man?'

'I think you're a great man.'

'But do you think I'm a *good* man?' She didn't reply.

'That's why I like you, Carla.' And he meant it. There was an honesty in her work that he admired. Sometimes he glimpsed other escorts staring blankly at the ceiling, or glancing at their wristwatch as they moaned beneath him in a parody of passion. Some clawed at his back and screamed so loudly that he felt humiliated by their theatrics, but Carla stoically endured his attention, at least showing him the respect of silence.

'You worry too much.'

'I think you're right.'

He stood up, trying to avoid the reflection of his portly naked figure in the wardrobe mirror, and pulled the robe onto his back. His eyes were reduced to narrow slits in his crumpled face, almost useless without the thick-lens glasses that cut a trough into his rounded nose. He was deathly pale.

'Do you want a drink?'

'It's a little early.'

'It's three o'clock,' he said, pouring himself a glass of port from a decanter, 'but ten o'clock in the evening in New York. How about a Manhattan?' She watched him from the bed without replying for a moment, then pulled on the dress that had been discarded on the floor.

'I didn't ask you to get dressed.' She hesitated, holding the straps against her shoulders. He let her stand there for a few moments before his face broke into a smirk. 'A joke…'

'Whatever you are drinking is fine,' she said, blushing, and joined him at the oak desk. He had already poured her a port. They took their drinks from the bedroom into the adjoining lounge. As they opened the door, a voice called through the intercom.

'Are you okay, sir?'

'It's fine, Julian,' he replied to his bodyguard. 'So vigilant,' he grinned at Carla.

The lounge was exquisitely furnished, and even bigger than the bedroom. The vast bay window overlooked Kensington Park, sleeping silently in the darkness beneath. He led her across the room to a couch. His paperwork was neatly arranged in folders beside it.

'I prefer to work here. I've had my fill of desk work.'

She sat next to him, careful not to spill her drink over the expensive upholstery.

'Surely someone could deal with this for you?'

'I have to justify myself somehow,' he said, picking up a folder from the floor. 'Plus, there are some things I don't trust anyone with.' He sat back and closed his eyes, enjoying the warmth of the port as it slipped down his aching throat. The folder was also reassuring on his lap. It felt good to have some semblance of order restored after the chaos. When he opened his eyes again, Carla was perched awkwardly on the edge of the couch. She hadn't touched her drink.

'Perhaps you could help me with some of this?'

'I don't think I could.'

'Why not?'

'I'm not the right person.'

'I think you could be,' he said.

Before she could reply, he had opened the folder and lifted a stack of papers from within. He laid them in a pile on the carpet, carefully pushing the sides together until they were aligned perfectly. He noticed her looking at a sheet of paper on top with a colourful logo in the corner.

'If you read that one, I'll have to kill you.'

'I'm sorry…'

'It's just a request for money,' he laughed, handing her the letter. 'Most of them are.'

She smiled, but he could see that she was still uncomfortable. She wasn't sure what was expected of her, and her awkwardness was appealing. The situation was somehow more intimate than sleeping together. She held the letter in her hand, self-consciously reading it in silence as he watched. The rain pounded against the window harder, and the concealed lighting hummed in accompaniment.

'I've read about your charity work.'

'Yes, that's one of the two things I'm now most famous for.'

She avoided his eyes, knowing full well about the other. 'It must be nice to be able to help people,' she said quickly, sipping her port.

'I help people, but it isn't nice at all.'

'Is that because of the… stories?'

'No, it's because of the responsibility,' he said. She blushed again.

'I can imagine. How do you decide?'

'It's arbitrary,' he said, staring across the room. There was no point in trying to pretend there was any kind of science to it. He read the letters, watched the news and reacted. He supported some causes because he wanted to, and ignored others that he didn't. There was no fairness or order to his thinking. Many of his contemporaries on the rich list amused themselves with their toys: car collections, bigger yachts, sports teams or even tropical islands — these things didn't interest him any longer. Others simply obsessed over the accumulation of wealth itself, driven by an insatiable desire to eclipse their peers. Some strapped themselves inside rockets, or plunged to the depths of the ocean in a relentless quest for further amusement and self-justification — but these egotistical indulgences gave him neither. The planet was suffocating. Children were starving unnecessarily every day, and it sickened him. In his darker moments, he questioned why he should care. He was merely conceding his own advantage by giving his money away, but he believed in judgement at the end of it all. A life of eighty years was nothing in comparison to eternity.

'I read that you donated a large number of your shares in the company recently.'

'It's true. Why do you think I did it?' he said, nestling back into the plump cushion of the couch, watching her.

'I've no idea. I don't take much notice of the newspapers.'

'That's why I like you, Carla,' he said again, smiling.

His reputation had been butchered in the press. His lawyers were working around the clock, pursuing multiple lawsuits, but the rumours persisted. Ironically, the internet was to blame for most of it. The hand that fed him now had him by the balls. It had been far simpler when he was running his own company, but since the takeover there were suited little college upstarts trying to undermine him in the boardroom. They were singularly wet behind the ears, but as dangerous as a pack of jackals together. He was still the CEO in name, although he now found himself on gardening leave — just until things died down a little, they said. There didn't seem to be anything he could do to placate them. Even when he donated his shares to charitable causes, it was seized upon as an indication of guilt. Whatever he did, the questions remained. It was only a matter of time before the allegations were revealed by the media. His lawyers could not hold back the tide forever. There was hope if his new solution could be delivered in time, but there was still so much to put in place...

'Are you okay?'

'I'm fine,' he said, rubbing his eyes. His head was aching, and he was angry again. He suddenly wished he didn't have to talk to her. She seemed to pick up on his change of mood, staring out of the window towards the park in silence. Her nose came to a slight peak at the end. He hadn't noticed before, and it was quite endearing.

'I think I should go.'

'Before you do, I need your help with something,' he said, becoming alert again. 'I didn't ask you in here just to read my begging letters.'

'I don't think I'm the best person to help you.'

'You're the perfect person to help me,' he said, standing up. He padded across the carpet, bringing back a briefcase, which he rested on his lap. 'I like you. More importantly, I know you understand what would happen if you betrayed my trust.' He studied her anxious brown eyes, making sure she had absorbed the full significance of what he had just said.

'I'm not sure I want to be involved... in anything,' she replied, hugging herself.

'There's nothing to worry about,' he said, entering the digital combination code right in front of her. The lid clicked open, and he pulled out a folder with several documents clipped together. 'I want you to read this and give me your opinion, that's all. I believe this is the answer to my problems.'

She hesitated, before taking it from his hands, and then slowly began to flick through the pages. After a few minutes reading, she looked up, more anxious than she had appeared before.

'Is this real?' she said.

Chapter Four

Joe tried to gauge the correct handshake pressure to apply, wary that he had already fallen short on another conventional interview measure by having dirty shoes. He was morbidly drawn to the crooked teeth of his interviewer, and quickly looked him in the eyes.

'Joseph Massey,' he said.

'William Fowler,' replied the interviewer, gesturing for him to sit, 'and this is Christine Thompson and Martin Knight.' Joe greeted them, before lowering himself into the chair across the table.

'You may be wondering why you are still here,' Fowler said, getting straight to the point. 'I have your selection form in front of me.'

'I wasn't certain if...'

'The elimination process was an exercise in thought,' he interrupted, pompously.

'And your reaction was rather unusual, Mr Massey,' added Knight. He had milky blue eyes that dissolved into a pallid complexion. He tilted his head slightly backwards as he spoke, peering past his narrow nostrils. 'Free thinking is something that Schelldhardt encourages to a degree, but more importantly, we need people who know how to obey rules.'

'I felt that we needed to make a statement. It seemed unfair.'

'By "we", I assume you are referring to yourself and Rachel Harding, whose form was startlingly similar?' said Fowler.

'That's correct.'

'Well, statement made,' said Fowler, clicking a ballpoint pen into action, 'but let's put that aside for a moment.'

They were sitting in the library of Marryfield House. The shelves on all four walls were laden to their capacity with dusty books that appeared older than the house itself. The chairs were upholstered in crimson leather, arranged around a desk that had been veneered in a Celtic parquetry design. The furniture sat on a large rug that almost covered the entire wooden floor. The rug looked extremely valuable, and Joe tried to make minimal contact with his shoes, conscious of the dried mud flaking from them. The windows were small, sacrificed to allow optimum storage space for books, making the room darker than the others in the house, and there was a rich orange light within.

He was relieved to move on from the initial awkwardness of the interview, and assumed his best listening face as Christine Thompson explained the details of the Schelldhardt graduate scheme. She spoke as if addressing a room full of people, focusing on a space somewhere over his left shoulder and never making eye contact, like a newsreader. This must have been an inevitable consequence of having to repeat the same information several times that day, but the temporary anonymity was very welcome.

They asked a series of questions about his past experience and qualifications. Fowler had a tendency to over-elaborate, and his colleagues often had to stop him when he strayed too far from the point. Some of the interruptions were for Joe's benefit. Thompson stepped in whenever he struggled with an answer, prompting him for additional information that would benefit his cause with a warm smile. Knight, on the other hand, seemed totally disinterested, and Joe felt as though he had already made up his mind. He repeatedly glanced at his watch, exposing an unpleasant expanse of hairy wrist each time.

'And now we arrive at the business end,' Fowler said, shuffling some papers. 'This graduate scheme requires a particular kind of person. Do you have close family ties, Mr Massey?'

'In what way, sorry?'

'Would you be able to commit to large periods of time away from home?'

'Are you in a serious relationship, Joseph?' Thompson added, before he could reply. It felt like a loaded question.

'I'd miss my mother, but working away wouldn't be a problem,' he said, hesitating for a moment, 'and I'm not in a serious relationship.' He noticed that Thompson was watching him carefully.

'We require a certain amount of sacrifice from our new recruits. For the first twelve months of this scheme you would be working in a controlled environment where you would have no contact with your loved ones. Is that a problem?'

'No, that would be fine,' he said, clearing his throat.

'And you have no other work or social obligations that would jeopardise your application to this end?'

'No, none. May I ask exactly where I would be working?'

'We can't say at this point. The location varies. It's a global company. I'm sorry I can't be specific.'

'In this country?'

'Not necessarily, but possibly.'

'The company would provide all travel, accommodation and living expenses on top of your salary. Plus, of course, Schelldhardt welcomes all new recruits by clearing their student debt on day one, subject to certain restrictions,' smiled Thompson.

'Though you can't leave for three years without paying back the money,' added Fowler.

Knight was now openly ignoring everyone, and appeared to be doodling on his pad. He moved his hand across the paper when he noticed Joe watching.

'The other important thing I need to mention is security. This entire interview process is subject to the confidentiality agreement you signed earlier. I need to stress that this is an area that Schelldhardt takes very seriously. If details are leaked through any media, the matter will be investigated thoroughly, and the company has a strict policy of prosecuting infringements,' said Fowler.

'This may sound heavy-handed, Joseph, but some of our candidates will be working on some highly confidential projects,' said Thompson.

'I understand.'

'You don't understand quite yet,' said Fowler, grinning horribly. Joe wanted to ruffle his neatly parted hair; he had rarely seen anyone looking so smug. 'You may find the final part of the selection process a little intrusive, if selected.'

'The final part?'

'Yes, there would be a screening procedure to complete, should you be successful.'

'A lot of companies perform similar checks,' said Thompson.

'Though ours is more rigorous than most, I think it's fair to say. They will delve quite intimately into your personal circumstances — much further than the standard disclosure tests you may be familiar with. Is that a problem?'

'I've nothing to hide,' he smiled, wishing that he hadn't.

'I'm sure that's the case, Joseph,' said Thompson. Joe was now starting to feel tired. It had been a long day, and he just wanted to get through the interview. He asked a few questions when prompted, but felt as though it was pointless. If Knight had any part of the decision-making process, he was wasting his time.

'It looks like we're finished, then,' said Fowler. He leant over the desk to shake his hand, affording a final close-up view of his delightful teeth. 'Oh, one last thing,' he said, riffling through the papers. 'You can have your sheep back.' He held up Joe's folded selection form, smiling. 'An interesting protest, and very impressive origami. We guessed that the sheep was some kind of pun about following the crowd?'

'That's right,' lied Joe. Sheep were Rachel's favourite animals.

It was beginning to feel like a day at a theme park, with long periods of waiting interspersed with short periods of excitement. Each time Joe moved on, the room he found himself in was smaller than the last. He had expected to be escorted from the premises after the interview, but after an hour of waiting in the stuffy reception room, things were looking more promising.

A man creaked across the wooden floor towards him. He was short and stocky, wearing a shirt and tie. He looked at Joe, then down at his clipboard.

'Mr Massey, please step this way.'

Joe wasn't sure what to expect, and what he found came as a surprise; he was led through the main kitchen of the house into a wide storage room, which was cold, and mainly bare. In place of the regular furniture stood a large white machine, similar to those he had seen in hospitals. There were several cooling units adjacent to it, and the larder had been partitioned off behind a glass screen at the back of the room. There were two nurses sitting behind the glass, studying a laptop. One of them glanced up and smiled at him.

'Congratulations on reaching the third stage of the selection process. I am Michael Brace,' the man said. He had close-cropped hair, and a short white beard. His handshake was uncomfortably firm. 'I will be running through the company screening process with you.'

'Here?'

'Yes, here,' Brace laughed. 'I expect your feet haven't touched the ground.' He led him to a desk where another laptop was situated, and tapped at the keyboard. 'I need to run through a few things with you.'

The questions were initially innocuous enough, confirming security details, and verifying the information he had written on his application form. Then, as Fowler had warned, they became more personal. Schelldhardt had already run disclosure checks and had compiled a report.

'First, let's clear this up right from the start. We are aware of two significant episodes in your past, first back in 2002 and then in 2009. I can't say that they enhance your application, but they don't necessarily guarantee that you will fail. There were extenuating circumstances at the time. Do you wish to discuss them now?'

'I can only say that I deeply regret both of them,' he stammered. 'I fully understand the serious nature of my actions, and they are something I have to live with every day.'

It was a shock that Brace had come straight out with it. He had understood that both matters had been handled off-record, but in truth he was in no fit state of mind at the time to know for sure. There was a moment of silence, and Brace watched him, pursing his lips, as he recorded some notes on the laptop.

'Let's move on. Your mother was declared bankrupt in 1997, two years after your father died.'

'Is that relevant?'

'Everything is relevant,' replied Brace, studying the screen. 'Please don't take this personally.'

Joe's medical history was next on the agenda, and Brace asked about the antidepressants he was prescribed for a short time as a teenager, before delving back into anxiety issues he had experienced in his early school years. Joe had no idea that the information was available in his medical records, and he was sure it was illegal for Schelldhardt to obtain it.

'Your social media footprint is, on the whole, acceptable, but we

31

need to discuss the activity at your home computer IP address. Did you share your house with anyone except your mother before university?'

'No, it was just the two of us.'

'And your mother is fifty-two, so it is unlikely she would download films illegally?' Joe nodded his head, sheepishly. 'I would say even more unlikely that she visited some of these pornography websites I have listed here.' He handed Joe a piece of paper, and he sunk in his chair as he read it.

'I don't look at this stuff any more.'

'The last access date was the fourteenth of November 2009. There isn't anything particularly worrying on this list, but as a Schelldhardt employee you need to be aware that this kind of activity, even in your leisure time, is carefully monitored by the company.'

'I understand.'

Brace typed a few more notes into the laptop, peering over the top of his glasses. Joe watched the nurses behind the screen. One of them pointed at their computer, and he was paranoid they were reading through the dubious Internet browsing list. One thing occurred to him, though: if Schelldhardt had already investigated his past and found all of the information they needed, then why were they proceeding with the checks if they were going to reject him?

'Right,' said Brace, standing up, 'you're probably wondering what this is for?' He pointed towards the mechanical elephant in the room. Joe nodded, also getting to his feet. 'It's an MRI scanner. Are you familiar with them?'

'I've seen them before.'

'These are a whole new breed,' he smiled. 'We need to run a few tests. It's a compulsory part of the screening procedure.'

'That's fine,' said Joe, eyeing the circular tunnel that ran through the centre of the machine.

'Great. Please remove all metallic items,' said Brace, holding a plastic tray in front of him. Joe fished out his wallet, keys and phone, and passed them to him. 'The ring, too.' He hesitated, but wrestled his father's ring from his finger, and placed it with the other objects. Removing his jacket, he climbed onto the soft table.

One of the nurses joined Brace. His head was positioned between two restraints at the end of the table, and the nurse placed a pillow under his legs. The table rose slowly, level with the entrance to the scanner. It sounded like a roller-coaster car clicking its way to the top of the track.

'It's important to keep still,' said the nurse. 'It will be very noisy inside the scanner, but there's nothing to worry about. Remember, it is only capturing images.'

'We're going to give you a light sedative to relax you. The sedation will be increased as the test progresses. You will remain responsive at all times during the procedure, but you may experience some memory loss. There will be images displayed on the screen, and you will be asked some questions. There's nothing more to it than that,' said Brace. 'I'm putting a controller in your hand. Use this to select your answers as they appear.'

Joe smiled weakly at the nurse, who rolled up his sleeve and injected him with the sedative. She placed headphones over his ears and pulled a plastic helmet over his head. There was a screen inside the helmet that displayed the word "Welcome". He felt the controller in his hand, moving a pointer around the screen. He clicked on a green button to continue. Brace and the nurse moved away into the partitioned area.

The sedative was beginning to take effect, and he felt calmer. The table whirred backwards into the mouth of the scanner, and the machine screamed into life. Despite the headphones, it was still incredibly noisy, and the electronic pulsing seemed to pass through his entire body. The sound constantly changed tone and rhythm, and just as he adjusted to one, a new pattern succeeded it. It was like being trapped inside the helmet with a maniacal violinist.

'Focus on the screen,' said Brace through the headphones. 'In a moment a series of categories will appear on the screen. I want you to position them in the order of importance to you, with the highest first.' As he spoke, the screen was filled with eight boxes, each a different colour. There was a different word in each: Family, Ambition, Relationships, Spirituality, Wealth, Health, Politics, Environment and Morality. 'If you hover over any box, you can see further details,' added Brace.

Joe moved the controller around the screen, with the machine still whining around his ears. As he hovered over "Relationships", it revealed other subcategories. Each of these divided further. The boxes could be rearranged on the screen. He immediately began to think how he could put himself in the best light for the interview, moving "Morality" and "Ambition" higher in the list.

'Please don't try to second guess the test. We can see when you do that,' said Brace. 'These categories must be arranged honestly, according to your own priorities. There are no right answers.'

Joe smiled to himself inside the helmet. It was a strange feeling having his thoughts exposed like this, and it made him self-conscious. "Health" seemed an obvious choice to include high in the list. Some of the other categories were far more difficult to prioritise, and he became worried that he was taking too long to perform the task. He switched the order around at least twenty times until he was finally happy, clicking on the green button to continue.

'That's excellent,' said Brace, barely audible above the pulsing machine. 'We are now going to resolve your top-line categories into a list. Once this has occurred, please pre-prioritise the individual list entries that are now out of place. For example, as you have specified "Family" higher than "Ambition", when these two categories are resolved, you may decide that you want to position "Second Cousin" from the higher category beneath "Career" in the lower category. Be totally honest with yourself.'

This was tougher still. More and more items seemed out of place as he studied the list, and he felt the positioning of some of his priorities reflected poorly on him. There was far too much sitting above "Climate Change", but he had considered everything truthfully.

It seemed to take an eternity to arrange the list to his satisfaction, and even as he accepted his choices there seemed to be a handful of items misplaced.

'Thank you,' said Brace. 'We are now going to increase your sedation level, and you will have the opportunity to alter your list if you wish.'

Joe's nose was itching. Wearing the helmet was worse than being in a hairdresser's chair. He was going to say something when the nurse touched his arm, but the increased sedation instantly made it difficult to speak, and he mouthed like a goldfish.

His list now seemed glaringly in error. Was his mother's health more

34

important to him than peace in the Middle East? Of course it was. Who had he been trying to fool? He rearranged the list effortlessly, smiling in satisfaction to himself as he completed the task in minutes.

'Excellent. There are some pictures of faces on the screen. I want you to click on the ones that best represented your emotions when you crossed the field today.'

The screen was blurring in and out of focus. He was dizzy, and the rhythmic pulsing now disoriented him. A confused face on screen. He didn't know whether to cross the field without her. An anxious face. He needed the job. There were a few random words exchanged between Brace and the nurse, but he couldn't make sense of them. He could even be imagining the whole thing. The last vague memory he had was of an image of Rachel on the screen.

'She's the problem,' said Brace. Or maybe he didn't.

Chapter Five
30th September 2014

Shendi instructed his bodyguard to pull over in the narrow country lane. The Bentley glided to a halt between two beech trees at the side of the road, crunching over a patch of loose chalk. The bodyguard turned round from the driver's seat, puzzled.

'I'm going to walk from here.'

'Alone?'

'I'll be fine. I'll call when I'm ready to be collected,' said Shendi, stepping out of the car. He stretched, pulling the tail of his shirt from his trousers, and he absent-mindedly stuffed it back into place.

It looked like it was going to rain. There was an oppressive grey cloud hanging over the hillside, shadowing the copse. The birds in the treetops grew frantic as he crossed the lane towards them. He stopped to fasten his blazer at the side of the road, assessing the wooden gate that stood padlocked before him. After three clumsy attempts, he hoisted his leg onto a wooden strut, and then heaved himself over the gate and into the neighbouring field. A nearby cow voiced her disapproval at the intrusion, before wandering away, chewing. His bodyguard continued to watch from the car, and Shendi waved him off, before settling on a familiar wooden bench beneath the public footpath sign. The words were still engraved on the brass plaque: "Spirit of the meadow". This was the place where it had all begun.

He muttered a silent prayer, breathing the scent of the wet grass deeply, and wiped his glasses clean with a handkerchief. He was home. The memories flooded back, bringing tears to his eyes, both for himself and for her. This was land he owned, and a view he once knew well; the hillside overlooked Swanton, nestled on the river Lyre below. He found it incredible that the town appeared unchanged after all these years, despite everything that had happened since. He held his hand out in front of him, pinching the houses in the gap between his thumb and index finger, and chuckled to himself. How different things could be now! Pulling the notebook from his blazer, he began to write. They wanted to know everything, and being here again would help him recount the smallest details.

Despite his failing eyesight, it was easy to pick out the most prominent buildings. By the river stood the church, Our Lady and Saint Joseph, where he was baptised, confirmed, married and would certainly have been buried had he stayed. The weather had been similar on his wedding day, and he could clearly picture his wife, Catherine, struggling to tame her dress beneath a willow tree at the side of the river. It was too cold to leave their guests waiting long for photographs, and there were only a handful taken to record the occasion, one of which he still kept in his wallet. He wished, particularly after what happened later, that he could have given her a better day.

A few streets away from the church was his school, known locally as the yellow house — a landmark whenever giving directions. The building was still painted primrose all these years later — the legacy of a cantankerous old priest practising during the Twenties who insisted that the colour symbolised divinity. Horse chestnut trees, now taller and more gnarled, lined the school playing field that was barely large enough to house a football pitch. It was the scene of many unpleasant sporting memories for him, and he could vividly recall the sting of a wet leather ball on cold winter days. He had stood shivering between the goal posts, an easy target for his more athletic counterparts who opted to pepper him with shots rather than score.

At the opposite end of the town was the biggest structure of them all — an eight-storey rectangular building with five turret-like structures poking from the roof, and a white clockface that looked down on the market square. This was where his real education took place. Now an empty ruin, it was once the site of their department store, Elliotts, the "Selfridges of the South", a business that had been run by three generations of his family. In its heyday, it was one of the biggest employers in the county, and the central hub of the community, with farmers and fishermen bringing their local produce to the food halls early most mornings.

Shendi remembered, as a boy, how he loved to race around the counters, studying the tanks that writhed with crabs and lobsters, and watched as the baskets arrived, full of glistening, silver fish. As a particular treat, the rosy-faced fishmonger, whose name now escaped him, summoned him whenever he was butchering live eels. He recalled peeking through his fingers, both unable to watch or turn away, as the eels slithered around the wooden board before being chopped to pieces with a cleaver. It both disgusted and fascinated him in equal measures when they still wriggled to escape with their heads and tails removed.

Elliotts survived the War unscathed. His father often joked how the bombers had missed the biggest target in the town by twenty miles. There was a family legend that his grandfather, a fearsome man, stood on the roof of the department store during the air raids, shaking his fist at the aircraft as they flew overhead, and they didn't dare hit the building. Shendi always wanted to believe it was true.

The company continued to grow from strength to strength in the Fifties and Sixties, adding electrical goods and a bed department to the ever-filling floors. Elliotts was the first department store in Europe to stock an exclusive range of waterbeds in the late Sixties: objects that had fascinated his father on a business trip to America. Shendi often hid inside a wardrobe or under a cupboard as the store was closing so that he could lie on the waterbeds and read once everyone had left — on one occasion triggering a full-scale manhunt when he fell asleep, only to be found snoring on a king-size deluxe, by one of the security guards.

Everything fell to pieces in the Seventies, and from the hillside, Shendi could see the store's fate was inescapable: to the right of Swanton snaked what he still called the new road — a bypass neatly constructed to circumvent the town, sucking traffic away with an irresistible gravity to the newly built shopping centres further south. He dearly wished his father could have planned his strategy dispassionately from this vantage point above the town, rather than from the middle of the battlefield, blinded by loyalty and pity. The only weapons at his father's disposal were old-fashioned service and antiquated payment terms; even the people he strove to help turned their backs on him as times became hard. Fundamentally, everything he sold could be purchased cheaper, only ten miles further down the road. A business that had been built up over the course of one hundred years was eaten away in ten, counter by counter and floor by floor. Should he have done anything to help? That was the question that haunted him for a long time afterwards, but there had been plenty of other distractions at the time. The thought sent a shiver down his spine.

Shendi adopted his mother's maiden name ten years after the store's closure, avoiding further hostilities with the town's residents. He still owned the building, and refused to allow it to be redeveloped, despite numerous protests. He had even resisted a petition that had been put before Parliament, signed by over eight thousand people. People called him the Miss Havisham of Swanton, and they claimed it was like living in a ghost town. They even hanged an effigy of him wearing a wedding dress from the clockface.

Leaving the store in its dilapidated state was his revenge on the people of the town who had betrayed his father. He still paid a local security firm to patrol the gated ruin at night, regularly catching vandals and graffiti artists whom he took great pleasure in prosecuting. In the scale of his business portfolio, the store value was negligible, but it was symbolic of everything that had gone wrong.

He wrote quickly in the notepad, the feelings still raw all these years later. It was important he remembered all the details. He didn't fully understand how they were going to use the information, but it sounded incredible. If they could deliver on their promises, he would put everything right.

He paused, looking away across the meadow with the pen poised between his fingers. Would anyone still recognise him if he walked down to the town? For a moment he was sorely tempted to find out, struggling to his feet, only to sit down immediately. He could not take the risk. These were feelings he had suppressed for far too long, and he had to be patient. If the information could be used as they had suggested, he knew the perfect person to clear his name, and maybe he could save both of them in the process. There had been too many lives lost already.

Chapter Six

It took a few seconds for her to register who he was, and then her eyes began to fill with tears. Joe hugged his mother, taking care not to drop the potted plant he had brought her. She held him against her chest for a moment, before studying his face at arm's length — searching for hidden clues to his welfare. People said that they looked alike. They shared the same hazel eyes, and her hair was once the exact same shade of brown as his own. She dyed it slightly darker now, making her complexion appear paler than his, and the freckles on her cheeks were more pronounced. Their noses were the biggest similarity, slightly flat against their faces, though hers was a narrower, more feminine version.

'Happy birthday! Are you going to let me in?' he said. She smiled, ushering him into the leaflet-strewn hall.

'This is such a lovely surprise. I'll put the kettle on.'

It was her fifty-third birthday, and the occasion had fallen in the same week that she had moved into her new flat. An early present to herself, she said. He was embarrassed by his own paltry gift, but he'd only been working part-time since graduation, barely covering his bills. She took the pot, admiring the flowers poking out of the top.

'They're beautiful.'

'It's a diascia. I know you like orange. I thought it would look nice on your new patio.'

'Thank you,' she said, kissing him. She led him into the lounge, where there was barely room to sit amongst the piles of crates and cardboard boxes. Apart from the couch and television, the only items unpacked were two framed photographs, sitting on a shelf above a modern gas fire: one was a picture of himself as a baby, with his parents crouching proudly either side of his pram. The other was a photograph of his father, not much older than himself in the picture, wearing a suit — his long fringe hanging to one side in a drastic Eighties style. Joe knew the picture so well, but the man so little. He was touched, but also saddened to see the photographs so prominently displayed already. She followed his gaze, and he felt he had to say something.

'At least Dad's settled in okay.'

'We don't move on well, do we, Joe?' she smiled. He didn't want to think about that for too long.

'It was a great journey down. It only took two hours.'

'That's good,' she said, reaching for her bag. 'Let me give you something for the train fare.'

'It's fine, Mum.'

'Here,' she said, pushing a twenty-pound note into his hand. 'You can pay me back when you get a proper job.' It was a half-hearted refusal, and he crumpled the money straight into his pocket. They both knew he needed it. 'Have you had any luck finding anything?'

'Nothing concrete yet,' he said, hesitating. Having only just arrived, it felt too soon to revisit such a contentious subject, but she had caught him cold, and he was forced to elaborate. 'I applied for the Schelldhardt scheme.'

'Joe, I thought we spoke about this,' she said, placing her hands on her hips.

'We did, but I still don't understand why you are so against it.'

'I just don't think it's the right company for you.'

'Mum, it's one of the biggest companies in the world. They're renowned for their great work.'

'So I've heard,' she said, picking up a jumper and folding it angrily. 'There are a million other places you could apply to, you know.' She didn't meet his eye, despatching another item from the pile of clothes in silence. 'You can do better than that,' she added at last.

'Better? Mum, there's nothing else out there. This is as good as it gets, trust me.'

For a moment neither of them spoke, but he could see that she was upset. It was Rachel, of course. His mother knew that she was applying, too. After all these years, she still didn't trust him. It was understandable after what had happened, but it hurt him all the same. He didn't want her to be sad, and smiled to defuse the situation.

'Anyway, it's not looking hopeful, so you don't have to worry.'

'Joe, I didn't mean to…'

'It's okay,' he said, reaching out to comfort her. 'I think I would have heard something by now. I know that some people have already been accepted.' In fact, he knew of one person who had already been accepted, and then rejected — all within the space of the three weeks that had passed since the interview. The man had stupidly posted some details of the recruitment day on social media when he received their offer, and within a few hours the posts had been removed, and he found himself unemployed again. Schelldhardt was not bluffing with its threats.

The conversation was soon forgotten. She brought two mugs of tea from the kitchen, and they squatted on the couch, separated by a pile of carrier bags, recounting other news. His mother had a new job, working part-time at a travel agency. The money was terrible, but the people were nice. She could get a discount with certain travel companies, though she couldn't remember which ones.

'Do you want the tour? It won't take long,' she smiled. He followed her around the tiny flat, making overly positive comments as they moved from room to room. 'This is the dining room, but I was thinking of using it as a guest bedroom. I can fit a small table in the kitchen. That's enough for me to eat on.'

'That's enough for you now, but that could change.'

'I know,' she said, smiling. 'Are you going to stay the night? You can sleep in here. I've still got the inflatable mattress.'

'Yes, I was hoping to. I was thinking I could buy you a takeaway?'

'Oh, I'm meant to be going out for a drink. I could cancel it?'

'No, that's great. You should go.'

'It's only the girls from work. I can call them?'

'No, really. I'll stay here and unpack some of these things for you while you're out.'

She smiled and kissed his cheek again. 'That reminds me. A few of these boxes are yours. I found them in the loft. You can check through those if you like,' she said.

His mother left the house at seven, after three changes of outfit and two large glasses of Pinot Noir. Joe's phone was running low on charge, and he needed some alternative entertainment. The television didn't work. He spent ten minutes trying to tune the channels, before he realised that the aerial cable wasn't connected to the roof. Her laptop wasn't an option without a password either — vainly he tried several combinations of his own name without success, and even his father let him down. He finally managed to find an old portable CD player, buried under a pile of coats, but her music collection left a lot to be desired.

His mother's landline rang an hour after she had left, and he was unsure whether to answer it. When he did, he was certain there was somebody at the other end, but they didn't reply. A secret admirer of hers, or just an erroneous call from a handbag or pocket? He ignored it, but then the same thing happened three more times in succession.

Intrigued, he started to unpack the boxes his mother had left him, keeping the telephone close at hand in case it rang again. The first box had a photograph on the top. It was a picture of himself aged thirteen — his least glamorous era — standing overweight and spotty in the sea at Brighton. He quickly moved on, delving deeper into the box, where he fished out another photograph of his father. This was his personal favourite, still creased from where he had kept it beneath his pillow all those years ago. He had read so much into that blurry image, trying to deduce a personality from his quizzical face, frozen in time. It had been difficult growing up without him, never sure of exactly what he should be without his guidance, and for a time he had resented him for not being there. Later, when he had come to terms with his absence, he imagined his father looking over him, judging his decisions and actions with that same ambiguous expression in the photograph that seemed to fit any situation.

A letter fell out of the box. He had no idea how it had got there, but knew exactly who it was from. Only one person in his life had ever sent him a letter: Jenny Flynn. He wondered if his mother had found the letter amongst his belongings during the university holidays, and had put it there. Maybe she had even read it, which would have given her little faith in his ability to soar triumphantly from the nest.

Jenny was a second-year English student, who had taken it upon herself to fix his problems, and in the process had supposedly become infatuated with him. She encouraged him to express his emotions, and he had foolishly complied, on one occasion, fuelled by tequila slammers, explaining his feelings for Rachel. How this had endeared him to her, he did not know. He suspected she was drawn more to the tale of unrequited love, somehow superimposing herself into the picture and forming a tragic love triangle. Her infatuation didn't last long, and a few months later she announced that she had fallen in love with the guy who worked the bar at the student union. The falling wasn't as passive as she made it sound — he later discovered that she had been two-timing him for weeks, but it seemed an apt conclusion to a baffling relationship.

He hesitated when he saw what was at the bottom of the box, pushing his fringe back through his fingers. His journals were poking through the newspaper packaging. It had been years since he had seen them, and they barely felt like his own any more. So many people had scrutinised them, including the police and an irritating psychologist, who seemed to have more issues than he did. What had once felt so harmless was later a source of great shame to him, but now he opened them with a sense of anger at how they had been interpreted. There were descriptions of what Rachel had been wearing each day, and detailed accounts of their conversations, analysing them at great length. These details were interspersed with painful poetry that was never intended for anyone else's eyes. Had things not transpired as they did later, he was sure there wouldn't have been so much meaning attached to their contents.

The telephone rang, startling him. Again, he could hear the faint sound of breathing at the other end. After several seconds the caller hung up.

This time it spooked him. Perhaps it was because of the memories stirred up from the past, but he felt uneasy. He grabbed a glass of water from the kitchen, peering through the curtainless window into the street, and wished his mother wasn't out alone.

There was a figure beneath a tree on the opposite side of the road.

The reflection of the light on the window made it difficult to see anything, but it looked like a man, and he was staring right up at him. He slowly raised his arm to reveal what looked like a mobile phone in his hand, shining in the darkness. The man maintained the bizarre salute for a few seconds before lowering his arm, and calmly striding away into the night.

Had he imagined that he was looking up at their window? He left a message on his mother's mobile anyway, telling her to get a taxi home. He wasn't about to take any chances.

He returned to the spare room to continue sorting through his things, but was too distracted to concentrate. Instead, he pushed the boxes to one side to inflate the bed. The plastic foot-pump was an old adversary, and it repeatedly outfoxed him again as he chased it around the carpet until there was just enough air in the bed to lay on. There he finally rested, watching a cobweb drifting across the ceiling, while he anxiously awaited his mother's return.

His phone vibrated in his pocket. It was a text from Rachel. Had he checked his emails? She had been accepted on the Schelldhardt scheme.

He read the text a few times, still dreamy, but sat bolt upright when he finally grasped the meaning of the words on the screen. His fingers were unable to move fast enough to open his emails. There was a discounted pizza offer, and some information from his credit card company. Beneath them, there was one more unread message. It was from Schelldhardt. He could barely look as he opened it, squinting at the words from the corner of his eye.

He had been accepted.

Chapter Seven

Everything moved quickly in the next few weeks. Joe received a formal contract of employment in the post, with yet another confidentiality agreement to return. He was instructed to report to Portsmouth docks at ten o'clock on his first day, bringing his passport and luggage. There were no details of the onward journey, or any indication of where he would ultimately be based. Rachel had received identical instructions, so he hoped that they were heading to the same place.

He spent the last few days at his mother's flat. It would have been a difficult few days anyway, but she was still vehemently opposed to him starting the job. One evening, just after they had eaten, it seemed as though she might finally open up to him, but despite his coaxing, she held her silence, simply telling him to be careful. It made him uneasy. He was also disturbed by the bills that were piling up on her doorstep, but she was equally uncommunicative on that subject. On the Sunday evening before he left, she cooked his favourite meal, and they said their goodbyes. He hated leaving her, particularly as he would have no way of contacting her over the coming months, but he walked out the door without looking back.

It was raining heavily as he waited for Rachel in his car outside their flat. He tried to clear the windscreen, but the rear wiper moved much faster than the defective front blades, and he seemed to be fighting a losing battle against the elements. His battered Nissan could only accommodate two of them with their luggage, and Ryan and Dixon had made other arrangements to get to the docks. They had also received offers on the same day as Joe and Rachel, making it a clean sweep for their flat. Dixon triumphantly announced that they had won the Schelldhardt postcode lottery. Rachel locked the front door and dragged her suitcase down the path, with an overnight bag dangling from her shoulder.

The car spluttered up the road from their flat. The head gasket was leaking slightly, and the engine constantly seemed to be at the point of stalling. He cursed when he had to stop at the top of the hill, unable to pull straight out onto the main road at the junction. The rear wiper flayed wildly across the window, and the car edged backwards and forwards on the slope as he over-revved the engine, like an angry cat waiting to pounce on the traffic.

'I'd forgotten what it's like to be in a car with you,' said Rachel. Joe didn't reply, swearing under his breath as he missed an opportunity to pull out in front of a delivery van. He finally shuddered away, the engine roaring impotently. They had just reached the high street when Rachel asked him to stop just before some traffic lights. Without warning, she jumped out of the car and disappeared across the road. He pulled over to the other side of the junction and switched on his hazard lights, trying to spot her in the rear-view mirror through the driving rain. After a few minutes, she reappeared. She was smiling, waving a piece of paper in her hand. He instantly knew what it was: Schelldhardt had cleared her student debt as promised. In the troubled weeks to come, this is exactly how he would remember her, laughing in the rain.

They reached the port an hour early, and waited in the secure lot as instructed. The rain was clearing, and the sun intermittently shone through the clouds. There was only one ship currently in the dock, but they could see no tell-tale company logos from where they were sitting. Seagulls screeched overhead, fighting over scraps of food littering the car park. Joe was desperate for a coffee, but he didn't want to deviate from the instructions they had been issued by visiting the terminal building. Dixon and Ryan hadn't arrived, but there were other cars flooding into the secure lot. Just after ten, what looked like a large golf buggy pulled through the car park gates, and crawled to a halt at the front of the other parked vehicles. The driver stepped out, holding a placard with Schelldhardt written on it. They hurried to meet him.

'Welcome to Schelldhardt,' he said, checking a list on his electronic notepad. 'I'll take you from here.'

There was a strong crosswind, and the buggy felt as though it might tip over as it whined along the quay. They could see the Spinnaker Tower in the distance, and there were several military ships docked in the nearby naval base, as grey as the sea. Two Customs officers stopped the buggy and checked the driver's paperwork, before waving them onwards towards a gangway that led up into the ship. There were several people already assembled there.

'How do you like your new office?' the driver smiled, looking upward.

The ship towered above them. She was named *Ananke*, and was larger than a normal passenger ferry, over six hundred feet in length, with ten decks rising from the sea into the cloudy sky. The ship looked new, immaculately white and unblemished, with rectangular tinted windows on every deck. There was a helicopter pad on the top, adjacent to an array of aerials and radar equipment, turning slowly at the apex.

'I'll take your luggage. That gentleman will help you board,' he said, gesturing towards a sturdy-looking man in a suit who was wearing an earpiece and security badge.

'Names and passports, please,' the guard said, also checking an electronic notepad before taking their documents. He breathed heavily, looking from the passport photographs to their faces, and finally seemed satisfied. 'That's fine, thank you. Please report to reception,' he said, gesturing up the gangway. He was still watching Joe when he glanced back over his shoulder, but quickly looked away.

The reception area was much bigger than they had anticipated. It was lavishly decorated, with the ceiling painted as intricately as the Sistine Chapel. The centrepiece of the atrium was a beautiful statue of a woman, twenty feet in height, holding a length of chain in her left hand and a hammer at her side in the right. Joe recognised a few of the people queuing at the reception desk from the open day, but they were separated from the rest of the room by a glass corridor that led through to a security area.

The security procedure was more stringent than boarding an aircraft. They removed their shoes and emptied their pockets, before being scanned and searched. Their hand luggage was examined in a separate area by a small team of people wearing gloves, and their mobile phones and Rachel's laptop were separated from the rest of their belongings. An elderly lady with a kind face noticed Rachel's concern.

'We'll keep them safe. All electrical goods are quarantined,' she smiled. '*Ananke* is a carefully controlled environment, but you're going to be sick of hearing about that soon enough,' she added, lightly touching her hand. Their photographs were taken, and instantly embossed onto security passes, which they were told to keep with them at all times. The cards controlled their access to doors and facilities around the vessel, and they had individual profiles and privileges dependent on the working areas they were assigned to. Their passports and money were quarantined alongside their phones, and they were told they had no need of them aboard the ship.

'How do you feel?' Joe asked Rachel, as they queued at the reception desk after leaving security.

'Excited, and a little scared,' she said. He knew what she meant; they had talked at length about what they were going to do once they arrived, but actually being here was something different altogether, and he suddenly felt very small.

They checked in at reception, and were given a starter pack and allocated their rooms.

'The ship is minimally locked down on embarkation days. You'll find that you'll be able to move between decks and help each other unpack,' said the receptionist. 'One request — when security is increased, please don't contact reception if you find your pass doesn't work where it previously did. We get a lot of calls on transition days, and it's hard for us to deal with them all. You'll be clearly notified when the changes occur. Is that clear, sir?'

Joe was suddenly aware that they were looking at him. 'Our rooms are on different decks?'

'That is correct. You will be staying on deck four, which is the one below this one. Miss Harding's room is on deck six, but you will be able to visit deck six before security is increased. You'll understand more after attending your orientation sessions. For now, it's best if you think of *Ananke* as a giant office block with many different departments. It will all become clearer,' she said, already focusing on the next man waiting in the queue.

They wandered away towards the lifts, juggling their overnight bags and the various pieces of literature they had been issued. Rachel paused beneath the statue, sensibly rationalising her load into one bag, but Joe didn't bother. He looked up at the statue, defiant and unyielding, and tried to imagine what lay in store for them. The first orientation session was due at three o'clock, so they had a couple of hours to unpack and eat. They agreed to unpack first and explore later.

'I'm lost without my mobile. Hopefully, there are telephones in the rooms. If not, I'll meet you at your room at one,' said Rachel.

'Old school. I like it,' he smiled.

The door from the lift opened, and a naked man burst out.

It was so unexpected that the scene didn't register as being real. He charged straight towards Joe, who instantly braced himself for the collision. The man grabbed Joe's shoulder with one hand, and forced a piece of red plastic into his hand with the other. His face was scarred, and his eyes were distant. He closed Joe's hand around the piece of plastic, and smiled.

'I knew you would come,' he whispered, before rushing past. Rachel spun sideways as the man tore towards the centre of the atrium. He repeatedly ran round the statue in bizarre circles, briefly evading two security guards, before they grabbed him at each elbow. He was quite emotionless, and accepted his capture without a struggle. The guards escorted him away from the reception area through the crowd of dumbfounded new arrivals, some clapping and cheering. He looked back towards Joe, holding his finger to his lips, before he was led through a glass door. In seconds, the atrium returned to its normal activity as if nothing had happened.

'What did he say to you?' said Rachel.

'I didn't catch it,' Joe replied, feeling the ridged plastic in his hand. He didn't know why, but he didn't want to tell her. One of the security guards who had apprehended the man was watching them through the glass door, and another was wandering towards them.

'Are you two okay?' said the guard.

'Fine, thank you. What was all that about?' asked Rachel. The man watched Joe as she spoke.

'A party that got out of hand, that's all,' smiled the guard.

'Funny time for a party,' said Joe.

'Oh, I've seen it all here,' grinned the guard, sounding very much like he hadn't. He was still watching him suspiciously.

Joe smiled and slipped the piece of plastic into his pocket.

Chapter Eight
4th June 1993

Arnold Shendi couldn't tell Catherine the real reason he didn't want to go to the beach that day. He had been working ridiculous hours for months, and his wife's immediate assumption was that he didn't want to sacrifice the time. She couldn't understand it. They had more money than they had ever dreamed of, and had just moved into a beautiful new home in Surrey. Why wouldn't he take a weekend off with their friends?

He was happy to let her believe this was the case, but she had reacted so badly when he refused to go that he needed to embellish his excuse. He tried to play the elitist card, questioning why they would want to spend a cloudy weekend on the south coast of Britain when they could be strolling through the Piazza San Marco in Venice, or sipping a Martini in a Manhattan cocktail bar. Her reply left him little room to manoeuvre: Philip and Jane would not fly with their baby. He tried to argue that a fifteen-month-old child was no longer a baby, and that he didn't see why they should be casualties of their over-protective parenting. This only inflamed the situation, and he was shocked at Catherine's depth of feeling on the subject. Ordinarily, she accepted his absence from social events with resigned weariness, but on this occasion seemed determined to have her own way. It was going to be an awkward day for him.

There was a strong westerly breeze as they stumbled over the large pebbles towards an oasis of sand on Worthing beach. They shared the load of infant paraphernalia with their friends — a human caravan of brightly coloured plastic wobbling across the stones. The beach was almost empty, apart from a young couple huddled by the shoreline, their hair standing on end in the wind. Shendi hammered the windbreak into position, applying the primary survival principle of shelter as a priority, while the others arranged the camp and optimistically applied sunscreen. Sonic slept soundly throughout, curled under a blanket in his pushchair. His nickname originated from the popular video-game hedgehog who shared the habit of spinning his legs at an alarming speed. The longer he slept, the better, as far as Shendi was concerned. His awakening would only initiate a new round of questioning about his own ambitions of fatherhood.

'Isn't it lovely out of the breeze?' said Jane, stretching out on the blanket, her pale stomach exposed as she reclined. As chief instigator of the trip, Shendi understood why she was overplaying the loveliness, and underplaying the hurricane.

'I adore the beach,' said Catherine. 'I would come more often, but Arnold isn't keen.'

'What's not to like?' said Jane, wiggling her painted toes in bliss.

'I don't like swimming, I don't like the sun, and I despise exposing my body,' he said with a deadpan delivery that they had once encouraged in jest, but was now just accepted as a facet of his personality.

'I suppose that limits the appeal,' Jane smiled.

In the case of Jane and Philip, familiarity didn't so much breed contempt as brutal honesty. He had spent most of the last eight years locked in an office with his business partner, Philip, and there was little to say to each other that hadn't already been said. As entrepreneurial widows, the same was largely true of Catherine and Jane, but they still placed importance on their joint outings. It had been weeks since they had socialised together. The baby had provided a convenient excuse at first, but recently it had been more difficult to disguise the change.

'How about some champagne while Sonic is sleeping? It's in the cooler bag, Philip,' said Jane, shading her face from the sun. Philip was unusually quiet, and seemed reluctant to get the drinks. When he did, he rose in one abrupt motion, ripping open the zip in silence. Jane watched him with mild amusement, as he unceremoniously uncorked the bottle and poured four drinks, allowing the glasses to overflow onto the sand.

'Arnold?' he asked, not making eye contact.

'Just a drop.'

'Of course, you're driving,' he muttered.

'Champagne on the beach. Aren't we lucky!' said Catherine. 'To the continued success of our business,' she added, raising her glass.

The words grated with Shendi. He could barely look at her when she spoke of his company in that way. All the hours he had spent. All the things he had to do. Catherine knew this, of course, and that was why she said it. Irritating him was now one of her few remaining pleasures in life, and she luxuriated in the sanctuary of the group.

'Who would have thought that we would be in this position now,' said Jane, smiling. 'Mobile phones have moved on so much from those monstrosities you sold in the early days. And you think they will become smaller still, Arnold?'

She was patronising him, of course. So desperate was she to instigate social interaction that she would even encourage one of his impassioned business sermons, inflicted too many times over the years. Anything was preferable to awkward silence.

'I do, and I also believe they will be able to do far more,' he said, compromising.

'Arnold believes they will take over our lives one day,' smirked Catherine.

He ignored the sarcastic remark, but wasn't inclined to elaborate his prediction any further for their amusement. In truth, he was extremely excited about the recent advances in mobile technology. In December of the previous year, the first text message had been transmitted to a mobile handset, and IBM were working on a personal communicator that could send and receive faxes and electronic mail. Not to mention the emerging possibilities of the Internet. His company was perfectly positioned to exploit the new opportunities, if they could just endure the next six months.

Sonic started to cry and wiggle his legs in trademark fashion, sparing him from additional comment.

'I'll get him,' said Philip, too eager to leave the bosom of their group. He stood in the wind, with his son clinging to his chest, rocking backwards and forwards.

'Isn't that lovely,' said Catherine, watching them. Shendi did his best to ignore her, sipping his champagne. He braced himself for the conversation that would surely follow.

'Philip, keep his ears out of the wind,' called Jane, squinting into the sunshine. If he heard her, Philip didn't respond, and continued to nurse the child in exactly the same way. Catherine looked at Jane awkwardly.

'Why don't I take him for a walk?' she said.

Catherine and Philip held a hand each, as Sonic battled to stay upright in the hostile conditions. He stood like a gunslinger, his bowed legs inching past his nappy from side to side in a ridiculously inefficient motion. Jane clapped as he flashed her a dribbling smile, before almost collapsing in a heap.

Shendi felt uncomfortable alone with Jane. He always struggled to think of things to say to her, but today was more difficult than ever. She had married Philip five years ago, just as the business was beginning to flourish, and Shendi initially had doubts about her intentions. At the very least, their romance was an unwelcome distraction at a crucial time, and it had often caused conflict between them.

'Is everything okay with Philip?' she asked, as Sonic staggered out of view behind the windbreak.

'I've noticed he doesn't seem himself today.'

'He's been acting differently at home recently, too. I wondered if anything was wrong at work. You're his real wife, after all,' she smiled.

Shendi examined the shells in the sand by his hand, choosing his words carefully. 'We've been under a lot of pressure.'

'I know, but it doesn't usually affect him like this.'

'We've been under *a lot* of pressure,' he said, still looking away. She sat up straighter, eager to hear more.

'Why won't he talk to me about it?'

'It's been tough recently. I wouldn't judge him too much at the moment.' Just talking about their work situation made his stomach churn, and he shifted uncomfortably in the sand, reaching for an indigestion tablet in his pocket. He was desperate to leave the beach.

'Okay, fine,' she sighed. 'Maybe you could just tell him that I'm here for him,' she added, turning to watch the grey waves breaking on the shore.

The windbreak billowed in a sudden gust, flicking sand over them. Shendi stood up and brushed himself down. He took his car keys from his pocket, pointing the remote in the direction of his Aston Martin parked on the promenade. How he longed to be inside it! The car chirped back, and he stood looking at it, calming his breathing for a few seconds, before sitting back down on the blanket.

'You love that car, don't you?'

'There has to be some rewards for all of this work.'

'Yes, sometimes you have to wonder whether it's all worth it.'

He really couldn't bear to sit there any longer. He was a fool to think they would leave him alone, and he shouldn't have come. Sonic poked his head around the corner, laughing, propped up by Catherine behind. He charged on top of Jane, who wrestled him from side to side, before lifting his giggling body into the air. Shendi watched Catherine smiling at the pair of them, and felt sorry for her. Jane was right — he had been so blinkered and focused on what he was doing that he hadn't stopped to consider whether it was all worth it, until it was too late. If only he could turn back the clock. Catherine had never aspired to the wealth he had brought her, and he knew that it did not make her happy. The business had developed a life-force that was all-consuming, and it was too late to change course. The decisions he now made were simply a logical succession of necessary acts.

Jane placed a baseball cap on her son's head, and she wandered down to the shoreline with Catherine, taking a bucket and spade with them. After a few minutes, Philip returned, sitting in the same spot on the blanket. He sat watching his wife and child with his back to Shendi, his sinewy arms supporting his body. Although only a few feet away, the distance between them had never felt greater, and Shendi wished with all of his heart that things could have worked out differently.

'You have a wonderful family,' said Shendi. 'Sonic loves the sea.' Philip didn't acknowledge him, and continued to squint at the animated figures splashing at the water's edge. The wind howled loudly, sending a carrier bag tumbling across the pebbles right next to them, but he remained motionless, staring at the waves. 'He's such a happy little boy,' Shendi said, casually leaning closer on the blanket. Again, Philip ignored the comment. His cheek pulsed with a tension that appeared to be running through his entire body, and he studiously remained fixed in the same position. 'He'll grow up to be a fine young man,' Shendi added, trying one last time to initiate a conversation. The silence was getting awkward.

Philip finally turned to face him, with an expression that he had never seen before. 'I know what you've done to me, Arnold.'

Chapter Nine

He wondered if there had been a mistake. When Joe opened the door, he was unprepared for the size of room he entered, and it instantly lifted his mood. The spacious lounge led to a bedroom with a king-size bed in one direction and a kitchen diner in the other. The bedroom had an en suite bathroom, complete with a full-size bath, as well as a separate shower. His case had been delivered to his room. The security department had left a list of quarantined items on top, and he noticed that his adaptor plugs had been removed, but strangely his electric razor remained.

He reclined on the bed with the piece of red plastic he had been given in his hand. The writing was difficult to read, but it appeared to have the word "Anteros" etched into it. It meant nothing to him. He studied the object for several minutes, trying to work out what it was for, but was none the wiser. The way the naked man had looked at him was unnerving, and the guard's flimsy party explanation had failed to reassure him. He tucked it safely inside the lid of his case and started to unpack.

When he opened his wardrobe, he was surprised to discover that it was already nearly full, and then he found an explanatory note that the clothes were for his use. There was a tuxedo and a dress shirt in his size, as well as a selection of shoes. He wandered over to his window, which didn't open, and tried to look out. The glass was tinted, with an amorphous world of light and shade beyond. The ship was still in the dock, and he guessed that he wasn't missing much of a view.

He took a quick shower, then explored the rest of his cabin. The kitchen was fully equipped with a refrigerator and a small freezer. He opened it to find a selection of groceries, including beer and wine. All of his favourites were there. In the lounge, there was a disproportionately large television. He switched it on to find a channel dedicated to the Schelldhardt company. There was a cabinet beneath it, stocked with a generous selection of spirits, liquors and mixers. He poured himself a mineral water, thinking better of drinking before his meetings, and reclined on the couch with the telephone on his lap.

He called Rachel, who was equally ecstatic about her room, but still busy unpacking. They agreed to meet at two instead. Grabbing a bowl of fresh fruit from the kitchen, he flicked back to the Schelldhardt channel, keen to absorb as much information about his new job as possible. The headline reported that Schelldhardt was now officially the largest company in the world, having completed the acquisition of a major energy company that very week. The company's commitment to improving the world was reiterated at every opportunity, their initiatives ranging from eradicating Third World disease to reducing plastic pollution, under the customary slogan, "Business for good". Schelldhardt's interests were diverse, spanning half a dozen sectors, including financial services, engineering, technology and energy. The company had been taken over two years earlier, and had undergone a prolonged period of restructuring since. *Ananke* was the new corporate headquarters, but there were several other office locations, including a purpose-built centre of excellence in India that housed most of the operation. He grabbed a pad and paper from his case and made a few notes before orientation.

Orientation was held in the ship's main conference room, with a table long enough to accommodate forty people around it. They were shown a short safety film, and taken through a muster drill. *Ananke* was unusual: there was no passenger access to the upper decks, and no opening windows or balconies on any of the passenger floors. Schelldhardt had designed the ship this way to further safeguard company privacy. In an emergency, doors could be opened to access lifeboats and reach the upper decks. As they had already been warned, confidentiality was key to life aboard *Ananke*. There was restricted Internet and telephone access throughout the ship. Once at sea, the integrity of their operation was completely secure — something that set them proudly apart from their competitors.

Shortly after the safety briefing, the ship's engines rumbled into life, and there was an announcement over the broadcast system that they were leaving dock. A man asked where they were going — a subject that they had all been speculating about earlier. The answer was simply "to sea".

The meeting continued for another hour. After watching a slick video introduction about the company, an organisation chart was displayed on the screen, with each of their names shown in their respective new roles. It was worse than Joe had envisaged; although they were working on the same programme, he was not only working in a different department to Rachel, but also in a completely different business sector. He had been assigned to financial services in the compliance and audit department, and Rachel would be working in technology research and development. It seemed a fairly arbitrary scattering of people, and he wondered if he could request a transfer. The thought of a whole year without her was difficult.

Dixon could barely contain his excitement when Joe spotted him at the welcoming party. He had a glass of champagne in one hand and a canapé in the other. His sandy hair was slicked back, and he had removed his glasses — liberated from intellectual angst by the merest sniff of Bollinger and a bow tie. He looked like a boy dressed up as a man in his tuxedo.

'Unbelievable,' he grinned, sipping the champagne with his little finger extended. 'You have to hand it to them.'

'It's pretty impressive,' said Joe, surveying the opulent art deco ballroom. A band was playing jazz at the extremity of the room, and there was a crowd of people milling around the bar area. 'Have you seen the others?'

'Rachel?' he smiled, gulping his champagne. 'She's not here yet. Nor is Ryan. He made the schoolboy error of raiding the drinks cabinet before checking if it was a free bar. He was halfway through a bottle of vodka when I called his room.'

'Nothing like making a good impression…'

'I think he views their generosity as a challenge.'

They were interrupted by a man and a woman approaching them, laughing.

'How are you finding things, guys?' said the man. He was a little older, and had a strong European accent. Joe was drawn to the Mediterranean-looking woman — stunning in an olive-green cocktail dress that hugged her dramatic figure.

'Fantastic,' said Dixon, before he could speak. 'Is it always like this?'

'Schelldhardt treat you well. We work hard and play hard, so the old company cliché goes.'

'But try to focus on the play just for now,' said the woman, smiling at Joe. It took all his powers of concentration to avoid looking at her cleavage.

'Anyway, how rude of me. I'm Yann, and this is Marie,' said the man, shaking each of their hands. 'We are mentors assigned to guide you through the first few weeks on *Ananke*. Point one, I believe you both need new drinks.' He spoke with the confidence of someone who thinks their English is perfect, but fell just short of the mark.

Joe followed Yann to the bar, grabbing a couple of glasses of champagne. It was too noisy to hold a conversation, so he just nodded and tried to exude professionalism. Yann enjoyed talking, and Joe wondered if he even cared whether he could hear him. Marie was drawing plenty of attention from the men at the bar, and he felt awkward leaving her isolated for too long. He made his excuses at the first opportunity, and headed back to find Dixon.

The band had changed gear, and there were a few people starting to dance. It was becoming busier by the minute. He was about to move on when he was slapped so hard on the back that he nearly dropped the champagne.

'Joe!' Ryan shouted over the music. Joe spun round to see his friend, glassy-eyed and stupid. His black tie was already loosened halfway down his chest, and he was spilling the cocktail in his hand. 'We've hit the jackpot,' he grinned. Ryan's over-indulgence at parties was only matched by his inability to handle the aftermath. 'Is that for me?' he asked, noticing the second glass of champagne.

'It's for Dixon,' Joe smiled, pulling the glass from his grasp. 'We need to catch you up.'

Ryan laughed and wobbled away, leaving Joe to look for the others. He moved closer to the dance floor, finding a good vantage point to survey the room. There were a handful of people he recognised from the interview, but he couldn't see Rachel. He sensed the mood was beginning to liven, and was anxious to join the party. The thought was an instant kiss of death, and the music stopped abruptly. An announcer took the microphone.

'A buffet is now being served in the Babylon Room. Please keep all glass away from the swimming pool.' He had barely finished speaking before a tide of people began to sweep out of the ballroom through a pair of double doors. The rush was undignified, and Joe felt as though he should hold back before following. When he couldn't find Rachel or Dixon in the emptying ballroom, he changed his mind, but was now stuck at the back of the shuffling queue of shame.

It was worth the wait. The Babylon Room was even more spectacular than the ballroom, and it overwhelmed his senses. The aroma of cooking food was the first thing to demand his attention. Along the entire left-hand side of the room were tables laden with spit-roasting meats, exotic seafood, and a colourful selection of fruit and vegetables, all intricately prepared by the white-hatted chefs who stood proudly behind them. Dishes sizzled beneath silver serving domes, and the dessert stand boasted enough calories to power the entire ship — a mosaic of delicate sweets, fruits and pastries — most liberally coated in chocolate and cream. Plates clattered, cutlery clinked and the guests jabbered with excitement. The majority were heading in the direction of the food, and so he seized the opportunity to move against the tide, inching closer to the swimming pool. A bridge spanned the water, where a female singer was performing on a podium, surrounded by the spectacular shooting spouts of a fountain that was illuminated by multi-coloured spotlights. He recognised her from a reality television talent show.

'About time,' said Dixon, joining him at his side. He had a mountain of food on his plate. Joe noticed that the two glasses he had nursed all the way through the crowd were superfluous, as there was a waiter circulating with a tray of champagne flutes. Dixon was grinning like a fool, clearly a regular client already. 'Have you seen the pool? It's amazing.'

Joe stepped forward, peering down into the luminous turquoise water that shimmered the entire length of the room. It was immense. They were standing on the bottom deck of *Ananke*, and the vast oval pool had been built into the base of the ship. It was the ultimate glass-bottomed boat. The sides and base of the pool had transparent walls, filled with an incredible assortment of corals and tropical fish, swimming as if they were actually in the ocean. The submerged lighting shone out through the glass into the gloomy depths beyond, with streams of bubbles racing over the surface as the ship powered forward.

'That is quite something,' said Joe. He couldn't swim, and didn't want to move any closer to the edge.

'Yann said that he was swimming in the pool when a humpback whale appeared beneath the ship. It maintained the same speed as the ship for a full five minutes, watching him the whole time. Incredible,' Dixon added, shaking his head. 'Mind you, he is full of shit, isn't he?'

Joe smiled. 'Have you seen Rachel?'

'Over by that table with a brute of a man.'

Joe wandered in the direction Dixon had indicated, grabbing two glasses of champagne as he passed a tray. Rachel was sitting with a group of people he didn't recognise. She waved when she saw him approach, and he lingered at the edge of their table without a chair to sit on.

'This is my friend Joe,' said Rachel. The three others, two men and a lady, looked up and smiled politely. They didn't introduce themselves. One of the men, sitting next to Rachel, was indeed huge and ruggedly handsome, and was conspicuously focused on her. Joe stood awkwardly with the two glasses of champagne, trying to catch her attention again.

'Can I have a word in a moment?' he said.

'I'll be over,' she said, before returning to their conversation. Joe hesitated, before rejoining Dixon, positioning himself to watch Rachel's table over his shoulder.

'Did you find her?'

'Yeah, she's sitting over the back there somewhere.' He gave Dixon the spare drink, and then attacked his own.

People were starting to dance around the edge of the pool, drawn inevitably closer to the water by their folly. The singer launched into one of her hits, and there was a roar from the makeshift dance floor. Dixon watched, tapping his foot like an old man, still trying to maintain an air of sophistication that was diminishing by the glass.

'So, what do you think of your placement? You're in the technology area as well, right?' said Joe, leaning to be heard.

'Yes, odd really. Not what I expected with an economics degree, but they seem to pride themselves on their quirky recruitment policies. I suppose financial services makes sense with your background.'

'I guess,' said Joe, gulping champagne.

'It will be good for you, Joe,' Dixon said, intently. There was a sentimentality creeping into his voice that Joe recognised well. Drunken Dixon glowed like a Thirties actress, blessed with unrivalled insight into the human condition. He knew. He understood. He appreciated you. And like a benevolent creator, he would gently cajole more wonderment from his subject with an encouraging arm around the shoulder.

'Let's not talk about that now.'

'You're right,' Dixon replied, as if he had never witnessed such courage. He caught the eye of a passing waitress with a tray. 'Two more champagnes, please. And a couple of shots of tequila.'

It was amazing how quickly the polite cocktail party was degenerating. Despite the magnitude and variety of the assembled talent, the net sum was fast equalling dumb. Ryan, a prime exponent, appeared through the crowd with his arm around the shoulders of two girls.

'Hey,' he slurred. 'This is Chloe and Sarah.'

Joe and Dixon introduced themselves, but there was an unmistakable look of disappointment on the girls' faces.

'Joe,' Chloe repeated, as if repulsed by the word. She looked exactly like Ryan's last girlfriend — dark hair and even darker make-up. Sarah had an earnest face, and had joined Dixon at precisely the right point of the evening for a drunken analysis of life. Joe again found himself lingering at the extremity of a conversation, and consoled himself by chasing the remainder of his champagne with the shot of tequila. He immediately ordered more drinks for all of them. Craning his neck, he could see that Rachel was still sitting at the table next to the catalogue model. The man was far too close to her, defying all the laws of social convention, and obviously not accustomed to the niceties of a civilised cocktail party.

He lost track of the number of times he intercepted the drinks' tray, but he was not the only one. Inhibition had been the first casualty of the night, closely followed by sense, and now dignity was on borrowed time. He had given up any pretence of listening to the conversation and focused on drinking as much alcohol as he could in the shortest possible time.

The other guests on Rachel's table had left, leaving her alone with the man. Despite his new surroundings, he was beginning to feel a familiar sense of resignation. No matter how many times he experienced it, no coping technique could help him. He repeatedly told himself to look away, but just couldn't heed his own advice.

Her happiness was the most important thing. He should ignore her and immerse himself in the party.

But it was too difficult. The more he tried not to look, the more he looked — his neck twisting masochistically in her direction at every opportunity. The man had his sleeveless arm around her chair. A clumsy great pork chop of an arm.

'You've been watching her all night,' said a voice next to him. He turned to see Marie the mentor inches from his face. He could feel the warmth of her breath on his cheek.

'She's my friend. I'm just making sure she's okay,' he replied. The man appeared to be whispering something in Rachel's ear.

'She looks fine to me.'

'She does.'

'Maybe you should focus on enjoying yourself,' she said, reaching for a drink. He swallowed another shot of tequila and smiled at her. Ryan shouted something, but was distracted by the arrival of a waitress, offering him a silver tray with neat lines of white powder.

'Is that coke?' he asked Marie.

'It wouldn't be a Schelldhardt party without it. Don't look so shocked. You could be eaten by a lion in a shopping mall and our lawyers would prove it didn't happen,' she laughed. The waitress lingered patiently for a few seconds, but was called by a man nearby and wandered off. He turned round to see Chloe trying to snort a line from Ryan's feebly flexed biceps, but they were both hardly able to stand. Marie moved closer, whispering in his ear. 'Do you want to try something even better?' Joe looked across at Rachel, who was still deep in conversation with the man, and back into Marie's brown eyes.

'You're my mentor,' he smiled. Marie called the waitress, and she returned with two shot glasses filled with an amber liquid on the tray. Marie took one of the shot glasses and wafted it under her nose, savouring the bouquet.

'What is it?'

'You're going to love it,' she said, downing the shot in one go. She didn't move for a moment, then a wave of convulsion swept through her body. She looked at him and smiled. 'Your turn.' Joe took the glass and swallowed the drink in one mouthful. He wasn't sure if the colour subliminally influenced his thinking, but it tasted of oranges. He stood blinking at Marie, waiting for more of an effect, but was disappointed to feel no different. 'It can take a little while to hit home. Stay here, I'm just popping to the restroom, but I'll be back.'

Joe breathed deeply. Nothing.

Ryan and Chloe were dancing far too exuberantly to the latest song, and had cleared an angry pocket in the crowd. Some people were launching themselves into the pool, and there was a security guard simultaneously trying to fish them out. Joe wandered back to find his drink, where Dixon was standing toe to toe with Sarah, talking inches from her face.

'I always say the wrong things to girls,' slurred Dixon.

'You're right,' she said, and disappeared towards the buffet table. Joe placed his arm on Dixon's shoulder, who turned towards him, shaking his head.

'Where's your mentor friend? She likes you.'

'The bathroom,' said Joe, suddenly feeling dizzy. There were iridescent patterns at the periphery of his vision, swirling like amoeba under a microscope, yet evading focus when he tried to corner them. 'I think I'm tripping.'

'No one trips on champagne, idiot,' said Dixon, tipping his glass completely upside down to drain the last drop.

'No, she gave me something else. I don't know what it was.'

'Have another drink. You'll be fine.'

'No… I don't feel right. I think I'm going back to my room,' said Joe, grabbing the nearby ledge like a lifeboat.

'The hottest woman I have ever seen is trying to get you high, and you're going back to your room?' Dixon slurred, dissolving into giggles. 'Go and wallow in your own fuck puddle, idiot!'

Joe could no longer hear his words. The sounds in the room merged together, garbled and incoherent. He couldn't see his hand in front of him.

Out of pure instinct, he sat on the floor before he fell, and passed out.

Orientation

Joe was in total darkness, and his surroundings were completely silent. Most disconcertingly of all, he could not determine the position of his body — whether he was standing, sitting or lying. When he thrashed his arms and legs out in front of him, there was no sensation of contact or friction with anything. It was as if he was swimming in air, and in whichever direction he tried to move, the darkness stretched out infinitely before his eyes. All of his senses betrayed him; the place could be neither seen, heard, tasted nor touched.

'Where am I?' he shouted.

'It doesn't matter where you are,' replied a man's calm voice, startling him. 'It's just a place.'

'Who are you?'

'That's unimportant as well. Try to relax.'

The answer was as ludicrous as it was unhelpful. The more he peered into the blackness, the more isolated he felt. The sensation was perversely claustrophobic and agoraphobic at the same time.

'I need to get out of here,' he shouted, his fingers clawing at nothing. 'I can't breathe.' His heart was pounding, and he was terrified that it might stop altogether. Why couldn't he swallow? This seemed an integral part of the breathing process that he had somehow forgotten. How many times did he normally swallow in a minute? It must have been too long since the last. He was going to choke on his own tongue…

'Stay calm,' the voice insisted.

'I can't. Why am I here?' he moaned, feeling giddy. Everything was real and yet unreal at the same time.

'You're here to find something.'

'Find what?'

'I can't tell you,' replied the voice. 'Telling would guarantee failure.'

The notion that he was here for a purpose was calming, and one his anxious mind readily seized upon. In the absence of his normal sensual footholds on reality, he was more than willing to relinquish control. Especially if it allowed him to get out of here.

'What should I do?'

There was no reply, and for a moment he thought he had been left alone, panicking him again.

'I want you to focus on your happiest memory.'

'I'm sorry?'

'Picture your happiest memory.'

It was a ridiculous request, and one almost impossible to consider. He couldn't calm his mind enough to even try. Where was he?

'I can't remember.'

'You need to concentrate.'

'It's difficult!'

'A Christmas party. In your first year of university. A canal path walking home in the early hours of the morning.'

'Yes. Yes, that's it. How do you know about that? Did she tell you?'

'Just picture it. Feel it.'

The blackness before his eyes began to transform, as if it had been cloaking something beneath it the whole time, and it slowly swept away.

He was there again. He could feel the cold air filling his lungs, and the scene was shockingly vivid after the gloom; there was a path frosted in ice, sparkling under the orange street light. It crunched beneath his feet. He was staggering, his arm linked with Rachel's. She was wearing a thick grey coat with a Santa hat, and she was laughing. They were both laughing.

He lost focus and the image began to fade.

'Concentrate!' said the voice.

He tried harder, and saw her face turning to look at him. They had stopped walking. It was impossible to maintain the image, and it faded in and out of view. The effort was too much and he was in darkness again.

'I can't.'

'That's enough for now,' said the voice impatiently.

Chapter Ten

There were only a few seconds of blissful waking disorientation before his consciousness was dragged back to reality. Joe's discomfort was not restricted purely to his thoughts; it was hard to isolate the greatest physical source of pain, but his head felt as though it could burst like a pomegranate, and there was a stabbing pain in his ribcage that bore the hallmark of permanent internal damage. He tried to picture a cross-section of the human torso, running through a list of the candidates potentially needing major surgery or replacement. His liver was the obvious suspect, but he seemed to recall that this was slightly lower in the body. As far as he could remember, the kidneys were further back, but he could not account for the spleen. Yes, the spleen. Perhaps it was just wishful thinking, but spleen damage was the best scenario. He was sure it was a 'nice to have' extra, rather than an essential organ.

Grim reality unveiled itself by degree. He was naked in bed, and his clothes were scattered around the cabin floor. The low rumble of the ship's engines reminded him that he was at sea. He had awoken from an intense dream, but he couldn't remember anything about it. Unfortunately, he was starting to remember snippets of the previous evening too well.

There was a noise from the bathroom, and Marie walked in, wearing one of his T-shirts that barely reached the top of her naked thighs. She sat at the end of the bed and smiled at him. She was even more beautiful than he remembered.

'How are you feeling?'

'Terrible. Did you… stay here?' he asked awkwardly.

'Did I stay here?' she said, laying on the pillow next to him and stroking his head. 'I have never known a man like you. In the bathroom. In the bedroom. In the lounge. All night.' The shock must have been etched all over his face, and she smiled. 'You were sick everywhere.'

'Please don't say another word,' said Joe, pulling the covers over his head.

'I'm joking. Well, you weren't sick in the lounge,' she laughed, pulling the covers back down again. 'Seriously, it's totally my fault. I'm your mentor, and I should have known better. I slept on the couch to make sure that you were okay.'

'I am so very embarrassed. What was that stuff?'

'It was a liqueur. I'd forgotten how strong it is if you haven't had it before. If it's any consolation, they drink it as a rite of passage in some cultures.'

'I'm really sorry. What time is it now?'

'Eleven o'clock.'

'Eleven!' he said, slapping the mattress. 'There was so much I needed to do today.'

'Don't let me hold you up. You seem fine on your own now,' said Marie. He could not help but watch as she walked across the room to collect her clothes, and took them into the bathroom to change.

'Thank you, Marie,' he shouted after her. A few minutes later, she came back out wearing the olive dress he remembered from the night before, collected her handbag, and then waved goodbye, blowing a kiss before she left.

It was difficult to imagine a worse start to his career at Schelldhardt. He had humiliated himself in front of his new employers, and was completely unprepared to start work the following day. There was little time to read the background material for his new role or to explore the ship. Worst of all, he had no idea what had happened to Rachel.

He tried to sit up from the pillow, unable to dwell on the thought for a second, but it felt as though his head had been replaced by a bucket, swilling from side to side. He pulled on his boxer shorts, trying to dismiss the mental image of their undignified removal the night before, and shuffled into the kitchen. Fortunately, the kitchen sink had been spared his midnight redecorating spree, and he found a carton of orange juice in the refrigerator. He drained it noisily, acutely aware of the ship's rocking motion. Should he call Rachel? He was worried what he might discover. As he stared at the phone, it rang. It was Dixon. He had tried to knock on Joe's cabin door twice without getting a reply. He was coming down again.

Joe pulled on a pair of jeans and the T-shirt Marie had been wearing. It smelt of her perfume. He tried to ignore the stained towels lying in the bath, and studied his reflection in the mirror. He had rarely looked so bad; the colour was drained from his cheeks, and his hair was plastered to his head with a selection of fluids that he did not want to investigate further. He quickly cleaned his teeth and shaved the wispy hairs from his chin.

There was a knock at the door, and he opened it to see Dixon, looking equally unwell.

'You look awful. What happened to you?' Dixon asked.

'I was hoping you could tell me.'

Dixon walked into the lounge, scratching his head. 'The last thing I remember was your floor show before you were carried off.'

'Floor show?'

'Yes, you were unconscious, pissing yourself. Strangely beautiful...'

'Please say you're...'

'I'm afraid not. Then the hot mentor came back.'

'Marie.'

'Yes, Marie. She saw the state you were in and ran to find the other guy. They said they would take you to the medical centre and make sure you were okay. To be honest, I was too fucked-up to care by that point.'

Joe slumped into the leather couch with his head in his hands.

'To bring you fully up to date, Ryan spent the night in Chloe's room. He's not a patient man, is he? And I haven't seen Rachel today, before you ask. I woke up on the floor of my cabin, with my forehead balanced on a pint glass of water. Fortunately, it didn't break, so I consider myself the luckiest one of all.'

'I want to die,' moaned Joe.

'That's the spirit,' said Dixon. 'Wanting anything is the first step.'

Rachel phoned him at three, and they agreed to meet for a coffee in the snack bar. He was the first to arrive, and was alarmed to see the size of the queue. They seemed to have picked the busiest time of day. He ordered for both of them, struggling to be heard above the apocalyptic shrieks of milk frothing and clattering plates. His head was pounding.

70

Hell would be quieter. When he collected the drinks, Rachel was standing directly behind him. She was wearing a pair of jeans and a pastel blue jumper. If she was suffering, she hid it well.

'The flat white is for you. No sugar. I hope you don't mind me...'

'It's perfect, thank you.'

They sat at one of the last available tables, and could see the atrium through the glass partition. It was far emptier than it had been the previous day.

'How are you feeling now?' asked Rachel. It was not the question he wanted to hear. Either she had seen his fall from grace, or Dixon had told her about it.

'Better, thank you,' he lied. In reality, he had never experienced a hangover like it, and was mindful that his raw needs were barely concealed beneath the feeblest of guises. He needed to be careful what he said to her. A waitress collected cups from the table next to them, shamelessly staring. Joe smiled and she walked away. They waited a moment, and then spoke at the same time. It was like an awkward first date. Rachel gestured for him to continue.

'I was just going to ask if you enjoyed the party.'

'Yes, it was fantastic. My department sounds interesting. There is so much opportunity here.'

'This is definitely the place to make your mark,' he agreed, certain that he had already made the wrong one. He felt like he was relaying a company press release. She only smiled, and they lapsed into silence again. Every question that sprung to his mind seemed inappropriate, and he lacked the mental dexterity to direct the conversation the way he wanted to. He mutilated a sachet of sugar while he wrestled with his dysfunctional thoughts, eventually scattering the contents all over the table. 'It's a shame we won't be working together, though,' he blurted at last.

'I'm sure we'll be too busy to even think about it,' she replied, wiping sugar away from the table with her hand.

'True,' he laughed. 'We'll just have to make the most of things until lockdown. Do you know when it is?'

'Has no one spoken to you about it?'

'No, why?'

71

'It's today. I thought you knew.' His coffee was not sitting well on his stomach, and for a moment he thought he was going to be sick again.

'Today? How long is it going to last?'

'It varies, but apparently the first stint at sea is usually a long one. That's why so many people are here. Schelldhardt don't approve of company relationships, but they turn a blind eye on lockdown days.' As he looked around the room, he could see that it was true. He hadn't noticed that the snack bar was filled with couples of various ages, sneaking a few final moments together.

'Do you know how long this one will last?'

'Probably a couple of months,' she said, finally looking at him. 'I think we should go soon. We both have a lot to do.'

'We could meet up for a farewell dinner with Dixon and Ryan.'

'I don't think there will be time,' she said, standing up. His desperation must have been all too apparent, and she didn't look him in the eye. He knew that everything she was saying made perfect sense, but he didn't want to leave. 'You'll be fine,' she said, kissing him on the cheek.

Even as she walked away, he couldn't help but wonder if she had other plans.

He woke at two o'clock in the morning, dreaming that the ship was capsizing. His chest was covered in sweat and the bedclothes were scattered on the floor. It had taken him an age to fall asleep, and he was wide awake again. The engines droned in the background, and the ship rocked from side to side more noticeably than it had before. He took a mouthful of water, and fell back onto the pillow. A voice spoke on the communication system, quieter than the announcements during the day. *Ananke* was locking down.

A sudden feeling of panic hit him, and he jumped out of bed. He hadn't said goodbye to Rachel properly. The blood supply to his brain was unable to keep pace with his movement, and he nearly fell to the floor. When he reached the empty corridor, he decided it would be faster to call her, and hurried back into his lounge. The phone seemed to take forever to connect, before an automated message finally played. Lockdown was complete. Her number was unobtainable.

He had never felt so alone in his life.

Episode One: 2002

'What do you want from me?' Joe asked the voice, confused. The darkness that enveloped him had no end, and he could not feel his limbs.

'I want you to find something, but first you need to remember how this all started.'

'How what started?'

'Just concentrate. You are sitting in a classroom. You are ten years old.'

'I can't...'

'Concentrate. It's a rainy day in September, just before lunchtime.'

Even as he tried to fight the memory, the gloom began to distort around him. At first, the change to the darkness was almost imperceptible; shadows, barely distinguishable from their surroundings, stirred in the blackness. Then the world began to colour around him, like a vast canvas waking into life.

The classroom was filled with excited voices. He looked from the elfish face of Michael Abbott sitting next to him, to the crest-fallen teacher, slouched behind her desk. Their regular teacher, Mrs Robinson, was sick, and her substitute had lost control of the class.

'Silence!' she shouted again, only to be met with a chorus of jeers and laughter. She was roughly the same age as his mother, but her odd hairstyle and goofy glasses evoked the mood of another era altogether. They had sensed weakness when she first stepped into the classroom, and she had fatally failed to assert any kind of authority since. He turned to see the animated faces of the children behind him, their eyes alive with the possibilities of what might happen next. 'You will not be going to lunch unless you are quiet,' she cried. There was a momentary lull in their merriment as they assessed the threat, but then the noise rose louder still. She flustered with the papers on her desk, stacking them up, and then putting them down again in an impotent flourish of activity. She was in meltdown. The headmistress had already peered round the door once to check if everything was okay. It wouldn't be good for anybody if it happened again. 'Don't any of you want good jobs when you leave school?' she said at last, exasperated. The remark was obscure, but it momentarily quietened the class.

'I do, Miss,' said Billy Groves, the shaven-headed boy sitting two desks to his right. 'I want to be a solicitor, like my dad.' The laughter subsided. The teacher sensed the change of mood, seizing upon the tenuous connection she had made with her chief tormentor.

'That's an excellent idea. You'll need to work very hard, but well done.' What the praise was for was unclear — perhaps just for buying her some time. 'What does your father do for a living?' she quickly asked Rebecca Partridge, who was twisting her ginger pigtails around her fingers.

'He's a postman, Miss.'

'That must be a lovely job, outside in the fresh air,' she sighed, perhaps wishing she was there herself. 'Would you like to do that when you leave school?' Rebecca nodded enthusiastically, and the teacher smiled as if she had just been presented with a lottery win. 'How about your father?' she asked another, desperate to maintain the momentum. It had little to do with the arithmetic abandoned on the whiteboard, but their screaming voices could no longer be heard from the headmistress's office. Joe slid lower in his chair, praying that she would change the subject, but she was gaining confidence, moving from pupil to pupil with a renewed swagger.

Accountant. Policeman. Shop assistant. Computer programmer. Mechanic.

Strangely, she had no interest in their mothers' careers, possibly too frightened to deviate from her winning formula in any way. He knew what was going to happen, but was powerless to prevent it. The longer he waited for the inevitable, the weaker he felt — his body beginning to shake. He slid down in his chair as low as he could, but could not make himself disappear altogether. His cheeks were already burning in anticipation of the inescapable awkwardness to follow.

'And what does *your* father do?' said the teacher, looking straight at him. He was instantly immobilised, conscious of the other children watching him from the corner of his eye. Despite the anticipation, it was still a shock that the moment had actually arrived, and his mouth was instantly dry.

He said nothing.

'Speak up,' she said, smiling. It was a nervous smile, and he knew that there were only seconds left before it would leave her face. She was as vulnerable as he was, but there was nothing that he could do to save them both. The words would not leave his tongue.

She continued to stare at him in hope. The classroom was stirring again, and he could see the panic in her eyes. She pushed her glasses higher up the bridge of her nose, fiddling with the chain dangling from the frames. He smarted at the injustice of the situation, willing her to recognise his distress, but she didn't flinch.

'Well...?'

Silence.

The pause was embarrassing. Having lost control once, she could not let it happen again. He could only watch her fingers, playing faster and faster with the chain as she waited. He understood her situation completely, but she was totally blind to his. She was the adult, and he was the child: it was not the way their relationship was meant to be. He had lost the power to speak, and his lip was beginning to quiver.

Silence. Fingers moving faster. It felt like an eternity since anyone had spoken. She coughed. A nervous cough. The children around him were starting to chatter again.

'His dad is dead, Miss,' said Michael Abbott, bluntly.

Hearing the words spoken aloud was both crushing, and a release. He could feel the stares of the other children, and could not bring himself to look at the horrified teacher at the front of the class. Tears were forming in his eyes.

'No, he isn't!' he shouted, scrambling from his chair. It was the most ridiculous thing he had ever said. It felt as though he was floating as he rose, so pumped with adrenaline. His legs weren't his own, but they still carried him out of the room before he broke down, slamming the heavy fire door shut behind him. The crash echoed in the silence of the deserted assembly hall.

Sobbing alone, he could hear the gossiping children inside the classroom. He covered his ears, and tried to shut them out. Moments later, someone opened the door behind him, and he turned his head against the wall, hiding his face beneath his arm. The smell of plaster. The reassuring coolness against his forehead. Maybe he could stay there forever. He had no desire to speak to the teacher after her betrayal.

'Joe, it's okay,' said a gentle voice that he didn't recognise at first. He didn't want to turn away from his sanctuary to find out more. 'She's an idiot. She should have known better.'

He tried to speak, but only mumbled between his sobs.

'It was just bad luck,' she added. 'She's just as upset as you are.'

'I don't know what job he did,' he said at last, fighting to release the words. 'My mum never told me.'

He felt an arm around his shoulder, and he looked up, sniffing. It was Rachel Harding, of course. He had always admired her from a distance, but had never found the courage to speak to her. She looked like an angel.

'I'll get your packed lunch and we'll go outside.'

He smiled weakly, wiping away the tears. He didn't want her to take her arm away, but was willing to go anywhere that she wanted to. The further away from the classroom the better.

The bell rang as she returned with their lunches, and they had barely made it to the school exit when the other pupils began streaming past. Some of the children were sniggering behind her back. Encouraging each other, their sniggering turned to laughter, and the laughter turned to chanting.

'Rachel's got a boyfriend. Rachel's got a boyfriend…'

He only watched Rachel, her skinny frame pushing through them all with a look of absolute defiance on her face. He had never seen anything more beautiful in his life, nearly stumbling as they followed the concrete slope that descended from the school entrance to the playground. He steadied himself on the adjacent wall, his eyes still puffy and red from his tears.

'Let's find somewhere quieter,' she smiled, as they reached the bottom, with the other children still bustling past them. As she spoke, one of the older boys knocked her lunch box from her hands, scattering the contents all over the ground. She calmly bent down to pick up an apple, but as she did, the same boy pushed her over, her knees grazing on the tarmac as she fell. She looked up at Joe, trying not to cry, and something inside of him broke.

The capping brick on top of the wall was crumbling, and he instinctively reached out for a loose piece, feeling the rough edges in his hand. The boy was older, and much bigger, but he charged at him all the same.

The attack was a surprise, and the larger boy fell backwards, slapping down hard on the wet playground surface. Before he could gather his bearings, Joe was on top of him, and he smashed the piece of brick into his face with all of his strength. The boy's nose exploded, splattering Joe's white shirt with blood. There was screaming all around him, but he did not stop, bringing the piece of brick down again and again into the boy's face.

It was almost as if he was observing his own actions as an onlooker as the blows rained down. He could still hear the frantic voices and cries around him, but they converged into a single, numbing backdrop. The boy had landed in a puddle, and twisted to break free, but he was trapped beneath his body, squirming in muddy rain water and unable to avoid his fate. Joe wasn't even sure why he was attacking him any more.

The screams began to dissipate as he rested at last, his knees astride his moaning victim. He let the piece of brick fall from his hand, wiping blood from his face, and felt a strange sense of calm before he was pulled away. As he was dragged across the tarmac by two teachers, he stared into the sky, picturing the enigmatic face of his father in his favourite photograph. What was he thinking now?

'That's enough,' said the voice in the darkness. 'I need you to remember this feeling.'

Chapter Eleven

If a thirty-minute introduction could bore him so profoundly, Joe feared for the next forty years of his career. The office was nice enough — modern and open plan — and there was even his own nameplate on the desk. The people were friendly, too, but he was already doubting if audit and compliance was the area for him. William Fowler, one of the men who had interviewed him, introduced himself as his line manager. Joe recognised him instantly when he flashed his memorable teeth.

Fowler's job title was the senior assessor of audit standards, a position Joe could aspire to with fifteen years of hard work. Fowler assessed the junior assessors who set the standards to which the company audited obscure financial services, which were, of course, thin air themselves. He was divorced from the reality of actually making or doing something by at least twenty steps. It seemed inconceivable that a human being could become so abstract; he was the Salvador Dalí of the employment world. Joe was sure that if he blinked, he would disappear.

'We always have bacon sandwiches on lockdown mornings,' Fowler said, leaning back in his chair. 'I think we are satisfying a primeval urge to fatten ourselves up for the isolation.'

'Some of us need it less than others,' said Karen, a rosy-cheeked woman in her forties. She had piercing blue eyes that were softened by the roundness of her face.

'Thank you, Karen. Shall I put you down, Joe? Unless you are a vegetarian, of course,' he added, peering over his glasses accusingly.

Tom was the fourth person in the office, sporting thick grey sideburns and bouffant hair. He appeared oblivious to the march of fashion since the Seventies, evidently never finding a cure for the Saturday Night Fever. They were nice enough people, but a far cry from the glamorous crowd of go-getters that assembled outside Marryfield House. The four of them were isolated in their own room — a security door separating them from the main corridor. Much of the departmental work was paper-based, which struck Joe as odd for such a progressive company. There were vast flow charts documenting company procedures in minute detail, with a multitude of compliance points and regulations that needed to be followed. By the end of the first morning, Joe had been bombarded with so many acronyms and buzzwords that his head was aching. He hadn't enjoyed a decent night's sleep since arriving on the ship, and it was already taking its toll. He made the mistake of asking for a painkiller, not realising it was easier to score heroin than get an aspirin aboard *Ananke*.

By mid-afternoon, he was starting to grasp what was required. His role involved checking and filing reports sent from all over the world to certify that everyone was doing their job in line with the compliance charts. Whether they were actually doing what was written down on the pieces of paper appeared irrelevant; it was just the existence of a paper chain, absolving Schelldhardt of all responsibility, that was key. Once he realised this, he felt simultaneously relieved that he would be able to do the job, and despondent that it was going to be soul-destroying.

'Do you know what Anteros means?' he asked, when they stopped for a tea break. He was surprised he had blurted it out, and the relaxed atmosphere seemed to subtly change. Karen concentrated on stirring her tea, and Tom remembered he had to file an urgent report.

'I haven't come across that name,' said Fowler, cleaning his glasses. 'Where did you hear about it?'

'Someone mentioned it the other day. Maybe I misheard them.'

'Who was that?' said Fowler, still wiping the lens with a cloth.

'I can't remember. Sorry, ignore me.'

'You are suitably ignored,' he grinned.

Joe's second day at work wasn't quite as bad as the first. He arrived earlier than the others, and spent the time familiarising himself with some of the compliance work-flow charts, forcing himself to concentrate, despite another poor night's sleep. He had, again, been plagued by dreams that he could not recall in the morning.

'A little present from the company,' Fowler said, smiling. 'I know all of your own equipment was quarantined, so it may be of use.' It was an electronic tablet, and it had already been pre-loaded with music and films of his choice.

'I was going to ask how the company knew what I would like, but Schelldhardt seem to specialise in that.'

'Indeed, they do. I believe they have even transferred your photographs across as well to help you settle in. I'm afraid you still won't be able to access the Internet, but you will have access to some areas of the company portal on there.'

'The new model has bad reviews,' said Tom, dismissively tossing the manual aside.

'Personally, I don't trust reviews,' grinned Fowler. 'One could be selling the *Mona Lisa* online, and there would be a single star review saying that she isn't smiling properly. Take it with a pinch of salt, Joe.'

Fowler smiled, sitting back in his chair. He remained there for a few moments, watching him, with his arms folded behind his head. His expression was hard to read, and he appeared to be at a loss for what to do next.

'Oh, one thing I forgot to ask you,' he said at last. 'Did you remember where you heard the term "Anteros" from? Such a curious expression.'

It was obviously intended as a flippant remark, but there was a slight wobble in his voice, and his face was slightly flushed.

'No, sorry. Maybe I just imagined it,' smiled Joe. Fowler reciprocated the smile, but seemed to be waiting for him to elaborate. When it became obvious there was nothing else to say, he continued with his work.

Later that day, Joe looked up to see Fowler discussing something with one of the security guards through the glass panel. The conversation was obviously becoming heated. Fowler waved his arms vigorously, his neatly parted hair bouncing on his head. At one point the guard turned to face Joe. He stared for a few seconds, before his mouth turned into a smirk.

The compliance deck was a strange world within a world. There was a gym, a restaurant, a bar and a cinema. He visited the gym after work, pushing himself hard on the treadmill, before torturing himself further on the weight machines. He was out of shape.

The restaurant was apparently smaller than some of the others on the ship, but the head chef was Paris-trained, as Fowler had told him three times in just two days. There was a bar, but it was so bereft of atmosphere that Joe preferred drinking in his room. He had wandered in for a drink on his first night, and quickly learned to avoid the eyes of the handful of drinkers there who were desperate to talk to anybody.

He took a quick shower and changed at the gym, before heading back to his room. He was growing accustomed to the rumble of the ship and its disconcerting rocking as he wandered the corridors. He stopped at the lift. It was part of a fast-developing ritual to try to reach another floor whenever he passed it. Again, he inserted his pass, only to discover that access to the other floors was denied. There were stairs, but these were also electronically locked, and his pass wouldn't open the doors. He walked the length of the compliance deck, looking for points where he could reach an external deck, but again these were locked. In an emergency, access would be given to all floors, but the penalty for misuse was severe. The trigger point was entirely identifiable, and apparently twenty-five employees to date had lost their jobs raising non-emergency alarms. It didn't sound like a good move to push the red button.

His room was in a dimly lit corridor, along with five others in a row. Curiously, he hadn't seen any of the other occupants at any point since he had left Portsmouth. As he passed his neighbour's room, he could hear a voice from within. It sounded vaguely familiar, but he couldn't place from where. It was difficult to make out his words, so he moved closer, putting his ear to the door. The vibration of the ship distorted the sound, and he could only catch odd phrases.

'Is there a problem?' growled a hulking security guard, appearing in the corridor next to him. He slipped backwards in fright. The guard's vast frame obscured what little light there was in the corridor, and he edged forward menacingly.

'No, sorry, I thought it was my room.'

'Your room is next door. I suggest you go there right now. We're watching you very carefully.'

He didn't need to be told twice.

Episode Two: 2009

'I told you to focus,' said the voice in the darkness. 'You are seventeen years old. It's a humid evening in July, and you are waiting outside her house...'

The sensation was bizarre, but the blackness began to form a picture. He was standing beneath a tree, water dripping from its leafy branches. The sky was filled with grey clouds, backlit by the setting sun. It was getting late.

He leant his bike against the tree, and then walked along the street until he reached a chest-high bush lining the grass verge — his favourite spot to watch Rachel's house uninterrupted. She lived in a modest Thirties semi-detached build, indistinguishable from the others in the street to the uninitiated, but it was as familiar to him as his own face. Her bedroom window backed onto the street. The purple curtains were not yet drawn, so she was unlikely to have returned early. The neighbour's tabby cat was sprawled on top of the dustbin in the front garden. It rarely moved from the warmth of the black plastic lid.

He decided to walk the block, trying to kill time until she arrived. A few of the neighbours had seemed suspicious of him loitering in the street earlier in the week, and he didn't like to stay in the same spot for too long. It was a well-trodden route, and he often timed himself as he completed the loop, trying to shave seconds off his best time without breaking into a jog. He pulled a pair of headphones from his pocket, and selected a playlist to accompany the stroll.

On his seventh circuit of the block the playlist was complete, and he was becoming impatient. He hadn't anticipated waiting for so long. She was only meant to be going for a quick drink after work, and it was nearly dark. The street lights were flickering awake. Rachel was halfway through a month of work experience in a local insurance company, and her assistant supervisor, Daniel, was becoming far too familiar with her. He was seven years her senior, and Joe had taken an instant dislike to his brash personality. He wore obscenely expensive designer clothes and glasses, and strutted about with a confidence that belied his position. Initially, things seemed innocent enough: he offered her lifts to and from the office en route from his flat, and arranged social events outside of work to help her settle in. More recently, though, the after-work activities were exclusive to the pair of them. He tried to warn her, but she was naive to his intentions, always believing the best in everybody.

Daniel's car pulled up thirty minutes later, the stereo shattering the peace of the quiet neighbourhood. The headlights illuminated her front garden as the car chugged idly alongside the kerb. The exhaust pipe was wide enough to melt a polar ice cap. Rachel's carbon footprint was so important to her. Surely, she couldn't be impressed? He pushed harder against the prickly bush, straining to get a better view. Across the street, the tabby cat's eyes shone back at him in disapproval, and he wished that they could swap places; it was a far superior vantage point.

They seemed to be talking forever. Daniel was leaning towards her in the passenger seat, and he nearly stumbled as he strained to get a better view. He heard her laugh. Normally, the sound filled him with joy, but today it irritated him. He willed her to leave, but she continued to talk and talk. Daniel had never waited there so long before.

His calves were beginning to cramp, and he was now squashed flat against the sharp needles of the bush — rain water soaking his shirt. He would be seen if he moved too quickly, so he eased himself back onto his heels, his nose dropping just below the top of the foliage. As he adjusted his position, the car engine stopped abruptly, and so did his heart. The street seemed eerily quiet without the dull bass of the stereo throbbing in the darkness. They were *both* getting out of the car.

Rachel giggled, and Daniel guided her towards the front door, skulking behind her as she unlocked it with her key. Joe scurried across the road the moment the front door closed behind them. He drew level with his car, peering through the rear passenger window towards the house. Where were her parents? They weren't normally out on a Thursday. It was impossible to hear anything from his position, and so he crept into her front garden, taking care to stay hidden in the shadows. The tabby cat watched him, ears pricked, but didn't move.

He didn't know what to do. Should he ring the doorbell and pretend he was just passing? Her bedroom light came on, and he pressed himself flat against the front of the house, breathing heavily. He could see her elongated shadow flouncing across the front lawn as she drew the curtains. She must be changing after work.

A few minutes later the light was still on, and now he wasn't sure whether he wanted to see it go off at all. When it felt safe to move, he hurried back onto the grass, looking up at the purple-glowing window, and reassessed his options. If he rang her mobile phone, she would know that it was him calling. Having already made his feelings about Daniel clear, the interruption would probably have little effect. He could climb the gate into the back garden, and create some kind of disturbance there, but it would be difficult to get out again undetected. It was impossible to think rationally, and the longer he waited, the greater his sense of urgency.

He should walk away. It was none of his business.

He took a deep breath, and tried to heed his own advice, but every step he took away from the house felt like it was being taken by another person. All he could picture was Rachel with Daniel in her bedroom. The images played over and over in his mind until he thought he might die. The pain was almost physical.

He turned on his heels, sprinting back towards her house. This time the tabby cat was not so complacent, bolting away as it saw him approaching. As he reached the front garden, the light went out in her bedroom. He needed to act quickly.

There was a rusty watering can abandoned on the lawn. He ripped it from the tendrils of ivy that entangled it, spilling brick-red water over his jeans as he finally yanked it free. The car had an alarm. It was just a matter of setting it off, and running.

He dragged the half-filled watering can into the street, swinging it like a wrecking ball against the driver's window of the car. The trajectory was wrong, and it barely scratched the glass.

Nobody inside the house stirred.

The thought of them together in her bedroom steeled him to try again. This time he held the can flush against his chest, ramming the window with all of his strength. It shattered instantly, with fragments of glass exploding around his face and all over the pavement. The car alarm screamed out in unison, and he dropped the can, sprinting down the street without looking back.

There was a man blocking his path in the middle of the road, roughly twenty feet in front of him, and he slowed to a stop. If he was a neighbour, he didn't recognise him. They faced each other, motionless, like duellists, Joe fighting for his breath. For a moment, neither of them spoke.

'You are crossing a line that should not be crossed,' the man said at last. 'Trust me, I know.' There was shouting behind them further down the street. 'Go now,' he ordered, pointing at Joe's bike beneath the tree.

Joe nodded, grabbing the bike, and raced off into the night.

'That's all you need to remember,' said the voice in the darkness. 'The time has come for you to find it.'

Chapter Twelve
20th June 1993

When you fall, you fall quickly. There is precious little to grab hold of on the way down. That was the way things seemed to Shendi. Sometimes he struggled to piece together the decisions that had led him to this point in time, all seemingly innocuous and quite logical in their own right, but once linked end to end had formed a calamitous path.

He knew it was his last chance to resolve the situation amicably. When the letter from Philip's solicitor arrived at the office, he immediately hid it inside his briefcase. If anyone else in the company knew what was happening, there would be more trouble than Philip could possibly imagine.

He hesitated outside Philip's house, the same three-bedroomed property on the outskirts of Haslemere that he had lived in with Jane since they were first married. Philip had refused to move, despite their new-found wealth as the company had grown, and still took the long commute into their new headquarters on a daily basis. It had rained heavily during the night, but the sun was now burning through the hazy cloud. There were a few people wandering the street to collect their morning newspapers, their voices hushed when they greeted each other. Even the barking of the neighbourhood dogs was subdued, respecting the Sunday morning ambience.

Philip had stopped returning his calls, and so he had been forced to come to the house. This was the only time of the week that Shendi knew he would be at home. It was ridiculous to wait in the street any longer, and so he opened the gate and marched up to the front door, knocking vigorously on the oak panel. He could hear Sonic's squeals from within, and it made him feel even worse. He wondered if they had heard him, and was just about to try again when the door opened. Jane was standing there, bare-footed, wearing jeans and a T-shirt. She wasn't wearing make-up, and there was some of Sonic's breakfast stuck to her shoulder.

Shendi smiled, but her expression instantly changed when she saw him, and he thought that she was going to slam the door in his face.

'Jane, wait.'

'We have nothing to say to you, Arnold.'

'Jane, it is important that I talk to Philip. I know what you must think of me, but this is much more complicated than you realise.'

'He doesn't want to speak to you.'

'He *needs* to speak to me.'

She wavered for a moment, still holding the door ajar between them. He could see the confusion in her eyes, and he wished she hadn't become involved in the whole situation. If only Philip had listened to him…

'Despite what you might think, I have his best interests at heart.' She shook her head and backed further into the hall. 'You have to believe me,' he said, looking deep into her eyes. He could tell that she wanted to. Anything was preferable to her fears.

'Stay here,' she said. 'You can't come into the house.' She closed the door, leaving him standing on the step. A bee buzzed around the sweet-smelling lavender bush bordering the path. He edged away nervously, trying his best to look as inconspicuous as possible on the doorstep. An elderly couple tottered along the street, watching him carefully. He smiled, but they immediately turned away and continued their slow progress along the pavement. The wait seemed like an eternity, and he wondered if it might be a petty act of revenge to leave him standing there.

The door opened again, and Philip appeared in a towelling robe and a pair of moccasin slippers. He looked moderately healthier than when he had last seen him in the office, but there were still dark rings around his eyes.

'What do you want?' he asked bluntly.

'I need to talk to you.'

'My solicitor has advised against that.'

'Philip, there are things you need to know,' he said, edging towards the doorway.

'You're not coming into the house.'

Shendi had no idea what they thought he was going to do inside, but this part at least was clearly non-negotiable. He didn't know what else their solicitor had advised either — or, worse still, what Philip had told them about the situation. His solicitors were a mid-size local firm who would be torn to pieces in court, but they could still cause a huge amount of trouble.

'Fine, but your doorstep isn't the most discrete place to discuss this.' Philip glanced down the street, and at least seemed to agree with him on that point. He disappeared around the door for a second, and then returned with a bunch of keys in his hand.

'The car,' he said, nodding towards the BMW on the drive. Philip unlocked it with the remote, and Shendi followed him across the front garden. They sat next to each other, and for a moment neither said anything, staring out of the windscreen towards the garage. The leather seats were hot, and Philip turned the ignition to lower the windows.

'I should tell you from the outset that I won't be saying anything to incriminate myself,' he said, with his arms defiantly crossed. 'I'm scared you might be bugged, or have spies hiding in the bushes. Who knows what the hell you might do!'

Shendi massaged his eyes, too tired to even dispute the point. It probably explained why they didn't want him in the house.

'What have you told your solicitors?' he said, getting straight to the point.

'I've told them I have been set up.'

Philip sneezed after he spoke. It looked like he was about to add something, but then he sneezed another four times in succession, his eyes streaming. He suffered from hay fever, and Shendi was accustomed to the interruptions. He passed him a packet of tissues from the glove compartment.

'That was a mistake,' Shendi said, once he was sure he had finished.

'My solicitors think that I can avoid prison.'

'You can't. Not within the parameters we are working with.'

'Arnold, I'm not sure if you grasped the essence of our last conversation, but I'm not a willing party to your deal. These are your parameters.'

Shendi gritted his teeth. Philip had no idea how difficult it had been to strike the deal, and how much he had tried to consider him when doing so. He felt like exploding, but knew his best chance to resolve their differences was to speak calmly and logically. He sucked on an indigestion tablet, which slowly began to extinguish the fire beneath his ribs, and carefully considered his words.

'If I could guarantee that you would serve a maximum of three years, probably less, in an open prison, and when you came out, you would never have to worry about money again, how would you feel?'

'It sounds great, apart from the prison part.'

'We're talking about an open prison. These things are practically holiday camps. You might even receive a suspended sentence. Think about it: you would never have to work again. You could run that farm that you and Jane always spoke about.'

'Don't patronise me, Arnold. I understand what prison is. Do you really think I want to be absent for my son's formative years? When he starts school? What about when he learns to ride a bike, or starts to swim? What price can you put on that? I'd rather live in poverty for the rest of my life.'

'I think you are being overdramatic. If we play this well, it could be as little as one year. One year that he won't even remember, and a sacrifice that will set him up financially for the rest of his life.'

'You just don't get it, Arnold,' said Philip, slapping the steering wheel in frustration. 'The world is not all about money. Nothing is worth that to me.'

'There is no choice. We borrowed bad money, Philip. Not recently, but right at the start.'

'You mean *you*.'

'I mean *we*. Your signatures are all over the paperwork.'

'I'm sure they are. I trusted you! You know I always signed whatever you asked me to. You've been fucking me over all these years.'

'I've never asked you to sign anything I wouldn't sign myself.'

'Then remind me again, why am I the one going to prison? I don't believe this,' he said, on the verge of tears. 'This is just a mess. I can't believe this is happening.' Shendi watched him sadly. He could see Philip trying to rationalise the situation, like he had done himself for nights at a time during the last few weeks. 'We have accountants, don't we? They must have given you bad advice. We can blame them.'

'We signed the forms. We own the company. The responsibility is ours. Our accountants have actually helped us to cut a deal with the tax people.'

'They know about this?'

'They know some of it. They know there is more to find, but the investigation will end *if* we make certain financial commitments to pay back the tax and...'

'And throw them a scapegoat.'

'Philip, if it could be me, I would gladly take your place.'

'I'm sorry, why exactly can't it?'

'My connections wouldn't accept it. They will only deal with me.'

'Your connections? Are these the bandits that we borrowed the dirty money from? Are you now Don Shendi or something?'

Shendi tried not to smile, knowing it was inappropriate. He saw a flicker in Philip's eye, that he wanted to smile too. It made him sadder than anything else that had happened.

'You're making a huge mistake. You have no idea what kind of people you are dealing with.'

'If they are acquaintances of yours, I think I do.'

'They are nothing like me! These are ruthless people. Dangerous people. You have no idea.'

'That's your problem.'

'It's your problem, Philip! You have to understand that. I beg you to reconsider.'

A breeze blew through the open car window, and they sat in silence for a moment. Philip rubbed his eyes, the sleeves of his dressing gown falling down his skinny forearms. He looked ridiculous sitting there with his bony knees poking out behind the steering wheel.

'I'll take my chances,' he said at last, reaching for the door handle. Shendi grabbed his shoulder as he moved, and looked deep into his eyes.

'I can't let you do this.'

'Are you threatening me?'

Shendi continued to hold his shoulder and stare at him.

'I can't let you do this,' he repeated slowly. He released Philip's shoulder, before climbing out of the car. He poked his head back inside. 'You have until tomorrow morning to change your mind. Call me at home if you do.'

'I'm sorry about your commitments, Arnold, but I'm not promising you a single thing.'

Shendi walked away down the garden path, and into the awakening street without looking behind him. The sun was shining, and there were children riding their bicycles up and down the pavement. It was all so very familiar, but he knew nothing was ever going to be the same again.

Chapter Thirteen

Joe found it difficult to concentrate on his monotonous job. His mind continually wandered while he ploughed through the pile of paperwork in his pending tray, which filled like a clerical magic porridge pot each day. Fowler was spending less time supervising him, and more time on the telephone, and so he was forced to ask Karen and Tom for help whenever he came across problems. He wasn't sure if it was eye strain from using the computer, but he now suffered from headaches on a daily basis. When he mentioned the problem to Tom, he helpfully told him to stop wanking.

On Friday afternoon, it was unbearably warm in the office, and everyone seemed to be operating at half speed. Joe saw Fowler's head slide off his hand three times in a matter of minutes as he battled to stay awake after lunch. Joe seriously wondered if he could make it to the end of the week. A fly provided the only respite from the tedium when it buzzed into the office just after three, showing flagrant disregard for security protocol.

When he finally left the office, it was a bittersweet feeling. He was relieved to escape the stifling atmosphere, but he also felt empty. He associated Friday nights with drinks at the pub, or parties at the flat, and more than anything else, seeing Rachel. Leaving the office, in fact, constituted a three-minute walk along a couple of corridors to his room, and, luxurious as it was, the suite was beginning to feel like a prison cell.

When he arrived at the gym that evening, it appeared to be closed. There were no lights visible through the glass-panelled door, and the obligatory music channel had been silenced. He pushed the handle, and was relieved to discover that it wasn't locked. Flicking on the light switch, he found the air conditioning controls and randomly punched a few buttons. The unit groaned into action, and it was a relief to stand in the cool air pumping out into the room. He was still aching from his previous gym session, and the running machine was an unwelcome sight.

He sat on a yoga mat instead, and attempted to do some sit-ups. It felt like exercising with appendicitis, and after five minutes of writhing around on the mat, he finally surrendered. He remembered the steam room in the changing area. It was at least something different to break the monotony, and it might also help repair his mangled body.

The changing room was in complete darkness and he fumbled around the tiled wall for the switch. Unsure of steam room etiquette, he took a quick shower, despite there being no one there to care. The shower control required the dexterity of a safe-cracker to establish a temperature that wouldn't freeze or boil him, and it seemed to be a constantly moving target. After exhausting his repertoire of swear words, he gave up the fight, and headed for the steam room, wrapping himself in a white towel.

The steam room was surprisingly easier to operate, and he nestled into the furthest corner, resting his head against the wall that vibrated gently with the ship's engines. After initially worrying that he wouldn't be able to breathe as the room began to fill with steam, he relaxed. Only minutes later he jumped, realising that he was falling asleep, but the womb-like sounds of the ship were just too comforting and he didn't move, allowing the sensation to wash over him, and he remained propped against the vibrating wall.

There was a noise from the gym that awoke him again, but this time he sensed he had been asleep for longer. He was cold, and nearly all of the steam had dissipated in the room. He draped the towel around his shoulders and, as he pushed open the door, he noticed something different about the glass. There was something written in the condensation. Most of the letters had run, but he could just about read it.

What is the path, Anteros?

It occurred to him that the words were written on the inside of the glass. Someone must have been in the room with him.

'Hello?' he shouted, but there was no reply. He pulled the towel closer, tiptoeing across the changing room towards his pile of clothes, and hurriedly pulled them on. Once dressed, he poked his head around the corner of the door into the gym.

The room was empty.

When he eventually left his room for work the following Monday, he hurried past his neighbours' rooms, eager to avoid unwanted attention from any security guards on patrol. His colleagues were already engrossed in their work when he entered the office.

'Is there any way I can get Internet access?' he said, carrying a tray loaded with mugs of coffee to their desks. 'Just for an hour or so.'

Fowler looked up from his screen. 'It is possible, but you have to submit a request to the technology audit department. You would be supervised during the session. I have a form here. Would you like one?'

'Yes, please.'

'May I ask why you need it? I have to give my approval, you see,' he said, grinning. Those wonderful teeth again. Fowler loved moments like these when he was able to flex his limited authority.

'I want to check my bank account,' he lied. 'There seems to be a problem with my wages.'

'Not a problem,' Fowler said, reaching for his drawer. Joe was already wondering whether it was worth the effort of applying for the session. If he was going to be supervised throughout, there was a limit to what he could achieve.

It was amusing when they asked one another how they had spent their weekends, bearing in mind that the same limited options were open to each of them. He wanted to test the water about his experience in the gym, and seized on the opportunity.

'I tried the steam room Friday. Very relaxing.'

'Why do you need a steam room? It's hot enough in this bloody office,' said Tom. He didn't have the appearance of a guilty man.

'They are supposedly very beneficial for your lungs, so I really should find the time to try one,' Fowler said, coughing feebly. Karen didn't bother to comment, though it appeared this was more out of disinterest as she worked on a sudoku puzzle camouflaged in her pile of work.

'He's too busy in the red lounge,' she muttered, when Fowler left to use the bathroom. 'Who knows what they get up to in there.'

'The red lounge?'

'Yes, it's an executive perk. It's where all the high flyers indulge themselves without the other staff seeing them.' It explained why he hadn't seen Fowler around, but it seemed none of them had been near the steam room. He thought of the wide-eyed man he had met in reception on his first day, but had no idea how to find him. The Internet access request form was on his desk, signed by Fowler. If nothing else, he wanted to try to find out what Anteros was. It was the only place he could start.

Calibration

'Why am I here?'

'You're here to find something.'

'Find what?'

'I want you to focus on my words,' said the voice in the darkness, ignoring the question. Joe was unable to pinpoint the source of the sound. It seemed to emanate from every direction. He could feel nothing around him. 'You are standing at the edge of a railway line. The track stretches in both directions. The sun is shining into your eyes.'

The brightness was initially blinding. There was a railway track ahead of him. He could hear birds singing in the trees, and traffic rumbled unseen further away in the distance. The air was thick with diesel fumes, catching at his throat. He stepped forward, kicking away the loose stones beneath his feet, and noticed a fluorescent yellow shape between the tracks. It was a man lying on his side, and he wasn't moving.

He looked in both directions; there were three railway lines snaking into the distance. Two of the tracks were paired together with a mound of gravel separating them from the third, upon which the man was slumped. To his right, a dozen workmen, also in fluorescent jackets, were working on one of the tracks. They were too far away to notice him.

Joe edged out onto the track, giddy with a sense of wrongdoing, and scrambled over the gravel towards the motionless figure. He tugged at the man's shoulder, turning his face towards him. His forehead was caked in blood and dust. The man groaned and opened his eyes when he sensed Joe was kneeling over him.

'Are you okay?' Joe asked.

'Divert the train,' he mumbled, pointing at a lever poking from the ground beside the track. 'Quickly, it's going to hit the men,' he added, his eyes widening with fear.

Joe looked up, and in the distance, he could see a train approaching from the opposite direction. It hadn't been there a moment ago, he was sure of it. The men were still working on the line in the opposite direction, engrossed in their work. One of them had wandered onto the paired track, and was stooped, digging something.

'There's someone on the other track. I'll flag down the driver.'

'He won't see you in time,' moaned the man, before slipping into unconsciousness.

Joe shook his shoulder again, but he rolled lifelessly face down into the gravel.

He stumbled to his feet, cursing. There was nobody else in sight to help him.

Running to face the train, he waved his hands madly above his head, but despite his best efforts, it showed no sign of slowing. Instantly abandoning the plan, he turned towards the workmen instead, shouting and waving to get their attention, but they continued to work on, oblivious to him and the imminent danger. The lone worker on the other track was still digging with his back turned. They simply couldn't hear him. The yellow façade of the train was growing in the distance, far too quickly for him to reach them before it arrived.

Sacrifice one man to save twelve. All you have to do is pull the lever and divert the train.

The voice seemed to fill the air around him. He spun in confusion, but could not determine where it was coming from. The train was still hurtling along the track.

Confused, he screamed at the men as loudly as he could, his voice breaking with the effort, but they continued to dig.

If you do not pull the lever, twelve men will die. This is your responsibility. You must do it now.

Again, the voice came from nowhere, and he stumbled as he turned. The train was flying towards the point where the track branched. There was little time to think of alternatives, and he screamed out again, jumping and waving his arms furiously, but the men's backs were still turned. He kicked at the loose stones by his feet, but nothing he did seemed to attract their attention.

Do it now, or it will be too late.

He yelled again, eyeing the single worker on the other track, who was wearing ear defenders. It was hopeless. Everything was happening too quickly to think clearly. The train would hit the men in seconds.

Act now!

Lunging at the lever, he pulled it back with all of his strength as the train came screaming past. It changed direction at the last moment, hurtling towards the single worker on the track.

He closed his eyes.

Joe was in darkness.

He had no recollection of how he had got there or why he was there, but his heart was racing, and it was difficult to breathe. He had no idea why he felt so anxious.

'Where am I?' he said.

'I want you to picture something for me,' said a voice. 'You are standing at the edge of a railway line. The track stretches in both directions. The sun is shining into your eyes.'

Joe looked down at the injured man with blood caked on his head. He was wearing a police uniform.

'There are prisoners on the track,' groaned the man. 'You need to divert the train.'

As he looked away, he could see the problem. There were three inmates, chained together at the ankle, who were working on the line. A prison officer had wandered away from them, and was standing on the adjacent track, arms folded behind his back, looking in the opposite direction.

'There's someone on the other track,' he shouted, but the injured man had slipped into unconsciousness. If he diverted the train, he could save the three men, but the train would hit the prison officer. They couldn't hear his shouts and there was little time.

Will you save three men instead of one?

The source of the voice was impossible to pinpoint. He turned in every direction, but there was nothing around him. The handle of the lever vibrated in his hand as the train approached, but he couldn't bring himself to pull it.

Why are you hesitating? Is it because he is a prison officer? Is any one life worth three?

He stood, paralysed, with the lever in his hand, the train almost drawing level with his position. His fingers twitched against the metal shaft. There were only seconds left to decide. He shouted out again, but couldn't bring himself to pull it.

Pull the lever to save three men. It must be done now!

He froze.

The train raced past him, a warm gust of air rocking him on his feet as it headed towards the prisoners. It was too late. He removed his hand from the lever and closed his eyes.

Darkness.

There was a group of schoolchildren collecting something in jars on the railway track. On the other track was a solitary woman watching over them. It was such a stupid place to let them play. He could feel the rumble of the train approaching, and was about to pull the lever as the injured man had instructed, when he had the sudden sensation that something was very wrong.

Why are you hesitating? Are you going to let those children die?

He ignored the voice. There was something about the woman that disturbed him. He climbed to his feet, shielding his eyes from the sun to get a better view. She was familiar to him, but it didn't make any sense. He stepped forward, squinting harder to focus on the slight figure standing on the track, trying to absorb every detail of what he was seeing. Her hair was familiar. Her stance was familiar. Everything was familiar.

It was Rachel.

He shouted her name, but she couldn't hear him. The children, possibly fifteen or more of them, were still milling around the track, absorbed in their games. They were no more than five years old.

'Rachel!' he screamed again, so loudly that the words tore at his throat.

Pull the lever now. You must save those children.

He should pull the lever. He knew that he needed to pull the lever, but his hand wouldn't move. The children would die if he didn't act quickly. But if he pulled the lever...

Do it now!

He could not decide to do it. He would not decide to do it.

'This isn't real,' he shouted, as the train thundered closer. 'I don't

99

accept it!'

As he yelled the words, the ground shuddered violently around him, as if he was standing at the epicentre of a powerful earthquake. For a brief moment, everything froze, including the train on the track, and then exploded into the minutest particles of colour.

Darkness.

He had no idea where he was, or why his heart pounded so violently in his chest. The blackness seemed to stretch on forever, and for a moment he thought he was totally alone.

'You are failing,' said a voice somewhere in the gloom. 'You won't find it like this.'

Chapter Fourteen

Joe woke up with a strange sense of sadness and yet another headache. At first, he was convinced that he couldn't remember what Rachel looked like, creating a frightening mental montage of her features that bore no resemblance to her face. Even her voice was hard to imagine, and it scared him that he could forget her so quickly. It felt like an eternity since they had been at the flat together.

He filled a frying pan with eggs and bacon. Even the sizzle of frying food made him nostalgic for his friends. Ryan always cooked a big breakfast at the weekend, affectionately known to them all as the weekly smoke alarm test. He wondered what they were all doing.

His appointment for internet access was at nine o'clock. He waited outside the door of the compliance security office in an uncomfortable wooden chair. He had his banking details with him in case all else failed. It would be good to see that his student loan had been cleared at least.

The security guards on the ship looked like genuinely tough characters. Isolated at sea, there was a necessity to employ real muscle; a stark contrast to the congenial old guys that had patrolled his university, barely offering any kind of crime deterrent. Fowler told him there was quite an armoury on board, and the ship's security staff were more than capable of dealing with trouble until they could dock or external help could fly in. It was almost like living in a military state. The guards seemed to revel in the situation, and kept him waiting outside the office fifteen minutes after his appointment was due to start. He could see that they weren't busy, leaning around in their chairs, laughing about something. Probably him. Despite his annoyance at their tinpot authoritarianism, he was nervous all the same.

'Joseph Massey,' said the shorter of the guards, opening the door.

Joe sat in front of the computer screen with his host's chair directly next to him. The taller guard stood across the room, watching him as though he had been beamed down from a different planet.

'Where's your authorisation form?' said the man, clearly hoping that he had forgotten it. Joe produced the piece of paper from his pocket, and the guard almost snatched it from his hand, sniffing loudly as he read through it. 'Fowler,' he said, looking up at his colleague, 'he's from the red group.' Joe had no idea whether that was a good or bad thing. 'Which websites are you going to use?'

'For this bank,' said Joe, handing him his bank statement. 'Unless I can check the football results while I'm here,' he added, risking a joke.

'Emergencies only,' said the guard sternly. 'I assume the banking requirement *is* an emergency?'

'Yes, absolutely.'

'Do you have an email request form as well?'

'No, I haven't.'

'Then you can't contact the bank.'

'No need. I just need to move some money. For my sick mother.'

He instantly regretted bringing his mother into his lies, and hoped it wouldn't bring her bad luck. The guard nodded towards the keyboard, seemingly satisfied. His colleague had seen enough, and wandered out of the room, leaving them alone. As the door closed behind him, Joe opened the bank website on the screen. The keys clicked loudly as he typed, giving him an idea.

'I need to enter my security details now,' he said. The guard begrudgingly looked away, and as he did, Joe typed the word "Anteros" into the customer identifier box, using the copy key to store the value before over-typing with his correct code immediately afterwards. When the guard turned back again, he was already inside his bank account.

It was exciting to see that the loan had been cleared, but he had something else in mind. 'I won't be long,' he said, clicking on the transfer button. He hesitated for a moment, pretending to read something on the screen. 'Did you say I need a separate form to email the bank?'

'Yes,' said the guard, already enjoying the potential problem.

'Looks like I need one. Do you have a form here?'

'It will need to be re-authorised.'

'I know. I just want to get things moving.'

The guard sighed, as if the request was beyond the realm of all reasonableness, before grunting towards a drawer at the base of the desk.

At that exact moment, Joe flicked to the other open search engine tab, and pasted the word in with one click. An image appeared of a winged cherub with a bow and arrow, similar to the statue of Eros in Piccadilly Circus. Beneath it was the text, "Anteros, the god of requited love. The avenger of unrequited love." There was no time to read anything else, and he clicked the page closed before the guard sat up again with the form in his hand. Joe's bank account details were displayed back on the screen, and he made a point of slowly signing off and closing them, before folding the form into his pocket.

'Make sure you're more organised next time. This is a very busy department,' scowled the guard.

Joe thanked him and left the office, more confused than when he had entered.

He had a light meal in the restaurant, never feeling comfortable eating alone for too long. What he really felt like was a drink. The bar was surprisingly busy when he arrived. The regulars, mostly at the end of their careers, were, as always, slumped in the corners of the room against the flower beds with their drinks. The bonsai trees and clever planting could not deflect from their collective vibe of stagnation. The barman was busy with the party of visitors that had just arrived. They were all on their best behaviour, and their order was a horrifying assortment of soft drinks, half pints and compromises.

It was good to be away from his room. After a few drinks, and glowing with happiness, he noticed that someone was watching him from one of the tables. He didn't stare too long, fearing it was one of the regulars. The merest flicker of acknowledgement could drag him down a cul de sac of conversation with no means of escape for hours. He glanced up from his glass on three occasions, consciously timing a few minutes between each, and the man was watching him every time. He was sitting directly under a light, and it made it difficult to see who he was. When he glanced up the next time, he had gone.

After another drink, he needed the washroom. As he was about to use the urinal, one of the cubicle doors sprang open, and the man who had been watching him stepped out. This time Joe did recognise him; it was the same scarred face that had confronted him in reception when he had first arrived. His hair was shorter than the last time Joe had seen him, but his eyes had the same slightly crazed look. He must have been in his mid-twenties, and had a taut, muscular jaw. He was wearing a dark T-shirt and jeans.

'Sir, I'm sorry to approach you like this, but I need to speak to you,' he said.

'Who are you?' said Joe, backing away. He opted not to take the extended hand. 'Have you been waiting in there for me?'

The man smiled, and slowly shook his head.

'You're good,' he said, wagging his finger. 'That's why you will succeed where I failed.'

'What are you talking about?'

'I need to warn you.'

'Was it you in the steam room?' said Joe, edging towards the door.

'I'm sorry, I didn't have much time. I knew they were coming.'

Joe studied his earnest face, and he wasn't joking. Drunk as he was, he felt uncomfortable trapped in the confined space with him.

'Who was coming? I'd like to help you, but…'

'It will start soon. You know that, don't you?' The man looked at him with real fear in his eyes, and it unnerved him.

'What will start?'

'Everything so far has just been practice. You need to be ready,' he said, his eyes looking towards the door. 'I don't have long. They will know I'm here. I need to meet you one last time to give you something.'

He stared so intensely that Joe was reluctant to deny him. Better to agree and just get out of the room alive.

'Okay.'

'The spa room isn't safe now. Somewhere new. How about your room?'

'No, not my room.'

'The cinema, then. At seven tomorrow.'

'Seven is a little early…'

'It has to be seven! We will only have an hour.'

'Okay, I'll be there.'

'Thank you, sir. You have no idea what an honour it is to serve the prophet Anteros.'

The Lifeboat

The voice dissipated. Darkness coloured.

The lifeboat bucked a wave — swell flooding over the wooden sides and drenching them all within. The freezing water triggered another collective cry of misery. There was no longer any doubt they were sinking; it wouldn't be long.

Joe pulled his sodden clothes tighter to his body, trying to conserve his remaining body heat. The wind howled around them, and the miserable faces of the other passengers stared back at him — pale, drawn and hopeless. In the distance, their ship stood on end, inching downwards into the blackness. The ghostly glow of its extinguishing lights illuminated the night sky.

'We're sinking, Captain. The lifeboat is too full,' said the white-haired man, blinking water away from his eyes. Joe suddenly realised that he was talking to him.

'I know,' Joe replied, as another wave washed over the side of the boat, adding to the pool of freezing seawater that sloshed around their ankles. The thought terrified him.

'You need to do something,' shouted the man against the wind. 'We can't use the oars with this many on board.' He was right; the lifeboat was designed for thirty people and there were far more. Their only chance was to row for land before they sank, but it was impossible in the overcrowded conditions. 'We need to lighten our load,' the man hissed, leaning closer, out of earshot of the others.

'We might be rescued,' Joe said, unwilling to contemplate the implication.

'Not in time. We need to lighten our load now.'

'I can't force people over the side.'

'Then you will be responsible for the deaths of us all,' said the man, as another wave hit the boat hard. 'You are the Captain, and you have the pistol, after all,' he added.

Joe looked down. A gun was laying in his lap, cold and heavy.

It is time to decide. What will you do?

The voice carried on the wind from all directions, and he was certain that he was losing his mind.

'You must save whoever you can,' the man said, shaking him back to his senses. Joe turned to the faces huddled in the darkness. There was a mixture of men, women and children, shivering in misery.

'Help will come.'

'Help won't come in time!' the man insisted. A huge wave pounded the hull, nearly tipping the lifeboat on its side. When the boat steadied, the ship had disappeared from the horizon, and they had taken on more water in the lifeboat. Their faces were illuminated by the ghostly glow from a single lamp in the centre of the craft.

'We should ask for volunteers,' Joe said.

'What if the strongest rowers volunteer?'

Yes, what if the strongest rowers volunteer? What chance will your motley crew have of reaching land?

The voice from nowhere again. The other passengers had become aware of what was happening, and were arguing amongst themselves.

'What about the children?' a woman shouted.

'We save all of the children,' Joe shouted back.

'The children cannot row,' hissed the man beside him. 'You have to consider the majority.' A scuffle broke out in the back of the boat, and they rocked precariously from side to side. 'You need to take control or we will all drown,' said the man, sidling next to him again.

'We should vote.'

'They will never reach agreement.'

Act quickly. You could have a mutiny on your hands. If you do nothing, everyone will die.

'This one!' shouted a woman. 'He's taking the place of five.' Another passenger grabbed the lamp, and it was handed down the boat, until it illuminated the cowering figure of an obese man, spread across the entire back seat of the boat. Each portly leg alone occupied the space of two children.

'No, I can't swim,' he whimpered.

'You don't need to,' the woman sneered.

'We want volunteers!' Joe shouted back at them.

'He's not worth five others,' someone else said. 'He's no good for rowing, either.'

Another wave hit the boat, sending more water over the side, and it instigated a scuffle at the rear of the ship. There was shouting, and the boat rocked precariously.

'Take control,' the man next to him insisted.

A difficult decision is necessary. Doing nothing is not an option.

Joe fired the pistol into the air, and the scuffling stopped. Their faces were turned towards him again.

'If you fight, we'll sink for sure,' he shouted.

'The big one has to go!' the woman shouted. 'Do the right thing.'

All eyes were upon Joe. The boat was already listing low in the water, and the children were crying.

'Over the side,' Joe commanded, pointing the revolver at the quivering figure at the rear of the boat. His eyes were wide with fear in the pale light of the lamp.

'Please, I can't swim,' the man wailed again.

'Over the side,' Joe repeated, his finger on the trigger.

'I won't.'

'Shoot him,' said the man beside him. 'You'll give the children a chance.'

'Shoot him before it's too late!' screamed a woman.

Joe closed his eyes, the gun trembling in his hand. He couldn't look at the wretched face in front of him. His finger rested on the trigger, but he couldn't squeeze it. The waves battered the boat, and he felt the chill of the ocean running down his neck. He opened one eye, and the man hid behind his hands, with the crowd leaning aside to allow him a free shot.

Shoot now. Save the others while you still can.

'We need volunteers,' he said, lowering the gun. His failure immediately sparked uproar in the boat, and it rocked more violently than it had done previously, as fights broke out everywhere. They spun in a wave, and there were bodies thrown all over the boat.

'I volunteer,' shouted a female voice in the midst of the chaos, barely audible at first. Joe stood up, peering into the gloom to find the source. 'I volunteer!' she shouted louder. The fighting began to subside, and the other passengers slowly took their seats again. Eventually, all that could be heard was the roar of the wind, and all faces were turned to the woman in the darkness.

Joe knew the voice. Before the light shone in her face, he knew exactly who he would see. The lamp was handed from person to person until it paused in the middle of the boat, beside a slight figure, huddled against the side. A man held it up to illuminate Rachel's face staring back at him.

You have your volunteer. This is what you wanted. Accept her sacrifice to save the majority.

'No, you will not!' he shouted. 'I don't accept that this is happening!'

A huge wave rumbled across the ocean, towering above the boat. The passengers screamed and pointed as they saw it curling overhead. The wave came crashing down, and the scene obliterated into fragments of colour.

Darkness.

'It won't work if you keep doing this,' said a voice.

Chapter Fifteen
20th June 1993

Arnold Shendi had always wanted his own office. He attached importance to the word from a young age whenever visiting his father's department store. Whether the office was whispered in a revered tone when the staff collected their wages on a Friday afternoon, or in apprehension when they were summoned for pilfering goods or upsetting the customers, he realised its great significance even as a child. In a small town like Swanton, the shop was important, and the office was its command centre. Behind the sturdy walnut desk, which was as old as the building itself, his father sat like a God. He was the only man in town who wore a suit to work, even on Saturdays — a habit which Shendi had adopted as his own.

Now he had his own home office — a spacious and well-equipped working space on the ground floor of their newly acquired country estate. From the window he could see the meadows that sprawled in every direction, dotted with wild flowers, and undulating over the chalk hills beneath the summer sky. It was land that he owned, and there was so much more of it hidden by the contours of the landscape. Horses grazed beyond in the paddocks — animals that he had never taken the time to visit, tended by a local teenage girl who treated them like her own. The meadows bordered woodland that he had never walked in, coppiced by the village tree surgeon whose name he did not know. Moored by the river was a boat named *Catherine* that had never once left the jetty, pretty as a picture beneath a gnarled old oak tree. One day he would be able to enjoy the fruits of his labour, but not yet. He slid open the window, allowing the fresh air to permeate the stale atmosphere of the room, and tried to plan what he should do next. His nightmares had kept him awake all night again, and he shivered as he recalled the place he saw in them, so damp and cold. He could not bear the thought of her there, but the day was far too beautiful to be sullied by his dark thoughts.

There was a knock on the door, and Catherine entered nervously. He felt ashamed when she looked at him that way, but he understood that it was impossible for her to anticipate the state that she would find him in. His recent behaviour had been erratic, to put it mildly, and he had acquired a taste for good port — drinking his way through an entire crate in the last week. He was extremely particular about the vintage, allowing him to gentrify the habit in his own mind. Catherine collected the tray with his half-eaten dinner congealing on the plate, and began to gather the cups and glasses scattered around the room, many abandoned there for days. He picked up two himself, balancing them on the corner of the tray in an effort to show his willingness to co-operate. Today at least. She thanked him, which made him feel worse, and she seemed anxious to leave the room as quickly as she had entered.

'Catherine,' he called after her, 'are you okay?' He had no right to ask, but there was nothing else to say. He couldn't bear it if she disappeared in silence today.

'I'm fine.'

'No, really.'

'It's a beautiful day. I'm glad you opened the window.'

'Please stop for a moment.'

Catherine rested the tray on the top of a filing cabinet, and turned towards him. She had a thin, severe face that looked old before its time, but Shendi had always found her beautiful. Her mother was Italian, and they shared the same stern expression that most people found unwelcoming, but he had grown to love. He couldn't remember the last time he had stopped to look at her like this, and it was almost like observing a stranger in the room.

'I should be asking you the same question,' she said.

'Things have been better.'

'You haven't shaved for days, and you've barely eaten.'

'The advantages of working from home.'

'You haven't been working either, Arnold. Every time I come into this room you are either staring into space, or drinking yourself into oblivion.'

'It's a difficult time.'

'That seems to be your stock answer for everything.'

It was a fair point. He could hardly expect her to open up when he was keeping so much to himself, but it was impossible to let her know what was happening. She wouldn't understand.

'Things will improve soon. I need to get through the next couple of weeks.'

'I hope you know what you are doing.'

'What does that mean?'

'It means exactly that. If you won't tell me what is going on, then I hope that you are in control of the situation.'

'Have you been speaking to Jane?'

'What has Jane got to do with this?'

'It's a simple question.'

'No, I haven't. Why do you ask?'

Shendi breathed deeply. It was unlikely Jane had spoken to her. If she had, then he doubted whether she could have kept it to herself.

'I just wondered, that's all.'

'You're scaring me, Arnold. I've never seen you act like this before. I haven't spoken to Jane since we went to the beach. Are you in some kind of trouble?'

'It's nothing I can't handle.'

'Does it involve Jane?'

'No, I was just making conversation.'

'You never make conversation.'

'Forget I mentioned it.'

'I've told you we can sell this house if that's the...'

'It's not about money!' he shouted, startling her. He instantly felt terrible when he saw that she was beginning to cry.

'Then what is it?' she sobbed. He tried to speak, but it was impossible to construct a meaningful sentence. Words danced before his eyes — taunting him to tame them. Catherine waited, a pained expression etched deep into her face. He had to tell her now, or she may never trust him again. He tried hard to focus, but it was the act of trying itself that distracted him further. He could only watch as she cried harder at his lack of response, before finally leaving the room.

He had to end this today. There was no way they could continue to live like this any longer.

111

His first instinct was to call Philip again. He had hoped that if he bombarded him with enough phone calls, then the reality of the situation would finally hit home. That was their business, after all, wasn't it? Communication. If he couldn't communicate with his own business partner, what hope did they have of spreading their evangelical technology message to the rest of the world?

It had truly meant something to him when they entered into business together. They had been so proud when the first orders were taken. If only they hadn't been so impatient to grow the business. The bank had played a part in their mistakes. The manager, barely out of school, had shown little imagination, and was unwilling to lend the money they needed to expand their operation. Shendi, mortgaged to the hilt, had been forced to look elsewhere, chasing the shadows of business angels and venture capitalists for months, who were more interested in having their egos massaged than helping the business. After a depressing series of breakfast meetings with the local chambers of commerce, he had all but given up hope.

He met Hayward on the train back from one of those futile appointments. It was a chance encounter, and he could sense that someone was looking at his laptop screen as he worked on a spreadsheet. Hayward apologised, and they struck up a conversation. It wasn't until their third meeting, in a bar three weeks later, that Hayward tested the water. He had already hinted that he might be able to raise some capital, and now revealed that he represented interests in Eastern Europe, but wouldn't be any more specific. The structure of the loan was complicated, but it would inject a substantial amount of capital into the business — far more than they hoped to borrow from their bank. Shendi knew full well that they were money laundering, but there wasn't another option. He also knew that Philip would be horrified if he found out, but he needed his signature on the paperwork. He dressed the loan up as venture capital from a city merchant bank, and they celebrated with lobster and champagne the very same evening with their wives.

What he hadn't anticipated was what would happen when the business became successful. They paid back the loan with interest, and he thought that it would be the last they ever saw of Hayward; but then the blackmailing began. Their dubious investors claimed to have spurious rights to the company's intellectual property, and threatened to expose their mutual dealings, unless they made other financial arrangements together. There was so much money passing through the company books that it didn't seem worth taking the risk to challenge them, and Shendi was more interested in growing the business than confronting his corrupt bedfellows. It was a mistake, and as their finances became further intertwined, so their demands increased.

When the company was initially being investigated, Shendi spent a week in a hotel in Calais, thrashing out a deal with Hayward. Hayward made it absolutely clear that if the company failed, there would be repercussions. He hadn't told Philip the whole story, but the essence of it was true. Their accountants could hold off the Revenue if there was a sacrificial lamb and they paid back chunks of tax that they had unwittingly evaded over the years. No one would ever find out about the bad money, and they could all carry on with their lives, including Philip after a brief jail sentence. It was the only way.

Shendi sat back behind his desk, listening to the birds singing in the trees. There was a message flashing on the answer machine that he hadn't noticed. He hit the play button, leaning back in his leather chair.

'Arnold, this is Philip. Do not call this number again. I have told you on numerous occasions that this is now in the hands of my solicitors. I have made my final decision. If you contact me again, I will tell them everything I know. Goodbye.'

He played the message twice more, pinching back the tears in the corner of his eyes. When it finished for the last time, he deleted it. He could no longer fool himself that Philip was going to co-operate. There were two possibilities left open to him. He could let the investigation run its course, and accept that it would incriminate him and that they would lose everything. Hayward would expose him in the process, and the full story would come to light. The implications of that extended far beyond the realms of their business, and it would cause more fallout than Philip could possibly imagine.

The other option was almost too surreal to contemplate. He reached for the briefcase and took out the mobile phone that Hayward had given him when they met in Calais. The number was registered to an address in Paris that could never be linked to his own, and there was only one contact stored on the phone. The quick solution to his problem, Hayward had promised. It was a number he prayed that he would never have to call.

He punished himself by looking at the photograph that stood on the corner of the desk. It was Sonic's christening, with the four of them standing around the baby. Philip had insisted that he become the godfather, despite his protestations. It was a miracle he hadn't been struck down by lightning in the church that day.

He wandered over to the window, watching the sun set lazily over the hillside. It really was a beautiful day. There was a wind chime hanging from the window. Tiny telephones were suspended from the metal strands. Catherine had bought it for him as a gift when they started the business. He normally tied the strands together, irritated by the sound they made when he was working, but he carefully unfastened the ribbon, allowing them to collide in the breeze with a gentle tinkling sound.

The mobile phone weighed heavily in his hand and heart. Perhaps there was a third option after all. Perhaps Hayward could be bought. He looked from the serene beauty of the meadow to the cold, uncaring digits of the handset and knew that he had to decide now.

Chapter Sixteen

Joe arrived at the cinema twenty minutes early. His hair was still dripping from his post-run shower as he strolled around the foyer, trying to spot the peculiar face of his stalker. There were half a dozen people waiting for the film — a re-screening of *Apocalypse Now* — but none of them looked familiar. He grabbed a coffee and picked up a copy of a movie magazine from the dispenser by the entrance. Flicking through the pages, he loitered by the door so that he could see any late arrivals from either direction. The other cinema-goers began to file through the door at five to seven, and he regretted not pinning the arrangement down further. Were they supposed to meet inside? He stayed there until five past seven, and then decided he could wait outside no longer.

He wandered into the auditorium, which was already darkened to screen the pre-film trailers. Standing at the back of the room, he counted the heads of the people in front of him. There were six — the same number that had been queuing outside. He wasn't sure what to do next. Should he try the washroom? It wasn't an appealing option after his last experience. He decided to sit in the back row, as close to the entrance as he could, and wait. He didn't even know why he had come.

The film had already started when he heard the door open behind him and sensed movement. He tensed, half-expecting a knife to cut his throat, but instead felt a hand on his shoulder as someone sat next to him.

'I knew you'd be here,' the man said, unsuccessfully trying to whisper above the sound of helicopters and explosions on screen. It was more than Joe knew himself.

'I didn't think you were coming.'

'It was difficult for me to get away. I know the patterns, but I don't have long.'

Joe waited for an explanation, but the man was silent, watching the film. His eyes appeared even more crazed as they reflected the violence on screen.

'Who are you?'

'Sandbox,' he said, still staring forward. Joe wasn't sure if he had heard him correctly.

'What do you want from me?'

'What do I want from you?' Sandbox said, laughing. It amused him so much that he laughed again, shaking his head. 'I want you to succeed. I know you can find it.'

'Find what?'

'The path, of course.'

'What's the path?'

'Telling would guarantee failure. You know that already, surely?'

Joe hadn't dealt with anyone with real problems like this before, and he wasn't sure of the best approach. Should he play along at the risk of encouraging him, or should he be straight with him? It would be better to leave the man's welfare to trained therapists.

'You said that you wanted to give me something?'

'I'm tired,' Sandbox said, ignoring him. 'Do you have headaches?'

'Yes…'

'They come to my room every night now. Like they do to you.'

'Who comes?'

Sandbox was staring blankly into space, and he wasn't sure if he had heard him.

'I only want to please them, but I don't know what they want. It's so difficult…' he said, mesmerised by the film again. In the half-light of the cinema, his eyes looked wilder and whiter. 'I want you to tell me what to do. I don't care what it is, I'm just tired of trying to get things right.'

'What things?'

'Everything. I don't want to fail.'

'Fail what? I can't tell you what to do.'

'It's too late for me anyway,' Sandbox sighed, slumping in his seat. 'I'm finished once they realise what has happened today. But you can still succeed.'

They sat in silence for several minutes, staring at the screen. Joe couldn't concentrate on the film, and he suspected Sandbox wasn't watching it, either. He was breathing heavily, and Joe wondered if he had fallen asleep with his eyes open.

'Do you have dreams?' Sandbox asked at last.

'Everybody has dreams.'

'Do you remember them?'

Again, the question disturbed him. Joe had woken from nightmares many times in recent nights, but couldn't recall any of them. An explosion on screen startled him as he was about to reply. He turned to Sandbox, who was becoming more and more withdrawn. He was muttering something under his breath, but Joe couldn't make out what he was saying. He gently shook his shoulder. There was a flicker of recognition in his eyes, and he smiled.

'They know what you are thinking. You can't hide anything from them; you know that, don't you?'

'Who are you talking about?'

'Take this,' Sandbox said, passing him a carrier bag. Joe removed the book from within. It was some kind of new-age spiritual guide. 'Call upon this in your hour of need,' he said. 'This is how I found out about them.' Sandbox looked at him so intensely that he couldn't decline the gift. 'I'm sorry, I can't tell you any more. You'll know why soon.'

'Thank you,' Joe said, not wishing to offend him. Sandbox seemed pleased he had taken it, and was silent again for a moment. He appeared to be looking straight through him. Another on-screen explosion startled him back to his senses.

'Don't tell anybody about this. Anybody,' he repeated. 'I have more things in my room, but I couldn't bring them with me. It was too risky.'

'Okay,' Joe replied, without the slightest intention of investigating further. He was relieved if this was to be their last meeting.

'You'll have to collect it quickly,' Sandbox said, looking around him. 'They will know about this soon.'

'Where is your room?' he asked. Sandbox didn't respond, and appeared to be in a trance again. There was a smile on his face, as if he was thinking of something completely different. 'Where is your room?' Joe repeated. Sandbox stared into space, and started to move his mouth, though, at first, no sound was made.

'It's next door to yours,' he said at last.

Joe was woken by shouting in the middle of the night. The room was dark — the only faint illumination provided by the alarm clock on the bedside table beside him. The men's voices were so loud that he initially thought they were in his room, and he cowered beneath the bedclothes, terrified to look up. After a few more seconds, he realised that the sound was actually coming from the adjoining cabin. He could hear two people arguing, and one of them sounded familiar. It was Sandbox.

He crept across the room, pressing his ear against the plastic wall that separated their two cabins. It was difficult to hear what they were saying, and the ship's engines vibrated loudly within the cavity of the wall. Sandbox was clearly in distress, whatever was happening. He slowly pulled on a pair of jeans, taking care not to trip over the pile of books by his feet. Sandbox shouted for them to take their hands off him. Joe slid down the wall into a more comfortable position to listen further.

The voices were quieter now, but there was more activity. Something heavy thumped on the floor, the vibrations carrying through into his own cabin. There was the sound of rummaging, but no one spoke for a moment.

'Anteros!' Sandbox shouted.

Did the guards know who he was calling? Joe slumped sideways in surprise, stumbling over the books by his feet. He hit a nearby cupboard as he toppled, knocking over a lamp on top of it in a catastrophic chain reaction. Meteorites hitting the earth had made less sound. Not content with smashing onto its side, the lamp proceeded to roll around the desk in a grinding circle as he watched, frozen in fear.

The room next door was suddenly silent — more terrifying than the sound of the previous shouting. He heard footsteps pounding across the floor, and then a door opened. Joe crept quickly towards his own bedroom door, where he could see through into the lounge.

There was a narrow crack of light beneath the cabin door shining through from the corridor. He watched it carefully, his eyes struggling to adjust to the brightness.

A noise outside.

At first, he wasn't sure if he had imagined it, but then the light under his cabin door darkened with shadow. He felt the hairs on his arms and neck stand on end, and he froze, unable to advance or retreat.

'They're coming for you!' shouted Sandbox, before he was abruptly silent.

Joe remained completely still. He was conscious of the sound of his own breathing. The door was darkened for another full minute, but then the light beneath returned to its full grinning width.

Everything was silent.

After a further twenty minutes of waiting motionless by the door, he slumped back on the bed, running through all the possibilities of what had happened. He didn't sleep for hours.

He struggled to wake up the next morning, but when he did his overwhelming emotion was guilt. He had hoped the whole episode was just a bad dream, but the upturned lamp in the corner of the room suggested otherwise, as did the concertina of textbooks fanned out on the carpet. In the cold light of the day, his failure to act was shameful. What had he expected to happen if he had opened the door and intervened? Everything had seemed sinister in the darkness, and he had taken leave of his senses. He had stood by and allowed a man with mental issues to be dragged from his bed in the middle of the night.

As he was about to leave for work, he noticed something on the lounge carpet. It was a thin plastic tube with a white stopper that resembled a perfume sample. The tube was empty, and when he wafted it under his nose there was a faintly sweet odour. He had no idea how it had got there. He hesitated outside Sandbox's door as he left his cabin. There was no sign of anything untoward. He didn't know what he expected to see. A bloody handprint on the wall, maybe a pile of broken teeth by the door? It was ridiculous. He knocked lightly at the door — certainly not loud enough to draw anyone's attention. Unsurprisingly, there was no reply, and having made the token effort, he continued to work. He would phone the security department later to put his mind at rest.

When he arrived in the office, everything was reassuringly normal. Thankfully, no masked assassins were waiting behind the photocopier. Fowler's waffling voice had never sounded so good. He decided to delay the phone call to security and get as much work completed as he could first. He wasn't comfortable discussing the matter with the others, partly because of Sandbox's insistence on secrecy, but mainly because of his shame at not helping him.

He was given a new batch of forms to check from one of the branch offices in London. They were piled high, and it would take all of his powers of concentration to complete the task. However, trying not to think about Sandbox quickly developed into a state of only thinking about Sandbox. As he attempted to follow the compliance charts, he could vividly recall the shouts from his cabin the night before.

He put the forms to one side mid-morning, and decided it was a good opportunity to phone security. The telephone rang for so long that he nearly hung up. Eventually, a gruff male voice answered.

'Yes?'

'Oh, hello. My name is Joe Massey. I'm calling about a disturbance in the cabin next to me last night. Room number 425.'

'What kind of disturbance?'

'I'm not really sure. I heard an argument and then there was some scuffling.'

'Scuffling?'

'Yes, fighting, I think.'

'What time did this occur?'

'I'm not sure. Around one or two o'clock.'

'Did you report this at the time?'

'No, I didn't.'

'I see. Hold the line.'

Joe's shame was now public. The hold music started to play — an awful guitar track that sounded as though it should be playing in a euthanasia clinic. Why hadn't he reported the incident at the time?

'Hello?'

'Yes.'

'There were no reported incidents last night.'

'Are you sure? I assumed security had been called.'

'Not if you didn't call them.'

'Can you check if the occupant is okay?'

There was a pause on the line, and Joe began to think they had hung up.

'There is no occupant.'

'What do you mean?

'Room 425 has been empty for the last year.'

Phobia

'Focus,' said the voice in the darkness. 'You are sitting on a beach, facing the sea…'

As the blackness transformed around him, Joe could feel the wind whipping across the sand. Rays of sunshine filtered through the clouds, casting gangly shadows along the length of the shingle-covered beach. It was a place he somehow knew, but he couldn't recall being there before.

'I said, do you want a beer?' asked the bemused young man sitting next to him. He was wearing a wetsuit, with an expensive-looking camera dangling from his neck. There was a can of lager in his hand that he waved like a friendly glove puppet.

'Yes, sorry,' laughed Joe. 'I was miles away.' Dixon shook his head, exasperated, and passed him the can. Joe pulled back the ring, ducking to meet the frothing beer.

'I'm going to get some close-up shots,' Dixon said, clambering to his feet. He picked up a pair of fins from the sand, and limped through a patch of stones that separated them from the water.

Joe was taken aback when he looked up; there were seals and sea lions all the way along the shore, some playing in the breaking waves, some basking at the edge of the water. They were a variety of sizes and colours: a subtle spectrum of browns, greys and black. Their sleek bodies, powdered by sand, slipped effortlessly in and out of the waves — their grace in the water as pronounced as their clumsy blundering along the sand. As beautiful as the sight was, there was something that instantly disturbed Joe about it. His arms were covered in goose-pimples, though it wasn't the chill of the breeze that was the cause: he knew this place, and he knew that he didn't want to be here.

It was an irrational feeling. There was no one else on the beach. Dixon was crouched near the water's edge, his camera held in front of him in an exaggerated artistic pose. Everything was perfectly normal.

'*The peninsula Valdés is a unique nature reserve,*' said an unseen voice. Joe froze when he heard the words in the air — the familiar American accent, triggering fear deep in his subconscious. '*This sparse landscape is situated in the Argentinian province of Chubut on the Atlantic coast,*' the man continued.

Joe knew his voice, but he associated it with something else; it belonged to this beach, but in a different way that he couldn't quite recall. Something from his childhood. Something he had forgotten about. Had he imagined the words? There was no one else in sight for miles around them.

He hobbled barefooted towards the water, feeling every stone and shell underfoot. The hoarse barking of a sea lion stopped him in his tracks a few feet short of the water's edge.

'I think we should go,' he said to Dixon, who was further advanced, still taking photographs.

'Are you crazy? I've been waiting all day for this light. It's perfect now,' Dixon replied, not stopping to turn around. He continued photographing in his affected pose.

Joe stood by the water's edge, hugging himself. It was incredible how much colder it was just these few feet nearer the sea. He wanted them both to leave. Something was wrong.

'I've got a bad feeling.'

'About what?' Dixon laughed, still crouched.

'I don't know. Déjà vu. Something isn't right.'

'How can you have déjà vu when you haven't been here before?' Dixon replied, still snapping at his camera. It was a fair point, but there was something so familiar about the scene that he couldn't explain.

'*The peninsula Valdés is of particular interest because of the diversity of marine animals that frequent its waters; a variety of different seals can be found along the coastline, as well as dolphins, and additionally, southern right whales in the Golfo Nuevo. But it is the behaviour of one particular marine mammal that commands the greatest attention here,*' said the American voice, again from nowhere.

'Did you hear that?' said Joe.

'Hear what?' laughed Dixon.

'The voice,' Joe replied. But even as he spoke, something was changing. Dixon and the landscape were slipping out of focus, as though

122

there was static interference in the air, like old film footage. It was as if he was watching the scene on television, only he was immersed in the programme in some way. He could hear music. Background music that he remembered from his childhood nightmares.

'I can't get the shots I want,' said Dixon, pulling on his fins at the water's edge. 'I'm going to get closer to them.'

'I don't think that's a good idea.'

'I'm only going as far as the water's edge,' Dixon said, pulling the rubber hood of his wet suit over his head. 'Please don't project your irrational swimming phobia on to me.' He turned onto his stomach in the surf, waving the fins on his feet behind him. 'If one wants to photograph seals, one has to become more seal,' he laughed, before barking and clapping his hands together in front of the dangling camera.

'Don't do that!' Joe shouted, stepping as close as he dared. Dixon only barked more in response.

'*Two males taught the population this unique trick, and the knowledge has been transferred from generation to generation by these very intelligent, social mammals,*' said the American's voice. Joe recognised the words verbatim, and shook with fear.

'Get out!' he shouted at Dixon, who continued to wiggle his flippers in the air.

He was beginning to remember. A wildlife documentary when he was a young child. The voice of the narrator, the aspect of the beach, it was all the same, and it had stayed with him forever.

Joe could picture the scene before it happened. A large wave came rolling into the shore behind Dixon, exactly as he recalled it. As it rose to its greatest height before breaking, Joe could see a dark shape within it that chilled his blood. It seemed impossible that something so large could be so close to the shore, yet its arrival was inevitable.

'Get out now!' he screamed at Dixon, who turned at that exact moment to follow his terrified stare. The huge black and white head of the orca was now visible, larger than in his worst nightmares. The dorsal fin stood like a mast above the wave, as the whale launched itself towards the shoreline where Dixon was lying. The wave parted around the orca until its entire body was visible, beached in the shallows. The seals scattered in different directions, but Dixon couldn't scramble to his feet quickly enough, and the whale's jaws closed around his legs, shaking him from side to side, before throwing him into the surf directly in front of Joe.

'Help me!' Dixon screamed, extending his arm towards Joe, only a few feet away from where he stood. All he had to do was step forward into the water and pull him to safety, but he was frozen with fear. 'Please!' screamed Dixon, stretching his fingers towards him.

The whale wriggled on the shingle to adjust its position and turn towards them. It was so close, and so terrifyingly huge. He watched, petrified by fear, unable to step forwards or backwards. He *wanted* to save him, but he couldn't move.

'Don't worry,' said a familiar voice next to him.

Joe's mother was standing beside him on the sand. She crouched and put her arm around his tiny shoulder. He was crying.

'Can they come all the way up the beach, Mummy?'

'No, darling. And they only eat seals,' she smiled.

'Help me!' Dixon screamed, thrashing about in a crimson foam. Joe stood, watching helplessly, and in an instant the orca had Dixon between its jaws again, dragging him out to sea.

'I'm never going to swim, Mummy,' he said.

Joe was in darkness.

He had no memory of where he was or why he was there, but he was shaking violently.

'What am I doing here?' he said.

'I want you to picture something for me,' said a voice. 'You are sitting on a beach, facing the sea.'

Rachel was pinned beneath him in the sand. His shoulders heaved uncontrollably as he held her tightly, his face pressed against her wetsuit.

'What's wrong?' she said. 'You'll break the camera.'

'No more photographs. Not today,' he panted, as familiar music filled the air around him. 'We're going home.'

Darkness.

'We have a problem,' said the voice. 'I cannot allow this to happen again.'

Chapter Seventeen

Joe assumed there was trouble when Fowler called his room. He wanted to discuss something in private with him that evening. If it was regarding anything remotely work-related, he surely would have spoken about it in the office; but the fact that the consummate clock-watcher was giving up his own time to talk to him was unprecedented. Fowler arranged to meet him in the restaurant, which was also unusual, as he preferred to dine privately in the red lounge. It was all totally out of character, and Joe made an instant connection to Sandbox's disappearance.

The restaurant was far busier at nine o'clock, and nearly every table was occupied. He had arrived fifteen minutes earlier than Fowler's booking, trying to rehearse what he was going to say at the table, but it was difficult to know exactly what was going to arise. Maybe he should have reported the previous night's disturbance at the time, but surely the omission wasn't actually an offence? A more sinister possibility was a company cover-up. Perhaps security had indeed been too robust in their actions, and Fowler was going to warn him off delving any further into the matter. He wouldn't need to persuade too hard; Joe had too much to lose, and in all honesty, it was a relief that Sandbox wasn't still at large. It particularly bothered him why he had been in the adjacent unoccupied cabin at all. Perhaps he had been closer to disaster than he had even imagined, and it was better not to know.

Fowler arrived sporting a particularly horrific combination of shirt and trousers. His brick-red corduroy trousers, sitting a good four inches too high on his waist, met the lilac stripes of his shirt in a no man's land of colour. Even his smart blazer couldn't broker a deal between them, and the outfit was a mess. He smiled awkwardly, before joining him at the table, and for a moment neither of them knew what to say to each other.

'Have you ordered any drinks?' Fowler grinned. There were no clues from his expression; he grinned that same way whether he was commending or condemning.

'No, I was waiting for you to arrive.'

'I don't think it will hurt as we are celebrating, do you?'

'Celebrating?'

'I might be getting ahead of myself, but we'll see,' Fowler said, lounging back in his chair. He was talking in riddles, but it was a huge relief, regardless. A wine waiter appeared at their table — yet another benefit of the restaurant's later sitting.

'Can I see the *other* list, please,' said Fowler, flashing his security pass. As the waiter walked away, he leant forward again. 'The director's cut, as I like to call it,' he winked at Joe. Again, Fowler sat silently grinning at him, and Joe felt awkward. Fowler often appeared as if he was trying to convey a thought that he couldn't quite articulate, and hoped that if he stared long enough it would become clear. Joe sat patiently waiting for him to speak. The woman on the table next to them laughed raucously, clapping her hands together in appreciation of a colleague's joke, and it jerked Fowler back to his senses. Joe could almost see the cogs whirring as he retraced his mental footsteps.

'Yes, the reason I wanted to talk to you tonight was to discuss your position. It's a little too delicate for the office,' he said, sniffing officiously. 'You've made a good impression in the department, and your performance has drawn attention from other areas of the company.' Fowler poured water into their glasses, smiling. 'Do you remember Martin Knight?'

The name was vaguely familiar, but Joe couldn't place it. He shook his head.

'He was the other man who interviewed you at Marryfield House.'

'Oh, Mr Knight, yes,' said Joe. Hairy wrists. Arrogantly bored expression. He hadn't liked Knight at all, and the feeling seemed mutual.

'He wants you to transfer to a new position. It would be a significant promotion. Of course, I would be very sorry to lose you from my team, but it would be an excellent career move, and I wouldn't stand in your way.'

'This is very sudden.'

'Perhaps more sudden than you realise. He is looking to fill the role immediately, so if this were to happen, it would happen very quickly.

Naturally, there is no obligation, but I think you'll be interested when you know more about the role,' said Fowler, twirling his water glass. 'You would join the company higher executive scheme. I can't stress enough how difficult it is to become part of this programme. Knight is trying to build a team, with one of these executives operating in every area. He would like you to represent the compliance department. You would remain on our deck, but in your own office, I would imagine.'

'What about Tom and Karen? They've been here for years.'

'That is exactly why it was difficult to discuss this in the office. It's an awkward situation, but you have to think of yourself.'

The wine arrived before he could reply, giving him more time to consider his words carefully. Fowler tasted it with the ceremony of a ship launching.

'Excellent,' he said to the waiter, smiling. The waiter poured them each a glass.

'I'm flattered, of course…' said Joe, unwilling to wait for Fowler to pick up from the latest distraction. Fowler smiled, leaning closer again.

'Don't look so worried, Joseph,' he interrupted, luxuriating with the wine glass in his hand. 'Nobody ever feels ready for more responsibility. It's just something you deal with at the time. This role would command a salary double your current one.'

This was a real surprise; Schelldhardt already offered a generous package to their graduates, and anything even remotely close to double the amount would be a higher salary than most people retired on. He could help his mother get back on her feet.

'It sounds too good to be true.'

'And an executive position would come complete with access to the red lounge. It's quite a nice perk,' Fowler said, with a wine-stained grin. 'There might also be opportunities to move around the ship. Maybe see your friends in other departments occasionally.'

This was the one thing that he couldn't refuse. Fowler was watching him, and he sensed that he knew as much.

'How would I apply?'

Fowler grinned and topped up their glasses.

Things progressed rapidly as Fowler had promised, and three days after their meal together, Joe moved into his new office. Knight's people dealt with the logistics, and the transition was seamless. His office, previously belonging to one of the chief auditors, was awkwardly situated only four doors away from the main compliance department. The room was large and luxurious. Joe knew how valuable space was on the ship and at least three other people could have shared the room comfortably. He spread his things out to occupy it as best he could, hanging his jacket on a chair near the door, with his folders and charts piled at the opposite end of the office, near a selection of exotic potted plants. He sat somewhere in between them in a deep leather chair with enough levers to position each of his vertebrae individually. Fowler poked his head around the open door, knocking ironically.

'I just wanted to wish you good luck. Two pieces of advice from my many years in management — look busy and deny everything.' He grinned, then disappeared.

There was a training schedule on his desk. He had been booked on a series of courses commencing that afternoon. Hopefully, his new role would become clearer as time progressed. He bluffed his way through to lunchtime, organising everything in his drawers twice, before jotting down some notes from the training schedule. As he was writing, he sensed there was someone else standing in the doorway, and looked up to see Martin Knight. He recognised him instantly from the interview, but there was something different about him that he couldn't fathom at first. He was smiling… or at least trying to.

'I hope you've settled in.'

'Yes, thank you. I'm still finding my feet with the work.'

'That's understandable. It will take time. We are hoping for good things from you.'

'I'll do my best.'

'I'm sure you will. Which reminds me, I have something I'd like you to deal with,' he said, reaching for a sheet of paper from a folder. Joe tried not to panic as he was handed the form. Was his incompetence going to be unearthed immediately? 'As part of our ongoing commitment to good causes, we are introducing a new charity payroll giving scheme. Employee charitable donations will be made at source, before tax is deducted from salary. Do you think that's a good idea?'

'I think that's an excellent idea. We're all well paid, after all.'

'I'm glad you agree,' Knight said, pulling up a chair. 'What do you think would be a fair individual percentage contribution?'

'I don't think I'm the best person to ask,' he laughed. Knight smiled, but it appeared that he actually expected an answer.

'Well, would you agree that one hundred percent of one's salary is too much?'

'Of course...'

'And zero percent is a little mean?'

'Yes, it is...'

'So you acknowledge that there is a number, somewhere between the two, that would be perfect. Perhaps four percent?'

'Four percent sounds reasonable, yes.'

'Don't agree so readily,' he said, sliding nearer. Joe could smell his sour breath. 'Are you sure three percent would not be better, or even twenty? It's important to get this right, Joseph. We will be implementing this initiative globally.'

'I don't think I'm qualified to say.'

Knight nodded, watching him from his chair. There was something unsettlingly familiar about his line of questioning, but he didn't know why.

'These are exactly the kind of decisions our higher executive team need to make. You are part of that team now. Please think about it carefully,' he said, climbing to his feet.

'Yes, of course.'

'Sleeping on it may help,' he smiled. There was an odd expression on his face. He was gone before Joe could ask any more questions.

In the afternoon, he attended the first course in one of the conference rooms on the compliance deck. There were three other attendees — two women and another man, all roughly the same age as him, though their age seemed to be the only thing that they had in common. Each of the others had an Ivy League or Oxbridge education behind them. Not only were they better educated, but most of them had successfully run their own businesses, or achieved astronomical success in other areas of their personal lives. They wore similarly intense expressions, each appearing as though they had spent far too much of their lives in front of screens and books on summer days. He was embarrassed to introduce himself, and mumbled through his own meagre achievements as quickly as he could.

The course was run by one of the senior executives, Nathan Williams. Williams was mid-fifties, and had a calm and reflective demeanour. He was tall and slim, with a bronzed complexion, and his hair was neatly parted in a slick, silver wave. Dressed in a navy blazer and chinos, he could easily pass as a local councillor.

'Congratulations on reaching the pinnacle of corporate life,' he said, standing beside a vast digital screen at the front of the room. 'You are now members of the Schelldhardt higher executive team. As of this month, Schelldhardt officially became the largest company on the planet, which makes your roles even more significant. You will truly be changing the world in the course of your work.'

He paused, and the over-enthusiastic man beside him began to clap, before stopping, embarrassed. Williams waited, biting his lower lip.

'Now that might sound like pure hyperbole, but the decisions made by this team will have a profound effect on the global economy and wider world around us. We are entering a new period of human history, where commerce influences the direction of mankind's development like never before. Big business knows no geographical boundaries and it transcends race, religion and nationality. Companies like our own are now, without doubt, becoming the most important players on the world stage. If corporations are the new super-continents, then CEOs are the new world leaders. In time, presidents, prime ministers and monarchs may be considered as ceremonially insignificant as a town mayor,' he said, clearing his throat. 'Should we fear this new age? I say, "no",' he snapped, waving his finger at an imaginary dissenter. 'As you are aware, at Schelldhardt we pride ourselves on our commitment to improving the world in the course of our business activities. Our mission is today, and always will be, business for good.' He paused, pressing a button on his hand controller, and the familiar slogan, "Business for good" appeared on the screen. Joe glanced around the room at the other faces glowing in captivation.

'Maintaining our position as the foremost company in the world is an ever-evolving challenge. In order to facilitate our good work and perpetuate our mission, sometimes difficult decisions need to be made. As a member of the Schelldhardt higher executive team, your absolute focus must always be on company growth. Growth maintains our advantage over our competitors. Growth attracts the investment we need to thrive. Growth allows us to remain global agents of goodness.' He paused to show an unnecessary slide with the words "Growth is everything" on it.

Joe was feeling tired. His lack of sleep was beginning to tell, and the rhythmic resonance of Williams's voice was too comforting. Williams went on to explain in minute detail how growth had been achieved over the previous five years, preaching his message with evangelical zeal. The facts and figures were supported by dazzling graphics on the screen, and the bombardment was relentless. Joe wasn't the only one who appeared to be flagging under the onslaught, and even the most industrious note-takers were beginning to look jaded.

'And now we come to the real reason that you are in the room today,' Williams said, freezing in mid-sentence. He remained there, motionless beside the screen, watching them. 'I must emphasise that what you are about to see is highly sensitive, and completely confidential. While you may find this news unsettling, please take comfort from the fact that some of the greatest minds in the company are already tackling this problem, and I know that you will be able to further contribute to their efforts,' he said, clicking to the next page of his presentation. 'Cloudburst,' he grimaced. 'Our analysts have estimated that Schelldhardt is no more than five years away from a point at which the company will not be able to grow any further via conventional means. Cloudburst is the point at which there may be no more companies that are strategically desirable for acquisition. It is the point at which we have mechanised, automated and consolidated our operations to such a degree that we cannot reduce our cost-base any further. New business is the remaining hope, but in the face of the rising unemployment predicted from increased automation of lower-paid jobs, it would seem an unlikely Messiah. Factor in a growing and ageing population, and we have a perfect storm on the horizon. Obviously, the implications of this extend way beyond the confines of the company to the wider world itself.'

The presentation had switched dramatically from inspirational to worrying, and there were a few nervous coughs from some of the delegates. Joe paused with his pen in his hand, wondering if he should be recording the bad news. Williams hesitated, watching their reaction.

'If Cloudburst is the problem, then you are the solution. Each and every person in this room has been selected because of their ability to think outside of the box. We are looking to you to provide innovative ideas to challenge the way that we do business. At times, the task will not be easy or pleasant, but you must not shirk your responsibility. The single most important thing that you must take away from this meeting is that you must do whatever it takes for the company to continue our noble endeavours. Good is whatever is necessary to grow.'

Prognosis

'You're failing,' said the voice in the darkness. 'I cannot tolerate this any longer.'

'I'm sorry...' Joe muttered, disoriented. He had no idea where he was, or how he had got there.

'I ask you to define a percentage, and you make her the focus of your thinking yet again. Don't you have a mind of your own? A simple question and you regurgitate her ideas. You will never succeed while this happens. It must end now.'

'I don't know what you're talking about.'

'I am referring to your inability to deliver what I need. You will never find it, blinkered like this. We are running out of time,' said the voice, breaking up in frustration.

'What do you want from me?'

The voice sighed, and there was silence for a moment.

'Do you know how many people there are like you in the world? You can walk into any bar, in any city, on any night of the week and you will be there. You are *that* friend watching from the side-lines, noticing too much about her. You remember the things that she likes — what she eats, what she wears, how she cuts her hair. Her music taste is remarkably similar to yours, and coincidentally you love the same books and films. You know her opinion on a subject before she opens her mouth — but worse still, you adopt it as your own. You know more about her than her lover.'

'Why are...?'

'But I know everything about you. I know everything because I can see you here. There is nothing you can hide from me. You walk where you think you might meet her. You lie just to steal moments alone together. You cannot sleep at night, worrying what she is doing. You try to remember amusing things to say to her. Whenever you achieve anything, you imagine she is watching. Her approval is everything to you. She thinks you are a friend, perhaps her best friend — but she is wrong.'

'This has nothing to do with you...'

'This has everything to do with me! You fantasise about dying for her, because you cannot live with her. You hold on because you think you will succeed in the end. Every day is a fresh opportunity to try again.'

'I don't...'

'How much of your life are you prepared to waste waiting? You pride yourself on your tenacity. Your struggle is heroic in your own mind, and you fight. You fight, and you fight, but nobody wants you to win. You realise that, don't you? Nobody, especially not her. It is a hopeless, hapless cycle of failure.'

'Enough.'

'Exactly, enough. This isn't a game. You cannot reject the reality of your surroundings any longer. I am going to take you to a place that you *will* believe in. We need answers, and she cannot keep you from your task any longer. I need to know what *you* think is right and wrong if you are going to find it.'

Chapter Eighteen
16th July 1993

Arnold Shendi didn't intend to make a scene at the memorial service. He waited in the garden of remembrance, listening to the hymns carried on the summer breeze. It was a glorious day. He had overheard several mourners console themselves with that very fact, and he agreed that Philip may well have approved as they said — without his hay fever to consider.

Shendi had never cried so much in his life. There were elements of self-pity in his grief, he knew, but he was overwhelmed with sadness at the loss of his friend. When he thought about what he had done, it weakened him, and he sat on a bench beneath an arched trellis of pink roses, wiping the tears from his eyes. He couldn't bring himself to look at Philip's flowers. Catherine had sent a large wreath, omitting his name from the accompanying card. Even so, Jane had still accepted it with great reluctance — his wife tainted by guilt because of her association with him.

The service had been delayed for weeks because of the inquiry. Although Philip's death had been the result of a tragic accident, Jane's allegation that he was previously threatened by Shendi, coupled with the ongoing tax investigation into their company, had led to a full inquiry into the circumstances around his death. It transpired that the driver of the van that hit him was a recovering alcoholic, and it soon became obvious there was nothing linking him to Shendi in any way. He had been arguing with his ex-girlfriend on the morning of the accident, before taking the wheel with five times the legal limit of alcohol in his bloodstream. He didn't even know that he had knocked Philip down. It was a strange and shocking turn of events.

Philip had been true to his word, and hadn't mentioned anything to Jane about the company's early financiers. Shendi had no doubt this would have been investigated fully in the inquiry if he had, and from a business perspective, things had actually turned out well. The Inland Revenue had been sympathetic to the situation; providing the tax penalties were paid as agreed, there was no need to take further action against any of the other company directors, namely him. Hayward had barely acknowledged Philip's death on their call. His condolences were particularly insincere and revolting. Even though the tax investigation was over, it was already clear that his demands would continue. There was just too much money at stake. The world seemed a far worse place today. His friend was dead, Sonic no longer had a father and Jane was a widow.

He was disturbed by movement, and he saw that the doors of the crematorium had opened, with a stream of people emerging, wearing various shades of blue and lilac. Jane had chosen the colour scheme to symbolise Philip's love of bluebells. Apparently, he spent his weekends in spring, wandering alone through the woods to enjoy them. Shendi was completely unaware of this interest, but had worn a blue tie out of respect for her wishes anyway. It was a gesture he hadn't intended her to know about; he realised too late that the funeral party was heading for the garden of remembrance to see the flowers, and the only path out led directly towards them. He backed away through the trees until his shoulders were pressed against the spiky branches of the hedge that bordered the garden. The mourners were now funnelling through the iron gate and congregating around the wreaths that had been arranged in a long line. Jane rested her head on the shoulder of an elderly lady in a violet dress and hat, who had taken the day's dress code too far. If they followed the flowers to the end of the line, he would surely be seen. He considered walking into plain view. He could try to pass them all with his head bowed. They were distracted by grief, and busy looking at the flowers. But what if Jane did see him? He knew that she held him as accountable for Philip's death as if he had been behind the wheel of the van.

He decided that discretion should be valued above personal dignity in this particular situation, and started to push himself backwards through the hedge. It was only a few feet wide, and with a bit of effort, he should be able to get through.

The hedge was far denser than he had anticipated, with a network of tiny, needle-like twigs at its core. They clawed at his face and hands, and ripped at his shirt and suit. Once fully immersed within the foliage, he became jammed, pedalling his legs without moving, like a cartoon character that had run off the edge of a cliff. He twisted violently to free himself, and the hedge cracked and snapped around his body. A twig tore across his eyelid, and he could feel blood trickling down his face. With one last vigorous twist, he dragged himself out the other side, falling onto the grass as he emerged into the sunshine.

Jane was looking down at him.

He slowly rose to his feet, brushing the twigs from his clothes, and straightened his tie. Her eyes were red and puffy, but she was dressed immaculately in a blue skirt and white blouse.

'I knew it was you,' she said, sniffing.

'I'm sorry…'

'I'm glad you came, for two reasons.'

'I didn't mean to intrude…'

'Firstly, because despite everything, and God only knows why, I think Philip would have wanted you here,' she said, ignoring him. 'You had some kind of hold over him that I will never fully understand…' Her voice trailed away at the thought, and she stared at the grass. When she looked up again, her eyes were full of anger. 'Secondly, I wanted to say to your face that I will never believe what happened to him was an accident, and that you had no part in it.'

'Please, Jane, you need to…'

'Shut up, Arnold,' she said slowly and deliberately. 'I don't want you to come near me or my son ever again. I don't want to see you. I don't want to hear from you. I don't want to correspond with you in any way. Do you understand?'

'We need…'

'Do you understand?' she said, dissolving into tears. She shook so hard that he wanted to comfort her. It was only weeks since they had been laughing and joking together, but now they were conversing like strangers. Everything was his fault.

'I understand,' he said, wiping the blood from his face.

Jane turned to walk away, but he needed to reassure her about the business. He couldn't just let her go like this.

'Philip has a lot of money tied up in the company,' he said. She stopped walking, and he knew that she could hear him. 'He would want you to have it. I want you to have it,' he added, holding out his hands towards her.

She turned fully to face him again. 'That's all the more reason not to take it. I don't want your money.'

'Philip worked hard for that money.'

'I don't want your blood money, Arnold. Not a penny. I'm sure it will bring you great pleasure.'

'For your son, then,' he said, fighting back the tears himself. He couldn't bear that everything they had done should be meaningless.

'We would rather starve. Keep your money, and never contact us again.'

She slowly walked away to the car park, and he felt utterly helpless.

'I'll look after it for him in case you change your mind,' he shouted after her. 'I'll keep it in a trust fund, I swear.'

She was gone before he had finished speaking.

Chapter Nineteen

Knight cornered Joe in the corridor as he was heading to get a sandwich.

'I wanted to give you this,' Knight said, handing him a security pass. 'You now have access to the red lounge. I'll show you around later.'

'Thank you. Does this mean I can visit other decks?'

'Why do you need to visit another deck?'

'I... wanted to catch up with my friends.' He didn't want to repeat Fowler's promises, knowing that the man tended to open his mouth too much. Knight sighed, and Joe instantly sensed that he had disappointed him.

'There will be opportunities, but that shouldn't be your priority right now. You have an important new role in the company.'

It was a mistake raising the subject, and he felt like a spoiled child.

He arranged to meet Knight at seven-thirty that evening. The entrance to the red lounge was at the far end of the compliance deck. He had tried to open the door with his pass on several occasions before, but the access light above the handle had remained defiantly red. It was a thrill when the green light appeared.

The first thing he noticed was that he had stepped into a false corridor. The real entrance turned immediately to the left, and he assumed the decoy route was to maintain privacy; passers-by, himself included, often craned to peek inside whenever someone entered the room, but all they could see from the outside was the bland vestibule he now stood in. He followed the corridor to the left, accompanied by the sound of a classical piano piece, piped through a concealed speaker overhead. When he reached the far end, the corridor opened into a reception area that looked as though it had been styled around a nineteenth-century gentleman's club, complete with dark oak panelling and red upholstered seats, not unlike the rooms in Marryfield House. He wasn't sure if it was his imagination, but the light itself within seemed tinged with the faintest hue of red. A middle-aged man in a waistcoat and bow-tie came to greet him.

'Can I take your jacket, sir.'

'No, I'm fine, thank you.'

'As you wish. Will you be dining this evening?'

'I'm not sure. It's actually my first time here. I'm meeting Martin Knight.'

'I see. I believe Mr Knight has arrived already. Would you like me to call him?'

'Yes, please… No, actually could I have a minute of your time?'

'Of course, sir.'

'Any tips for how I should conduct myself here?'

The man smiled. He had world-weary eyes that had obviously seen many new arrivals like him before. 'I'm sure your conduct will be perfectly acceptable.'

'So there are no specific rules?'

'There is only one. That is to respect the absolute confidentiality of the red lounge. I'm sure Mr Knight will tell you more. In the meantime, let me get you an aperitif.'

He waited in one of the leather armchairs, nursing a chilled dry sherry in a stemmed glass. He felt like an extra in a period drama. Knight appeared five minutes later, casually dressed in a short-sleeved shirt, and blue trousers.

'Let me show you around,' he said.

Joe followed him from the reception area into another corridor which was unlike any other he had seen on the ship, again appearing to have been transplanted directly from a stately home. It was about thirty feet in length, and several rooms branched from it. Paintings were hung along the walls on both sides. Joe looked at the nearest one — a portrait of a white-haired man with blue eyes and a jolly expression. The plaque beneath revealed he was one of the previous Schelldhardt directors. Knight noticed him looking at it.

'Somewhat kitsch all of this, isn't it? Our visitors love it, though. So English, they say.'

'What kind of visitors come here?'

'Our major clients. We have also had politicians, celebrities, even royalty. One thing you must appreciate is the absolute discretion needed at all times when visiting the lounge.'

'I was warned about that earlier.'

'Not sufficiently,' said Knight, eyeing him sternly. 'Everything that happens in the red lounge...'

'Stays in the red lounge?' Joe quipped.

'No, it doesn't happen at all, Joseph. Do you understand?' Knight's expression was odd, and he wished he hadn't interrupted him. 'Schelldhardt take an extremely dim view of any transgressions.'

'I understand.' And he did. After the way Sandbox was treated, he didn't want anyone taking a dim view of him.

'Wonderful,' said Knight, smiling. 'There's somewhere I'd like to show you.'

The gaming room came as a surprise. Joe could see that there were at least thirty people inside, some gathered around a roulette table, others playing blackjack, and the last group involved in some kind of dice game he hadn't seen before. The air was foggy, which was unexpected, as there was a smoking ban in most areas on the ship. There was also a level of laughter and noise that he hadn't heard since the welcoming party.

'Do you play?' asked Knight, leading him into the room.

'Not really. I've been to a casino once before.'

Knight wasn't listening to his reply, his attention drawn by a stocky, bald man at the edge of the roulette table who had just spotted them.

'Come,' the man mouthed to them across the table, beckoning them as if he was marshalling a jumbo jet into the room. He hugged Knight like a long-lost son, but his hooded eyes watched Joe over his shoulder.

'Who's this?' he said to Knight.

'This is Joseph. Joseph, this is Andreas.'

They shook hands, but Andreas still eyed him with suspicion.

'Will you be visiting the annexe?' he said to Knight.

'Not tonight. Another evening I hope.'

Andreas moved closer to Knight so they were out of earshot, and Joe stood awkwardly looking around the room as they talked. Andreas seemed to be sizing him up as he spoke to Knight. Joe tried to ignore their conversation, and watched the roulette players. There was no indication of the table stakes, but large piles of chips were being won and lost. He recognised a few people, but it was surprising how many people he hadn't encountered before on the compliance deck. One of the audit directors — an Atkins-starved stick of a woman who lived on her nerves — was sitting at the table. A stack of orange chips was shovelled in front of her when she won, which she celebrated with a line of coke, eagerly snorted from the silver tray, held stoically by one of the cocktail waiters. She immediately scattered most of the chips randomly around the table for her next bet. Joe noticed a group of people standing beyond the roulette table, by a green velvet curtain. There was a security guard beside it who periodically pulled the curtain aside to allow entry into the room beyond.

Joe was suddenly aware of Andreas standing next to him. 'It's the annexe. Not for tonight,' he smiled.

They left the casino, and Knight lingered outside the entrance, staring at a painting of a Napoleonic Wars scene on the wall.

'The red lounge is the place where all the real business is conducted at Schelldhardt. You may find some of the activities here somewhat unorthodox, but it is vital that you embrace the culture in order to progress within the company. People need to be able to trust you.'

'Andreas didn't?'

'I don't yet,' said Knight bluntly. 'You have to earn that trust. Believe me, if you do, the rewards are waiting.'

'What is the annexe?'

'It's where the high stakes games are played. I will show you in good time.' Knight wandered off before he could ask any more questions. He was waiting at the next doorway.

'And this is the recreation area,' he said, walking through the door. Joe was clearly expected to follow.

It was a little disconcerting lying on the adjacent bed to Knight — naked apart from a towel around his waist. It was like a bizarre couples' day at a spa. A massage was apparently part of Knight's daily routine before dinner, and Joe sensed it was part of the trust process to join him. He was initially concerned that it was all some kind of homoerotic casting couch ploy on Knight's part, but was relieved when the two masseuses joined them in the room.

He sighed, breathing in the fragrant scent of tangerine oil, gently massaged into the small of his back. The masseuse's hands worked their way up his spine, kneading away the knots of tension. The room was lit by candles, and filled with the sound of Rachmaninov's Piano Concerto No 2 — Knight's selection.

Joe closed his eyes and tried to relax. Everything had been happening at such a rapid pace that he barely had time to take stock of it all. He wasn't averse to change, but his rapid rise into the upper echelons of Schelldhardt's management was both unanticipated and slightly absurd. He turned his head, and opened his eyes to see Knight staring at him from his pillow.

'Do you think that you can adapt to this life?' Knight said. Was it a self-congratulatory remark? Knight wasn't smiling, and so he took it at face value.

'I'm enjoying the challenge.'

'We work hard and play hard at Schelldhardt,' said Knight. 'It is important that you immerse yourself in every experience. Especially in the red lounge.'

'I fully intend to.'

'It's important because you will make other people uncomfortable if you don't. We thrive on solidarity.'

Knight turned onto his back, meeting the dark eyes of his masseuse standing over him. She smiled, and began to massage his stomach, rubbing oil upwards through the matted white hairs of his chest. Without saying a word, he pulled at the cord of her robe, and it fell open, exposing her naked body.

'Be quick,' he said to the girl. 'We are eating shortly.'

At work, Joe tried not to think about the previous evening, but Knight's encounter with the masseuse stayed with him most of the morning. The mental image of his director's coming face was certainly not conducive to departmental planning. While he was prepared to maintain the confidence of the red lounge, he didn't want to be any part of Knight's activities there.

There was a meeting invitation in his calendar at one o'clock that was intriguingly marked as private. He was unable to see the other attendees, but it was scheduled in his own office. He finished his lunch and rushed back to find Knight and Nathan Williams, the man who had run his first course, already waiting for him. They were sitting behind his desk, faintly ridiculous in their identical poise and demeanour. A huge screen had been installed on his desk, filled with brightly coloured graphs and figures that continually flickered with updates.

'The company is embarking on the biggest restructure in its history,' said Williams, getting straight to the point. 'We must delay Cloudburst for as long as possible. Schelldhardt needs to leverage the synergy of different global workstreams and reduce the cost-base of its core activities to grow and continue our great work.'

Good is whatever is necessary to grow, Joe thought. Williams had said it far more succinctly in the classroom.

'We need your help, Joseph,' said Williams. 'We are forming a steering committee to lead us through this exciting transition. At times it will be challenging, but we must never lose sight of the bigger picture. Incredible new projects will be funded as part of this initiative. Schelldhardt must strive to remain a shining beacon of virtue in these troubled times, bringing hope to the hopeless.'

Williams unconsciously slipped into a sales pitch whenever he opened his mouth. Rather than reinforcing his message, it made everything he said feel like a lie. He seemed to be at the point of moving himself to tears with his own words.

'How exactly can I help?'

'We want you to be part of that committee. We intend to hand you full control of the audit and compliance area. Much of the operation is based in the Caribbean, but, of course, it includes our corporate headquarters here. We need your recommendations on how best to streamline our processes,' said Williams, fiddling with a pen in his jacket pocket. 'You must identify areas of weakness to ensure continued profitability. We will give you complete access to the information you need to make an informed decision,' he said, gesturing towards the screen.

'I don't understand. The company has just announced record profits.'

'Our investors must see an increasing return on their interests. Cloudburst is coming, and we need to consolidate our position,' said Knight. 'This is a delicate equation. We need you to determine the optimum number of reductions, without impacting productivity. It's a balancing act, Joseph, but we know you can get that number exactly right.'

'Please don't think about this in the wrong way,' interrupted Williams. 'Without the growth we need, wonderful projects, such as our innovative new irrigation scheme, simply won't happen. This will bring fresh water to thousands of desperate people all over the world. Job losses are an unfortunate necessity to facilitate these initiatives, but any gardener knows that a spot of judicious pruning encourages new growth. We are simply passing you the shears.'

They were both silent for a moment, and it was hard to decide who had the most nauseating smile.

'Why me?'

'As we have said before, you have impressed us.'

'Please don't get me wrong, I'm very grateful for the chance, but surely there is someone more qualified and experienced who should do...'

'Yes, but you are young and talented,' Knight interrupted. 'We realise this is a steep curve for you, Joseph, but we know you can step up,' he added, leaning forward across the desk. His expression hardened. 'Plus, when the belt tightens, we must all ensure that we are not part of the excess slipping over the waistband.'

It was a thinly veiled threat. Williams coughed, rising to his feet as if he was no part of the remark. He strode across the office, reaching for a folder from his briefcase.

'There is something here that might interest you,' Williams said, passing him an envelope. 'Open it.'

'What is this?' he asked, looking blankly at the piece of paper.

'It's a bonus. A thank you for the good work you have put in so far. You'll notice the scheme is particularly tax efficient. Schelldhardt is the ultimate offshore company, after all.'

'It's very generous, but...'

'Is there something wrong?'

'It's just that I don't think I should accept this in the light of what is happening.'

'Interesting,' said Knight. 'Is it the amount? We can make it more or less, depending on what you think is appropriate. Just tell us the exact figure that you think would be fair.'

'It's the principle of taking a bonus at all when other people are losing their jobs.'

'It's your choice, Joseph, but I wouldn't beat yourself up about it,' said Knight, leaning back in his chair. 'Anyone would take it in your position. The company needs to retain talent, at times like this more than ever. You're worth it.'

'I'm flattered, but…'

'There is a second envelope,' interrupted Knight. 'Maybe you should take a look inside this one before you make a final decision.'

Joe, opened it, at first baffled by what he was seeing. It was a pile of bills, many of them urgent demands for unpaid services. It wasn't until he noticed the name and address at the top of the letters that he realised their significance. They were his mother's.

'How did you get these?'

'It doesn't matter,' said Knight dismissively. 'The point is, there are many conflicting principles at stake here. There must be a compromise we can reach between them all. You simply need to let us know exactly where that compromise lies. We know from your interview how important your mother is to you. Have a think about how we can restructure the department, and come back to us with an appropriate figure for yourself,' he smiled.

'Forget about the vulgarity of money for a moment, Joseph. Focus on the good we can achieve together. Think of the desperate people in the world we can help. This is your chance to make a difference,' said Williams, placing a hand on his shoulder. 'You *do* want to make a difference?'

'Of course.'

'Excellent,' said Williams, 'then it's settled.'

When he returned to his cabin, he listened at Sandbox's door, but there was no sign of activity, which only added to his guilt. He couldn't face the gym that evening because there was too much on his mind, even though he knew, paradoxically, that exercise would relieve the tension. His headaches were unrelenting, and he needed to find some way of relaxing without resorting to alcohol to ease his problems. He could see why drinking was an issue at sea.

He flopped on the couch with a glass of iced water and tried to plan what he should do. He half expected Knight to call him at any moment with an invitation to the red lounge. The thought made him angry. He shouldn't allow himself to be pressurised into doing things he had no desire to do. Schelldhardt didn't own him.

When Knight hadn't called him two hours later, he became paranoid. Was he out of the picture? Perhaps he should have shown more enthusiasm to be part of the steering committee. He skulked off to bed.

Chapter Twenty

The following days were unsettling. There were rumblings and rumours about the changes afoot, and wherever he went on the compliance deck he saw huddles of people whispering and looking over their shoulder. Even though he was part of the restructuring process, he began to wonder if he was being told the entire truth, and lapped up each new conspiracy theory along with everyone else. The steering committee was due to meet for the first time the following week, and there was speculation that some radical new policies were going to be introduced.

He had finally seen a doctor. His headaches showed no sign of abating, and he called the clinic before work when the pain had become unbearable. The doctor suspected that he was suffering from migraines. She would refer him to the on-board clinic for more tests if the headaches persisted. He was at least now equipped with some stronger painkillers that certainly helped.

That Friday evening, he decided that he needed to get out again. It wasn't doing him any good see-sawing between the office and his own room, and he needed a change of scenery. Knight had explained that it was management etiquette for higher-grade staff to drink in the red lounge to avoid any "embarrassing episodes" in front of staff. The irony of that was not lost on him, but he decided it was best to heed the advice. At least the visit would be on his own terms this time.

He locked up his office on time that evening. There would almost certainly be an urgent call after he left, but the word was losing its meaning. The entire department lurched from catastrophe to catastrophe anyway, if the frantic messages on his answering machine were to be believed. Dealing with the Caribbean was proving more problematic than he had anticipated, and it felt impossible to come up with the right answer. He was mindful that the lines on the graph were real people, with real lives, and it made him reluctant to intervene. Cutting jobs would create real hardship.

He heard children's voices as he walked along the corridor to his cabin. The door to the crèche was normally closed, but this evening it was ajar. The purity of the sound was cleansing after the events of the last few days, and he lingered by the door.

'Joe?' called the woman from within. He barely recognised her at first. Her hair was pinned back, and she was wearing glasses. Undoubtedly, she was as beautiful as he remembered, though.

'Marie? I didn't know you worked here.'

'This is my day job. Irresponsible mentoring is just a sideline,' she smiled.

She invited him inside, where a classroom full of children dressed in navy blazers sat at their miniature plastic desks. There were at least thirty tiny faces, none of them older than five years. Marie set them all a task, which they began to work through in stoical silence.

'School runs late here,' he said.

'School finished three hours ago. This is a remission session.'

'A remission session?'

Most of their faces looked pale and tired. What he had believed so uplifting outside the classroom was completely dispiriting within.

'These stakeholders have failed to meet their service level agreements for achievement in mathematics. These are the punitive measures in place for the contract breach.'

'Are you serious?'

'Well, that's how the company describes the situation. This is a very competitive programme, Joe. Parents join Schelldhardt just to get their children on the scheme. They want them to become the best of the best. Each child is benchmarked against a global standard, and the standard rises every year. It's tough.'

'What if they fail?'

'We operate a strict three-strike rule. On the third failed attempt to meet the required metrics, they are removed from the programme.' A little girl looked up, her big brown eyes full of concern as she overheard the conversation.

'They're all so young…'

'It's an intellectual arms race. The only remedy for failure is more tuition. But more tuition raises the standard and speeds up the treadmill for everyone. They all have to run faster and faster just to stay where they were.'

'It's crazy,' he said, shaking his head. 'I don't think I would want my child to go through this.'

'The world is changing, Joe. Schelldhardt is preparing the elite for the future. Our children are no longer only competing with their neighbours. If they won't apply the necessary effort, someone else in the world will. Would you be the one to let your child fall behind?' she smiled. He didn't reply, and when he glanced back up at her, she was still waiting for an answer. 'Well?'

'Well, I don't have children, so luckily I don't have to worry about it,' he grinned. There was something that bothered him about the way she posed the question. It felt as if he was talking to Knight. Her expression softened, and he sensed she realised as much.

'Anyway, are you going to ask me for a drink? I'll need one once this has finished.'

'I was heading to the red lounge.'

'That sounds great. I'll meet you there at nine,' she smiled.

He rinsed his face in the washbasin, and slipped a painkiller. The night was still young and he didn't want to spoil it by submitting to a headache.

The gaming room was busy when he passed it. He could just about make out the stout figure of Andreas at the back of the room, surveying his smoky kingdom. He hurried on, eager for a drink.

The bar in the red lounge had a livelier atmosphere than his regular haunt. He'd been unable to fully appreciate it previously — too stunned by Knight's behaviour in the recreation room. Today, he was ready to embrace the vibrancy. It seemed that cocktails were *de rigueur* on a Friday evening, and every table was loaded with a kaleidoscope of coloured drinks that lifted the mood — as did the live band playing on the stage.

It seemed rude not to participate, and Joe studied the cocktail menu, searching out the maximum spirit content to minimum paraphernalia combination. He settled on a Texas tea, which sounded like a potent stablemate of the Long Island iced tea — a favourite tipple from his university days. He selected a table at the edge of the room. The bar stool sacrificed all practicality for style, with the corkscrew-shaped chrome base meeting a narrow leather perch that appeared to have been designed for a small child. It felt as stable as a unicycle. He wobbled there self-consciously, sipping through his straw.

Again, there were so many people he didn't recognise in the bar. It seemed impossible that they could all be accommodated on the compliance deck. Their dynamism was in stark contrast to the air of desperation in the other bar. It either stemmed from the confidence of their position, or the nervous energy expended to keep them there.

'You made it,' said a voice behind him. He turned around to see Marie, equally stunning in her change of dress.

'My mentor. Not a moment too soon,' he said, greeting her. 'I was about to drink myself into oblivion.'

'What a great plan,' she said. 'I fully approve.'

'Can I get you a drink?' The old conversational customs held little weight at the Schelldhardt free bars, and all he was really offering was to walk eight feet to get them.

'As soon as humanly possible. Whatever you are drinking.'

They worked through the cocktail list in record time. Marie shared his agenda of sticking two straws up at the week, and was as unsettled by the restructuring rumours as the others he had met.

'My job isn't "business critical", so I'm screwed,' she said, poking at the olives in her Martini with a cocktail stick.

'I'm sure that isn't true,' he lied. If Williams had anything to do with the process, she almost certainly was. Marie was wearing glossy lipstick, and he couldn't stop staring at her mouth when she spoke. It was surreal to be drinking with such an attractive woman, and he found her even more appealing now he saw this vulnerable side. Her diminished confidence empowered him, levelling the playing field.

They drank for a couple more hours at the bar, and decided they wanted to move on. The last thing he wanted was to collapse in front of her for a second time, and he was already wobbling slightly. Perhaps he should have checked if the painkillers could be taken with alcohol. He had no idea how she managed to stay so coherent as he gradually degenerated into a slurring fool.

They ran through the main corridor of the red lounge, laughing. The disapproving portraits of Schelldhardt's past directors frowned down at them, which only amused them further. Before he knew it, they were pushing through the crowd to reach a roulette table in the gaming room. On another occasion, he would have been self-conscious of his inability to walk in a straight line, but he blended in with the other clientele perfectly. Marie stopped the "coke-man" as he passed them, and challenged Joe to a race. He protested weakly, but moments later his chin was propped at the opposite end of a silver tray to Marie. A timid start cost him, and their faces met only a quarter of the way along his line. Their cheeks brushed, and she turned her head to kiss his lips as they passed. It seemed perfectly natural. When he stood up, he thought he was having a stroke. His front teeth were numb, and reality seemed to have been diced up into a series of fascinatingly vibrant excerpts. He followed Marie to the table like a mad dog. She was somehow managing to converse with the croupier, and had secured a pile of chips.

'Wait!' he said. She turned her head, and he kissed her again, giggling.

He had acquired superpowers.

She grabbed him by the hair, pulling his mouth closer, and their tongues entwined. She dragged his head away again, and shoved him to one side like a discarded toy.

'I'm winning big,' she said, thrusting her entire pile of chips onto black, and nearly falling off the chair in the process.

She won. He ordered two glasses of champagne. They drank them. Two more arrived and he almost vomited. She challenged him to another coke race. This time he won.

The next moment, he found himself face to face with the security guard in front of the green curtains.

'Do you know who I am?' he shouted, stumbling backwards.

'What's the problem?' asked Andreas, appearing beside him.

'He won't let us in.'

'Mr Knight hasn't cleared you for the annexe.'

'Fuck Knight, and fuck Schelldhardt,' slurred Joe, wobbling off, 'and fuck you, too. I'm taking my business elsewhere.' He chased after Marie, who was already tottering out of the gaming room. 'Where are you going?'

'I'm hot,' she said. He stumbled after her through the corridor and they followed the narrow passageway into the recreation area. Marie opened the wrong door, disturbing the massage of one of the female directors. The woman was naked, with two muscular masseurs straddled across her. It wasn't just Knight who made the most of his time at sea. Marie apologised, giggling, and slammed the door closed. They would pay for that one in the morning, Joe thought.

He struggled to keep pace with her, rebounding off the walls of the hallway, despite his best attempts to run in a straight line. They came to a changing room, and he nearly slipped over on the wet floor. Two men at the side of the room grinned at Marie as she pulled her dress over her head and threw it on the nearby bench. She spun around to face him in her underwear, her hair dishevelled, biting her lip.

'Strip,' she commanded. 'Strip now!' He fumbled to undo the buttons of his shirt, not wanting to lose sight of Marie removing her underwear for a second. She stood, perfectly naked in every way, watching him. He nearly fell to the floor in his haste to pull off his trousers, dragging one trapped leg behind him like a wounded animal as he tried to reach her. She giggled, and turned towards the showers, and all that existed in the universe at that moment was her glorious body as she walked away.

She was waiting for him as he turned the partition into the showers, and she pulled his mouth onto hers beneath the powerful warm jet of water. He was terrified to get any closer, but when her breasts brushed against his chest, he thought he would explode, and staggered forward. Every nerve ending in his skin was firing in anticipation from the fleeting contact, and he ached with absolute desire for her. He kissed her again harder, and inched closer to her body, running his hand down her spine. She smiled, lightly pressing her fingertips against his chest, before following the flow of the gushing water down his stomach, lower to his groin. Her mascara was washing away, but this adulteration of her perfectly made-up face only made him want her more, stripping her totally bare. He finally dared to touch her breasts, and pulled their bodies together. As they touched, his legs weakened, the feeling so impossibly perfect.

At that exact moment, when he had never wanted anything more in his life, it happened. He thought of Rachel. His eyes met Marie's for a split second, and she immediately noticed the change.

'Don't think!' she commanded, slapping him hard around the face. He rocked back on his feet in shock, his ear ringing from the blow. She slapped him harder across the other cheek before he could regain his senses. 'Only think of me,' she said, arching her back against the tiled wall of the shower and parting her legs, the shower streaming over her glistening body. She grasped his erection and pulled him towards her.

Infidelity

'Don't frustrate me again,' said the voice in the darkness. 'You can't be unfaithful to someone you have no relationship with. Rachel is just your friend. You understand that, don't you? This is actually progress.'

'How do you know about her?'

'You can't hide anything here. I know everything about you. It's perfectly natural for you to sleep with an attractive woman like Marie.'

'I don't want to discuss this.'

'But I do. Do you accept that there has to be a relationship before you can be unfaithful?'

'Yes.'

'So you think that you are in some kind of mental relationship with Rachel?'

'I wouldn't call it…'

'Don't lie to me.'

'Yes, it is some kind of relationship.'

'But it is one that she does not wish to share with you. A very one-sided relationship, I think you'd agree?'

'But…'

'That aside, you feel guilty about what you have done, yet you fantasised about Marie before this.'

'That's different.'

'What's the difference? You were unfaithful in your mind, but you just made it a reality.'

'There's a huge difference.'

'Is there? You were merely replacing thought with flesh. At what point does infidelity begin? The first realisation you are attracted to someone? A smile? A flirtatious text? A fantasy? You tell me the exact point.'

'It's difficult to define.'

'Define it you must. I need to know the precise moment. Everything is a question of degree. Detail is our currency here. Is it the action or the potential consequences that disturb you the most?'

'I don't have to explain myself to you.'

'I'm afraid you do. That's precisely what is going to happen. You need to break this cycle of thought if you are going to find it.'

Chapter Twenty-One

Waking up with Marie and feeling like death went hand in hand. He resisted a Pavlovian impulse to panic when he saw her beside him on the pillow, trying to recall how he had humiliated himself this time. She was naked in his bed, still sleeping. The mattress was littered with their clothes, while the covers were discarded on the floor of the room with an empty wine bottle and two upturned glasses on top of them. He had obviously attempted to play some music through his computer tablet at some point, and had somehow managed to shatter the glass screen in the process. If he was more coherent, he would be mortified.

Images of the previous evening began to flash before his eyes, his own participation in the scenes almost impossible to absorb. They seemed like someone else's memories. He felt utterly spent, both mentally and physically. A familiar residue of despair endured all the same. It should be Rachel beside him.

Marie stirred, stretching with her arms draped behind her. It was impossible for him to imagine anyone more desirable, but everything seemed so wrong. He felt incredibly guilty that he had enjoyed sleeping with her so much, counterpointed by a shameful sense of masculine pride.

'Good morning,' she said, smiling at him. 'Is everything okay?'

'I've felt better.'

'Yes, we may have overdone it again,' she said, sitting up. She wrapped her arms around his shoulders and kissed him lightly on the temple. 'I need to go. I have to open up the crèche again today, and it's not the best time to call in sick. I'll be in touch.'

He spent the next few hours pre-cleaning his suite in preparation for the cleaner's arrival. The effort of staying on his feet was too much, and he climbed back into bed to nurse his head immediately after he had finished. He barely left the sanctuary of his duvet for the remainder of the weekend, still trying to piece together the events of Friday night, perpetually flummoxed.

Knight cornered him on the way to the office on Monday morning. There were important clients they needed to entertain that evening. It was the last thing in the world Joe felt like doing after his heavy weekend, but every attempt to extricate himself was swatted away. He decided his best policy was to leave the office at a decent hour and try to revive himself before the meal.

Thankfully, work provided a good focus for his attention that day. His feelings for Marie were difficult to rationalise, and he tried to push them from his mind. In the afternoon, he sat at his desk, dialling in to meetings where all of the problems seemed unsolvable. In fact, the entire intention of the calls appeared to be to discuss how insolvable the problems were, and to arrange other meetings where they could all despair further.

The screen flickered on the desk in front of him: the Dominican Republic office was under-performing again. Their numbers were down for the third successive week. Logically, something had to be done, but he knew Schelldhardt was such an important employer in the region, and it was a tough call to make. He began to compose an email three times, abandoning it on each occasion, unable to decide what to do for the best — ultimately, doing nothing at all.

He blundered through to the evening, and headed out to meet Knight, dosed up with painkillers.

The meal was predictably arranged in the red lounge, and he felt like a villain returning to the scene of a crime. He convinced himself that every smile was underwritten with unspoken knowledge of his dubious conduct on Friday night. He knew this wasn't rational, and bad behaviour needed to be fairly spectacular to stand out in the red lounge. Even so, he couldn't shake the feeling.

Like the next stacking Russian doll, the Schelldhardt hierarchy unveiled a new level of privilege at the meal. The red lounge restaurant was luxurious enough, but they were shown through a side door to the most lavishly decorated table he had ever seen. The cutlery laid out at each place setting stretched ridiculously in each direction. There appeared to be a different piece of silverware for every conceivable food they might encounter. Joe hoped that a broad strategy of working from the outside in for each course would hold him in good stead. Knight had pre-warned him to wear a dinner jacket and tie, and the other guests, two men and a woman, were also formally dressed. Knight was the only other representative from Schelldhardt, and they sat around a vast circular table, talking over the top of an elaborate candle arrangement. The stems of the wine glasses looked like they would snap if anyone dared to touch them, and Joe sat with hands on his lap, terrified to move.

To his horror, he was introduced as the company compliance expert. Knight dropped the bombshell in passing, and he braced himself for the humiliation to follow. Fortunately, their guests had other things on their mind, and the discussion seemed to bear little relevance to his department at all. From what he could gather, they were the representatives of major investors, with very different opinions as to which direction Schelldhardt should be heading. He wasn't sure what role Knight played in the proceedings, but he seemed to understand what they were saying. Once again, Joe had no idea why he was there. The woman, Helena, in her late forties, continually disagreed with the others on every subject. She seemed to value Joe's opinion above everyone else's, purely on the basis that he was young and therefore had his finger on the pulse. Perhaps she actually just felt sorry for him, or even believed she was a youthful kindred spirit. One of the men, whose name he missed, took great delight in aggravating her at every opportunity. It was already clear that it would be impossible for the group to reach consensus on any new direction, though amazingly they all managed to agree on drinking red wine.

Knight sent him to select a "nice" wine with the waiter. It wasn't a simple case of choosing from a list, and he was led to a cellar where the bottles were stored in a honeycombed lattice of shelving. It was cool and musty within, and the dust irritated his nose. There were cryptic notes scribbled beneath each wine — whose only purpose could be to humiliate the uninitiated. He had already come to realise that for Schelldhardt management, appreciation of wine had latent connotations of intellect — it was naive to consider it just a drink. Choosing the wrong wine in the red lounge would single him out as an idiot faster than anything else could. Their appreciation of wine, like the positions they held themselves, justified even the most unreasonable expense. They were worth it.

The wine waiter lovingly described the contents of his cellar. Some of the dusty bottles cost thousands, and he had no idea how much money he should be spending. One of the wines was ethically sourced, and grown in organic soil — untainted by chemical impurities. The waiter spoke about the production of the wine like a proud father. The South African farmers and workers received a fair price for their product in the face of challenging economic, social and political conditions. It wasn't just a drink, it was an epic family saga.

Joe picked up the bottle, but hesitated with it in his hand. The wine was twice the price of some of the others. He would be overstepping the mark to choose it. He put the bottle down and picked up a French wine, lower in price, but lacking the ethical promises of the other. The wine waiter again patiently talked about the wine, explaining about the grape, the vintage and the history of the region. Joe thanked him, convinced this was the correct selection instead. The French were renowned for their wines, and it was a much safer option in every respect. He would be hard pushed to make a fool of himself with this steady fellow, and would return to the table a conquering hero. The waiter was summoned to the restaurant, and left him alone to choose. Just as he was about to walk away with the French wine, the South African bottle caught his eye again.

Organic. Ethically sourced. Fair trade.

The ethically sourced bottle was surely worth the price difference. It was impossible to put a price on the welfare of the planet and the well-being of the farm's workforce. After all of the obstacles that had hampered its production, it would be churlish to quibble over the price difference. It was the right thing to do. Even as he changed his mind, the French wine caught his eye again.

Cheaper. French. Safer.

Schelldhardt was about to embark on a major restructuring programme. If everyone avoided unnecessary additional expense, they could save jobs. It was ridiculous to spend huge amounts of money on luxuries like this, and everyone loved French wine. He put the fair-trade bottle down again.

He swapped them over another half a dozen times in a manic cycle of indecision. His head was aching, and he felt dizzy, almost stumbling backwards out of the doorway. What would Rachel choose? Fair trade or job saving? He was frozen to the spot, unable to think.

It was impossible to decide.

'What are you doing?' hissed Knight, standing in the doorway of the wine cellar.

At first, Joe couldn't understand what he was saying, suddenly jolted out of his trance. He was conscious of his mouth hanging open, and wiped his chin with the back of his hand. It was like being woken up from a deep sleep, and he realised he still had a bottle in his other hand.

'I'm choosing the wine.'

'You've been in here for over an hour!' Knight screeched.

Over an hour. It couldn't be true. Yet, he somehow knew it was.

He felt his knees buckle, and knew he was going to faint. The bottle dropped from his grasp, smashing into a crimson bloom on the floor. He managed to stagger to the wall before he followed it down in an undignified heap. His vision was blurry, but he could just distinguish Knight's face above him.

Something was very wrong, but he had no idea what.

Chapter Twenty-Two

When Joe awoke, he was unsure where he was. The rumbling of the ship's engines was quieter than in his cabin, and there was an unfamiliar antiseptic smell that caught the back of his throat. As he twisted to one side, he could make out several blue lights flickering on the side of a machine. He stared at them in the gloom, mesmerised by the patterns they formed.

'You're awake,' said Knight, somewhere in the darkness. Joe jumped at the sound of his voice, unnerved that he had been present the whole time. He sat upright, trying to focus on the shadowy figure beside him. Knight switched on a lamp, and Joe was momentarily dazzled, before his eyes adjusted to the light. Knight was sitting in a chair, still wearing his dinner suit from the previous evening.

'Where am I?' Joe asked, blinking.

'You're in the clinic. Do you remember what happened last night?'

Joe rubbed his forehead, his hand shaking slightly. He remembered the awkward meal, and then choosing the wine. After that, everything was hazy.

'Not really. I hope I didn't upset our clients.'

'No, not at all. Just relax and concentrate on building your strength back up. You lost a lot of blood when you fell.'

'Fell?'

'You hit your head,' said Knight, gesturing to his crown. Joe tentatively fingered through his hair until he reached a small, smooth patch where he had been shaved, and he could feel the ridges of some stitches in the centre of it. The area was numb. 'You're perfectly fine now; the doctor just asked if I would sit with you as a precaution.'

Joe lowered himself gently back on to the pillow. He was nauseous and his throat was raw.

'How did it happen?'

'You fell in the wine cellar. Don't worry, I'll make sure you're fully compensated for the accident.'

'I don't remember.'

'It was quite a knock. I don't want to see you in the office for a few days. Take some time out to relax.'

'What about the steering committee meeting?'

'Fortunately, it has been postponed until next week. Plenty of time to get yourself fit and back in action.'

Joe's body was trembling, and he felt weak. He had woken up too many times feeling like death and he was frightened. Something was happening to him, but he couldn't define what it was. He wanted to be alone. Knight was watching him, and it made him uncomfortable.

'I'm sorry, but I don't think I can do this.'

'What do you mean?' asked Knight, leaning towards him.

'This job. I'm grateful for the opportunity I've been given, but it's just too much for me to handle.'

Knight sighed, folding his hands on his lap. 'It's understandable that you should feel like this. It has been quite a shock to your body and you need to rest.'

'I've felt like this for a while,' Joe said. Even as the words left his mouth, he could barely believe he was actually saying them to Knight. 'I'm not ready for a role like this.'

'Nonsense, you've impressed everyone with your approach. Even our clients last night commented on your excellent input.'

'I didn't do anything!' Joe said, more forcefully than he had intended. 'I don't understand why everyone keeps praising me. I shouldn't be in a position like this. It makes no sense.'

'We have worked you too hard recently, Joseph,' replied Knight calmly. 'I take full responsibility for the mistake. Trust me, the problem will be rectified. Have a rest, and then we can push on again next week.'

Joe managed to bite his tongue before he completely backed himself into a corner. The money he was earning was phenomenal. His mother's bills still played on his mind, and there was a limit to how much he should say. He had nearly mentioned Sandbox, but thankfully stopped himself. Knight was not a wise choice of confidant.

'Thank you. It has been difficult to adapt to so many things at once.'

'That's entirely to be expected,' said Knight solemnly.

They sat in silence for a moment, with the ship's engines rumbling in the background.

'Do graduates ever change departments? If they find they aren't suited to a role.'

Knight stared at him without replying. In the light of the lamp, his complexion appeared paler, and his eyes looked tired and sore. There was something else, though, cold and menacing deep within them. Joe almost expected them to roll over, like the eyes of a great white shark.

'Schelldhardt is extremely thorough when it comes to recruitment. Graduates don't change department because they are always assigned to the correct department to begin with. There are no mistakes, Joseph. You are here for a reason, and you would do very well to remember that.'

Joe hesitated, knowing that he was pushing the limits of Knight's tolerance. 'I think I'm a mistake. I think you knew it at my interview.'

Knight continued to stare, as if sizing him up, but then his expression softened. 'I can't offer you the chance to change departments, but you can see your friends if you think it would help.'

Joe relaxed on the pillow, surprised at the concession and change of mood.

'Yes, it would.'

'I'll try to arrange something. We need to get through the next couple of weeks first. There are some important tasks ahead for you.'

It took a few days to feel well enough to return to work. If his cabin had seemed claustrophobic before, then the feeling reached an entirely new level as he recuperated. He was unable to exercise at the gym, and spent most of the time reading in bed. The screen of his tablet had broken at an unfortunate time, but he didn't want to confess to the accident. Apart from watching television, there was little else to do. Marie had neglected to leave her phone number, and he felt uncomfortable visiting other areas of the ship while on sick leave — especially the crèche. He wondered what she must think of him. His meals were delivered to his room, and he left the empty plate by the door each evening, like a prison inmate.

When he returned to the office, the wiry bristles of hair poking through his scalp had grown just long enough to mask the stitches on his head. By the following week, he felt back to full strength, but he was still worried about the state of his mental health. It was a struggle to make even the smallest of decisions, and he was unsatisfied with whatever he finally chose to do. He couldn't decide what he should eat for lunch, or how much photocopier paper should be delivered to the office. He froze in the doorway of the staff restaurant, unsure whether it was appropriate to hold the door open for a female director. Was it sexist? Was it sycophantic? He finally let the door slam in her face, and immediately regretted it. It was difficult to understand why he was beating himself up so much over everything. He lay in bed at night, cursing about the things he had said and done during the day, and worrying about harmless mistakes, or words out of turn. It was affecting his confidence, and it was difficult to sleep at night. Worst of all, whenever he spoke to one of his colleagues, he found himself weighing up their value against a water ditch in Africa.

On the day of the steering committee meeting, his confidence was so low that he seriously considered trying to pull out altogether. Knight called him into his office, moments before he was going to phone.

'You look so much better, Joseph. It's good to see you back in action again,' Knight grinned, before his expression changed. 'I just wanted to warn you about something before the meeting. Your latest recommendations were a little off,' he added, handing him a report. 'You shot too low. I know it was empathy rather than apathy that made you cautious, but your inaction with the Dominican Republic office actually had a negative effect on the entire region. It's a valuable lesson to learn. The net result of our choices is more important than our intentions, wouldn't you agree?'

He was too mortified to reply at first, sliding lower in his chair as he read the report. A forty percent decrease in profitability across the CARICOM region. Food parcels for workers in Schelldhadt Belize. Three colleague suicides in Jamaica.

'Well?'

'Yes, I'm sorry. I really thought that…'

'Not to worry, though, you are still learning. If all goes well today, I'll arrange for you to meet up with your friends this week.'

He was so desperate to see Rachel that he didn't say a word.

The meeting was to be held in the red lounge conference suite, and the delegates were told to keep the evening free for drinks afterwards. He set off early in the hope that he could catch Marie beforehand, but he found that the door to the crèche was locked and the lights were off. He had no other way of contacting her, and was surprised that she hadn't been in touch. He skulked around the red lounge, looking for her without any success, feeling as though he was taking the grand tour of his mistakes.

When he arrived at the meeting room, he discovered that the tables had been pushed to the edge of the room and the chairs were arranged into an elongated ellipse, with Williams already waiting at the head. The room felt bare, with only an expanse of beige carpet separating the lines of chairs. It was as if they were about to play party games. Joe recognised some of the faces from his earlier training sessions, and the suited attendees sat stony-faced in silence on either side of the ellipse. There was a stir when Knight arrived in the room on crutches. His left leg was in plaster, and he hobbled in, smiling in apology. The accident could only have occurred in the few hours since they had last spoken. He lowered himself into a chair, propping the crutches at the side, with his leg extended in front of him.

Williams was carrying what looked like a photograph frame, but as he turned towards Knight, Joe could see a yellowing piece of paper beneath the glass. Williams got to his feet.

'Greeting, friends. I have with me, as I always do at these gatherings, the first Schelldhardt shareholder agreement, signed over one hundred years ago in a humble tavern on the outskirts of Shoreditch in London. Before we begin, let us remind ourselves how Benedict Schelldhardt and his companions emerged from that historic meeting, spying a young crippled lad on the pavement outside. They dug deep in their pockets for coinage, unknowingly setting the tone for a company ethos of good that has endured for generations. Let us begin by praying on this special historical document,' he said, holding the frame to his chest.

'We pray for year-on-year growth.'

'*We pray for year-on-year growth,*' the group responded, in mechanical unison.

'We pray that our cost-base may eternally reduce.'

'*We pray that our cost-base may eternally reduce.*'

'May our auditors always look favourably down upon us.'

'May our auditors always look favourably down upon us.'

'Give us the strength to do what is good.'

'Give us the strength to do what is good.'

'This we ask in the name of the shareholder. The shareholder is sacred. Amen.'

'Blessed is the shareholder. Amen.'

After the bizarre prayer, the meeting began with a series of routine announcements, before Williams dramatically declared that the serious business of shaping the company's future should commence. After all the mistakes he had made, Joe was determined to make a positive contribution. Despite his desire to speak up, it was intimidating voicing his opinions in a room filled with so many people, and they faced him like a jury from the opposite side of the ellipse. The agenda moved from one cost-saving idea to another, each sweetened by a token act of generosity to the wider world. His confidence was so low that he couldn't open his mouth at first, never quite finding the right moment to interject. There was finally a lull in the conversation, and he seized the chance to speak. He could barely spit out the words, but when he did, they were met with initial silence.

'Everything I have heard today does not address the long-term problem of Cloudburst,' he said. Mention of the word itself was sufficient to induce a state of palpable unease in the others, but he did not stop. 'The initiatives we have discussed only delay the inevitable, but will not prevent it. Growth cannot be infinitely sustained, it's obvious. If the primary need for growth is to satisfy external investors, then why don't we look at ways to change the company financial model? It just seems that the whole world is working harder and longer purely to perpetuate the wealth of a small minority,' he said, gaining confidence.

There was silence. It was clear from the horrified faces before him that his words were tantamount to heresy, but he persisted.

'I have some ideas of how we could achieve this by...'

'Thank you for your contribution, Joseph,' interrupted Williams. 'Your thoughts are interesting, if a little naive. These are very complex issues, and you are new to our company. Please stop there.'

Williams was clearly not alone in his disgust, and several of the other attendees were openly sharing a joke at his expense.

'That's the guy who screwed up in the Caribbean,' whispered a woman, loudly enough for everyone else to hear. He was saved from further embarrassment when coffee arrived for the meeting in true Schelldhardt style — an epic production on a silver tray with every base covered: there were separate jugs of cream and warm frothed milk, and piles of Belgian truffles thrown in for good measure. No doubt the coffee beans were ground directly from the arse of an Indonesian civet cat. The excess was shameless. He found himself shunned on the periphery of the group, sipping his flat white in isolation. He longed for the meeting to end.

Unable to avoid the post-meeting drinks, he joined the others in the lift that served the red lounge. It was as ornately decorated as the main corridor itself, complete with an elaborate chandelier that jangled above their heads as the lift descended. They reached the swimming pool area at the bottom of the ship, where the joining party had been held previously. It was much quieter than he remembered, and the place felt different in a way he couldn't quite define. Perhaps it was a worrying side effect of his headaches, but the slight redness of the lighting that he had sensed before seemed even more pronounced here. Relieved to escape the attention of his colleagues, he demolished so many consolatory cocktails that he was already unsteady on his feet by the time the food was served — a lavish selection of canapés and seafood.

'That could have gone better,' said Knight, reclining on a lounger beside the pool in the gloom. He was sipping a mojito, with the reflection of the water rippling on his face. 'Some very inspiring ideas, though.' Was he being sarcastic? He always gave that vague impression, and it was hard to tell. 'Please sit, Joseph,' Knight said, beckoning to the adjacent lounger. 'I'm afraid I cannot stand.'

'What's happened to your leg?'

'A possible fracture. The X-ray machine has a fault, so the doctor plastered my leg as a precaution. The perils of injuring yourself at sea. Anyway, enough of my problems. It took courage to speak up like that.'

'I think discretion would have been the better part of valour on this occasion.'

'Perhaps,' said Knight. 'However, I take some of the responsibility.

I pushed you hard when you joined the department, and your recovery was rushed. Your judgement may be impaired.' It sounded as though he was slurring. Joe noticed the empty glasses abandoned on the tray beside him. He had been hitting the cocktails hard, too. 'You must understand that this isn't a simple equation. You may not agree with all of their methods, but if Schelldhardt is not the dominant global force, then something far worse may replace it. Better the devil you know.'

'I understand,' said Joe. 'I appreciate the chance I've been given.'

'Excellent,' said Knight, tipping his glass so the ice clattered his teeth. 'There may still be time for both of us to turn this situation around. How about securing some more cocktails? Just to anaesthetise the leg,' he chuckled.

For once, they were on the same page — both drinking to forget their problems. Joe fetched two more mojitos, and then two more. He settled in the shadows with Knight, glad to be hidden from the other guests. Strangely, the person he trusted least in the world was the most reassuring company of all tonight.

He was awoken by Knight's shouts.

The room was in darkness, and as he sat up, he could see that the bar was deserted and silent. They had fallen asleep, and the party was over.

'He's drowning!' shouted Knight, standing at the edge of his lounger. He looked crazy in the half-light, propped on his crutch, and pointing at the pool. Joe stumbled beside him, rubbing his eyes. He could see a body, face-down in the turquoise water, illuminated by the pool lights. It looked like a man. He appeared to be trapped somehow, turning in frantic, jerking circles.

'I'll get help.'

'There's no one else here, Joseph. It will be too late. Can you rescue him?'

'I can't swim.'

'Then he's finished,' Knight sighed. 'I can't go in the water like this,' he said, tapping the plaster with the other crutch. He began to hobble away from the pool.

'Wait, we can't just leave him...'

'There's nothing we can do. There are signs everywhere warning about the dangers. We shouldn't risk ourselves because of his stupidity.'

'We at least have to try,' he said, pulling off his shoes and socks.

He stood at the top of the glass staircase, surveying the vast blue expanse of water in front of him. The drowning man was at least fifteen feet away from the last step, thrashing about like a dying fly.

'Don't do it, Joseph. This is not your responsibility. You may not even be insured to go in there.'

'I'm not going to watch him drown.'

Breathing deeply, he descended the first couple of steps into the warm water. He could feel the vibration of the engines beneath his feet, and froze when a large parrot fish swam directly beneath him inside the glass step.

'You have no obligation towards this man, Joseph. Why should you risk your life?'

He ignored Knight's whining, his trousers clinging to his legs as he submerged further. Each stride tested his courage, and when he left the last step he was waist-deep. The warm water fizzed around him. He could see the glass bottom of the pool beneath, and the darkness of the ocean beyond that. If the glass broke…

'Joseph, stay where you are. I'll let everyone know that this was not your fault.'

Knight's rationalisation was both distracting and seductive, but he edged forward, the water level rising to his navel. He was beginning to shake. There were bubbles racing beneath the ship, and fish swimming everywhere in the glowing glass walls of the pool. It felt as if he was in the sea itself, and his wet shirt fanned out around him like a jellyfish.

The drowning man twisted his head towards him and yelled, before being dragged face-down again. Joe instantly recognised him from the welcoming party. It was Rachel's mentor, the catalogue model.

'I think I know that man, Joseph,' shouted Knight, shuffling closer to the edge. He leant forward on his crutch, craning to get a better view. Joe tried to ignore him again, inching further into the pool. Water was now lapping around his chest, and he was terrified that he would stumble.

The drowning man twisted his head towards him again, barely making a noise as his open mouth filled with water.

'Yes, it's him! He's a mentor from one of the decks above us,' Knight said, rocking on his crutches. 'He's screwing one of the new graduates. You know her, I think. The man's a monster!' he yelled, the ripples reflecting on his crazed face.

Joe hesitated, and as he did, the reality of his situation came back into sharp focus.

He couldn't swim. He was surrounded by water, and when he looked beneath him, the ocean stretched out into infinitely below. He gasped for breath.

'Let him die, Joseph. He doesn't deserve to live. He's screwing her night after night after night…'

'Shut up!' he yelled back at him, forcing himself to advance on the tips of his toes. The water lapped beneath his chin. The smell of chlorine was strong. Just another few inches and he would reach him.

'Turn back, Joseph. Don't be a fool…'

The pool darkened around him.

Something vast was passing beneath the ship, obscuring the lights that shone out from the water, and casting a dark shadow that was rapidly moving towards him. The feeling of fear was so overwhelming that he completely froze where he stood.

Yann's whale. It had to be.

He slipped, his head ducking completely beneath the surface, and came up gasping for air. The world was a succession of flashing lights and sounds, and he had no sense of which way to turn.

'You're drowning, Joseph!' Knight screamed.

He tried to yell out, swallowing water in the process, and thrashed his arms about him to stay afloat, the weight of his clothes dragging him under. The ship's engines thundered in the distance, mummifying him in sound, and for a moment he lost his bearings completely. He twisted his head downwards, to see a huge clump of seaweed passing beneath the ship.

Only seaweed.

The relief gave him strength to regain his composure, and he managed to scramble back to the tips of toes. He had drifted to within a few inches of where Rachel's mentor was floating, motionless.

'It's no good, Joseph. You're too late.'

Spluttering, he stretched out an arm, his fingers brushing the arm of the motionless man. There was no reaction.

The muscles in his shoulder burned with the effort of stretching further. This time he managed to get a firmer grip on his arm, yanking him towards him. His head bobbed above the water, choking. Momentarily free, he dived onto Joe's shoulders, dragging them both under again, where they swirled beneath the surface in a violent pirouette. Finally, they broke apart in opposite directions, before releasing themselves completely.

Wading to the side of the pool, he coughed and wheezed, before glancing up to see Knight watching him from the darkness.

'Well done, Joseph. Well done.'

Chapter Twenty-Three

Things were perversely normal the following day, but he felt a total sense of detachment from the events unfolding around him. He was struggling to maintain his grip on reality, and knew that he needed help, but had no idea where he should try to seek it. He punished himself all morning by reading reports about the suicides in Jamaica. There was a feature on the grieving families in the company newsletter, and a sorrowful little five-year-old girl stared up at him from the page. He should have closed the Dominican Republic office down when he had the chance. It was his fault.

He was summoned to an urgent announcement in the bar of the compliance deck at two o'clock. Pouring himself a glass of water, he perched at the end of a row of seats. The man and woman beside him were engaged in an almost hysterical bout of self-comforting. In fact, the entire room was agitated, and with good reason. Williams had painted a bleak picture. There was already plenty of speculation flying about in the ranks, and it was certain that jobs would be lost, though there were different interpretations as to where. Nobody seemed to know for sure what was going to happen. The announcement was being simultaneously transmitted to all Schelldhardt offices around the world, and a significant fraction of the global population was holding its breath.

Joe felt shamefully disconnected from the anxiety. He had offered his recommendations, and was party to their misery. He scanned the room for his own colleagues, and noticed that Fowler was sitting alone, his body language a curious mix of defiance and insecurity. He had once held a senior management position in the late Seventies, catching an early wave of the company's success. He was now flat on his stomach, paddling into shore on the last ripples. Would he make it?

When Williams finally took the microphone, it was a great relief; there wasn't anything he could say that could possibly be worse than the rumours. He was a slick public speaker — his rich and deep address strangely comforting, like a bedtime story. The goodnight kiss would follow for many of them, Joe thought. The positive spin, embellishing everything he said, took a few seconds to mentally translate into the bad news it actually was, and Joe could almost see the minds of the people around him whirring overtime to work out what it all meant personally. In summary, despite making record profits the previous year, Schelldhardt was shedding jobs in almost every area. Each department would be outsourced, downsized or rationalised. The relevant individual announcements would come later, but the purpose of the meeting was to prepare everyone for the worst possible news. The room was filled with an eerie low murmuring, punctuated by hysterical laughter. Williams assured everyone that the steps were absolutely necessary for Schelldhardt to grow. With growth, the company's good work would continue.

It was a huge relief to close the door of his cabin that evening, shutting the world out behind him. His elevated position into management had made him a sounding board for the entire department, and almost everyone seemed to be currying favour or looking for reassurance. It was exhausting, and he couldn't convince anyone that he knew as little as they did.

Joe started to run a bath when the phone rang. It was Marie, and she sounded upset. She wanted to meet him in the red lounge for a drink, but didn't want to discuss the matter over the phone. He suspected that her job had been a casualty of the changes, but could offer her little comfort in his exhausted state. She hung up the telephone before he had finished explaining how difficult the last few days had been, and he felt even worse about himself. He resolved to call her back the following day after a good night's sleep.

As the job losses in the compliance area had not yet been announced, he found it extremely awkward dealing with his former colleagues. Most of the time he kept the door of his office shut under the pretence of dialling in to conferences. He became exceptional at miming on the telephone. When he did leave the room, he tried to time his exit so that their paths wouldn't cross. He was still struggling to decide the smallest things. In the washroom, should he use a paper towel to dry his hands, or the electric hand dryer?

The footprint of recyclable paper production. The overhead of generating electricity.

He stood there, immobilised by indecision, until Fowler entered the room and he scurried away, his hands still dripping.

The successful steering committee initiatives were coming into force, and his computer was blitzed with incoming emails. Teacher-less classrooms. Self-driving taxis. Postal deliveries by drone. The workforce was about to be decimated. It was a future where executives and administrators worked side by side with machines — everybody else as extinct as the dinosaurs, though these very dinosaurs made up the vast majority of the company's client-base. It seemed that Schelldhardt was a serpent that was eating its own tail. The company was also planning to introduce "Total Time", to maximise output. The outdated concept of a weekend was dropping from the company lexicon. All religious festivals, such as Christmas, were to be referred to by their calendar date, and treated as normal days of the week. Employees' sleeping patterns were to be analysed to optimise the working day for each individual, and emailing facilities were to be installed in the restaurants and restrooms to eliminate dead time. In light of the current climate of insecurity, the committee felt that it was the right time to push their policies through.

There was a chart projecting the predicted impact on the share price, which climbed to infinity. It was quite clear that Schelldhardt's charitable intentions did not extend to their own workforce, but shareholders would at least see a return on their investment. The wealthiest one percent of the global population would become wealthier still, and Cloudburst would be delayed for another few years at least. That was all that mattered to them. Depressing as it was, he was just an impotent show pony who wasn't going to change anything. Though what was the show?

Knight stopped by to thank him for his courage the previous evening. He looked remarkably fresh, considering his over-indulgence on the night. The gesture was almost certainly triggered by guilt, particularly as a now-functioning X-ray machine confirmed that his leg was not fractured at all, and his cast had been removed. It was all very convenient.

As he sat in the sanctuary of his cabin, Joe noticed that an envelope had been pushed under his door. It was a note from Marie, who he had shamefully forgotten to call back. There were directions for where he should meet her that evening. The words "URGENT. COME ALONE" were underlined three times.

The park was actually a raised terrace, sandwiched between the rear of the crèche and the walls of the ship. He had no idea it existed, and followed Marie's convoluted instructions through a series of corridors to a narrow metal staircase that led to its entrance. It was obviously intended as a play area for the children, and the space was littered with plastic toys. The setting sun flooded the entire terrace in rich golden light along its length, where turfs of real grass had been laid to create a lawn. The walls were completely covered in climbing plants, flowering in a variety of bright, exotic blooms that quivered in the breeze of an open window. There was even a fountain that gurgled away through a pile of smooth rocks into a reed-edged pond, full of carp.

Marie was sitting on a bench, staring at the pond, and looked as though she might be tempted to throw herself in it. Her complexion was pale, and her hair that normally cascaded over her slender shoulders was tied back and greasy. She hadn't even noticed him arrive. She stood up the moment she saw him, hurrying across the grass towards him.

'Are you okay?' he asked, seeing the panic in her eyes.

'Something is wrong, Joe. I wanted to warn you.' She was shaking, and she continually looked about her.

'Warn me about what?'

'I don't understand fully myself. I was told to call you last night.'

'I know, I'm sorry I didn't come...'

'It's not that,' she said, looking confused. 'I was meant to tell you that I'm pregnant.'

'Pregnant? I don't understand... Are you?'

'No, how could I be? Look, I don't have much time. I told them I wouldn't do it, and I was threatened. I think that you might be in some kind of danger.'

'From whom? I don't understand what you mean. Why would anyone want me to think you're pregnant?'

'Look, there are things I have done that I regret. I'm sorry.'

'What things? What are you talking about?'

'It's better that you don't know,' she said, glancing over her shoulder again. 'Just remember that everything is not as it seems.'

'Tell me exactly what happened. We can speak to the security department.'

'No, it isn't safe,' she said, her eyes widening. 'The ship is going to dock to refuel in a week's time. You have to get off somehow.' She was starting to cry, and glanced around yet again. 'I'm so sorry, I have to go.' Before he could stop her, she hurried across the grass towards the exit.

He was stunned, slumping onto the bench. It had been convenient to dismiss Sandbox as a lunatic, but that wasn't so easy with Marie. To be warned twice was more than just coincidence, and he needed no further encouragement to believe that he was at the centre of some kind of conspiracy. But what? There was no linkage between anything that was happening.

There was a fog descending over his mind again. The park that had seemed so inviting now felt artificial and illusory, like a gingerbread house from a fairy tale. It was a garish imitation of nature, from the brightly coloured flowers, too sickly and sweet, to the perfectly manicured grass. Nothing felt right.

The wind howled through the window, carrying a fine mist inside the ship. He stepped closer to it, allowing the sea spray to blow over his face. The salt stung his eyes. Turning the ratchet clockwise, the gap became larger, and the wind blew fiercer still, each subsequent notch straining the mechanism closer to breaking point, like a fishing reel that had hooked a large game fish. As he wrestled to turn it to its limits, the window was soon tilted diagonally, exposing a gap at the top through which the sea wind blasted through unimpeded, almost tearing the plants from the terrace walls.

It was a gap big enough for a man to squeeze through.

Chapter Twenty-Four

He rammed his clothes into the suitcase. The act of packing was liberating, though he hadn't fully considered his next move. He needed to be ready to leave the ship when the time came, and somehow he had to persuade Rachel to join him. There was, of course, the small matter of reaching her first to have the conversation. He hadn't slept since returning to his room, tossing and turning as he tried to imagine possible scenarios that could explain what was happening, but without success. His headaches were unending, and he just wanted to be back home.

Fortunately, it was a Saturday — the last day until Total Time came into force, so he didn't have to face anyone at work. It gave him the opportunity to formulate a plan. He forced the zip of the case closed, and then dragged it onto the floor, the impact shaking the entire room. How had he been bought so easily? Wealth and luxury had dazzled him at the outset, and then he had sleepwalked straight into their arms. Today, everything was going to change — he just needed to work out how.

He made himself a coffee, rejecting the monstrous bean-to-cup machine sitting on the kitchen counter for the honesty of a spoonful of instant granules. He wanted nothing more to do with Schelldhardt's decadence. Curling up on the couch with a pad and pen, he began to jot down some ideas. The thought of climbing through the park window to reach Rachel terrified him, and he needed to be sure that he had eliminated all other possibilities first. The ideal solution would be to find a pass with no floor restrictions. Perhaps someone from the post room? They were always accompanied by a security chaperone when they visited his office, so it would be difficult to obtain, but he had to try.

That afternoon, it appeared as though the solution had fallen into his lap when Knight called at his room with some welcome news. He had managed to arrange a drink with his friends for that very evening. He apologised for the short notice, but he had only received authorisation that day. The only negative was that they would be meeting in the red lounge. It was a place Joe associated with disaster, but it was the sole venue that the security department would sanction.

It unnerved him that Knight continued to linger in the doorway, and he was conscious of his packed case sitting in the bedroom just a few feet away. His uneasiness must have been obvious, and he inched the cabin door further closed every time Knight glanced over his shoulder, without inviting him inside. It was almost as if he knew it was there.

'I hope you enjoy tonight,' Knight smiled, 'but please remember that everything you have experienced in our department is completely confidential. I will know if you betray my trust.' His smiled faded, and he stared at Joe with a familiar menace. It was a great relief when he finally left, and Joe immediately dragged the case further out of view.

They met at eight. Knight strode ahead, and he followed like his wretched hound, avoiding the austere old faces hanging from the corridor wall. Knight stopped at the lift with his back turned and waited; the red lounge bar wasn't to be their final destination tonight, after all. He inserted his pass into the control panel, acknowledging Joe's interest in the card with a smirk, before tucking it inside his jacket. Perhaps Knight had found the notes he made earlier in his cabin. It wouldn't be a surprise.

He assumed that they were heading down to the swimming pool, but the lift lurched upwards. They stood in silence, Knight staring forward with his arms clasped behind his back, smugly aloof. The redness of the light within the confined space seemed more pronounced than ever, colouring their faces. The chandelier rattled above their heads as the lift juddered to a halt. When the door finally slid open, cold air blasted in, shocking him out of his lethargy; they were on the top deck of *Ananke*, but it had been converted into some kind of fair. There were strings of multi-coloured light bulbs swaying along the length of the ship, brilliantly vivid against the darkening sky. At the centre was a carousel, pumping organ music out into the cool evening air. Large groups of people were milling around the deck. They were dressed in suits and dresses, laughing and joking with one another.

'There's been a change of plan,' Knight said, not bothering to make eye contact. 'Your friends will meet you here. It's a fundraiser, Joseph. Security will collect you at eleven and escort you back to the compliance deck. Remember what I told you. You will be watched,' he added, before pulling his jacket tighter and striding out into the wind.

Joe was reluctant to step out of the lift after him — a prisoner who had become too accustomed to his cell. His confidence was fragile, and it was difficult to know how to approach Rachel. As he rehearsed what he was going to say to her in his mind, he realised just how little he understood of what was actually happening. Alcohol had long since ceased to be his friend, but he still sought its solace all the same, making for a nearby bar tent with inappropriate haste. The cocktails were, as always, tempting, but seemed irreverent under the circumstances, the beer also too frivolous, and so he opted for a large Scotch, sitting solemnly in a sturdy glass with the necessary gravitas to accompany the difficult conversation to come. His hands were shaking. Perhaps it wasn't the best time to talk to her at all. It was hard to equate the happiness of the people around him with Marie's terrified face just the day before.

He stepped out of the tent with his drink, scanning the animated crowd. There were a few faces he recognised, but he couldn't see Rachel. Anyone who looked at him for a fraction of a second too long made him suspicious; were they one of Knight's spies?

An arm coiled around his neck, tugging him from behind.

'Surprise!' shouted Dixon, whose smile instantly dissolved when he saw Joe's expression. 'What's wrong? You look awful.'

For a moment he couldn't speak, shocked by his own overreaction as much as the contact. 'I didn't realise it was you,' he stammered. It was ridiculous that he had become so jumpy.

Dixon hesitated — for once at a loss for what to say. He had obviously been drinking, but it seemed he had yet to emotionally plateau. 'I see we've left you alone for far too long!' he grinned at last. He had regained his spectacles — one crumb of familiarity amongst all the unwelcome change. 'It's great to see you. Come and join the others.'

Dixon didn't wait for a reply, before wandering away. Joe discarded his drink on a nearby table, easing through a group of laughing men in pursuit. There was a huge banner billowing in the wind above their heads. It read, "Schelldhardt's planet Earth pledge". Male and female swim-suited models shivered beneath it, handing out leaflets to an unresponsive crowd. They passed the carousel, which he noticed had been customised to match the environmental theme. Dolphins replaced horses, their wasted riders clinging to fins and flippers, with drinks in their hands. At the centre, a mechanical polar bear sat on his diminishing ice cap, clashing a pair of cymbals together with empty-eyed madness. The colours and sounds were overwhelming after the stark isolation of the compliance deck, and he felt like a bewildered old man.

'Where are we going?' he shouted after Dixon.

'You'll see,' he laughed, still striding ahead.

There was a rowdy group of people assembled outside another bar tent, and one of them was Ryan — resplendent in his suit. He was draped around a young woman who didn't seem entirely impressed with the attention. She took the opportunity to slip away when she saw Joe approaching.

'Joe, it's great to see you,' Ryan said, shaking his hand. 'I've heard you've moved up in the world.'

'Hardly,' he laughed. 'Where did you hear that?'

'From Rachel. She's on the same management programme as you. The pair of you make me feel like a complete failure.'

'Rachel. Are you sure? I haven't seen her at any of the meetings.'

'Absolutely; she has told me all about it. Could you give me some tips on how to get to the top?'

Joe smiled, but was too disturbed by the news to comment. Dixon emerged from the bar tent at the same time, distracting him from the thought as he pushed a glass of champagne into his hand.

'Where is Rachel?' he asked, reluctantly accepting it.

'Oh, she's around. Have a drink with us first,' laughed Dixon, slapping his back.

He made small talk as best he could. Faces flashed by as they spoke, and he was convinced that they were staring at him. Occasionally, he spotted someone glancing back at him as they passed. He was starting to sweat, and loosened his tie.

'Does anything seem strange to you about Schelldhardt?' he asked Dixon.

'In what way?'

'I don't know. Have you noticed anything unusual since you've been working here?'

'Unusual?' Dixon laughed, throwing an arm around his shoulder. 'Same old Joe, always looking for the seams when he should be admiring the fabric. This job is more than I could have ever dreamt of.'

He looked positively euphoric, as did Ryan. There seemed little point in pursuing the subject further with either of them, particularly in their current state. They continued to exchange stories about their new positions, which seemed considerably less responsible than his own. He smiled and nodded, but was barely listening any longer. A woman in a lime dress caught his attention, pushing her way through the crowd towards him. It looked like Marie. She was blocked off by two men, and twisted sideways to ease through the gap between them.

'Joe,' she called, her voice drowned out by the sound of the carousel.

He stepped towards her, but as he did, one of the men turned and punched her full in the face. She fell backwards instantly, and the crowd closed around her.

He momentarily froze, unable to comprehend what he had witnessed. The man disappeared into the body of people, who continued to laugh and talk to each other as if nothing had happened.

'Did you see that?' he said to Dixon, who was too engrossed in his conversation with Ryan to notice. Joe ran towards the nearest woman in the crowd, nearly knocking the glass from her hand as he tried to get her attention. 'Did you see the woman in the green dress?' She looked at him as if was crazy, before turning her back, and laughing to her friend. Everyone he approached reacted in the same way. 'Someone must have seen that!' he shouted, but his voice was drowned by the carousel. There was no sign of Marie in the crowd.

'Joe, what are you doing?' said Dixon, grabbing his arm. 'You're making a scene.' Dixon looked at him so incredulously that it was impossible to trust his own judgement. Had he imagined it? Only one person could help him.

'Wait,' said Dixon, chasing after him. 'Where are you going?'

He didn't reply. Laughing faces blocked his path as he fought his way into a clearing. He could see Rachel across the deck, but was almost barged to the floor as he advanced towards her. He spun on one leg, but no sooner had he regained his balance when he was barged again. His faceless assailants stormed away through the crowd without looking back. It happened half a dozen times.

'Rachel,' he called, as he finally reached her. She looked stunning in her backless dress, but she had applied too much make-up, and he didn't like the transformation. She looked like a painted doll.

'Joe, how lovely!' she said, her lips brushing each cheek with fleeting indifference. 'It feels like *ages* since I've seen you.'

Everything was wrong: from the contrived greeting to her air of distraction. He almost laughed, thinking it a joke, but her eyes, heavy with eye shadow, were already looking beyond him.

'I need to speak to you, Rachel'

'Not now, Joseph,' said Knight, emerging from her side. 'We are negotiating a deal with an important client.'

The sight of them together was such a shock that he didn't reply. He sensed that his mouth was open, and Knight acknowledged the reaction with a grin. The situation instantly worsened when he shared a whispered joke with Rachel.

'Later, Joe,' she said, squeezing his hand.

He could only watch on the periphery as Rachel and Knight spoke with the advisers of the client. She looked perfectly at ease in their company. It didn't seem possible that she could have integrated into their world so quickly. And what about Marie? Had he actually seen her punched in the face? It was difficult to think clearly. In the distance, the polar bear at the centre of the carousel seemed more crazed than ever, bashing his cymbals together louder and more vigorously. Everybody around him was laughing and joking, their faces distorted in the fading light. Perhaps he really was ill.

He breathed slowly and forced himself to concentrate. From what he could gather, Rachel and Knight were discussing the new environmental initiatives. He caught random snippets of the conversation — the noise of the party around him deafening.

'Mr Andrada will only enter into this arrangement if Mr Gerrick is out completely,' said a fearsome-looking female adviser. Joe recognised their names from the Schelldhardt news channel. Andrada and Gerrick held two of the company's largest shareholdings, and there was bad blood between them. The mast of Gerrick's super-yacht had recently been extended to exceed Andrada's by two metres in a tit-for-tat escalation of their spat over mineral mining rights on the moon. At the last board meeting, they had each refused to enter the room first until the other was seated, delaying proceedings by two hours until a second door was unlocked, enabling them to enter at the same time from opposite ends. This had infamously left no time to discuss the company's child poverty initiative on the agenda.

'I'm sure we could accommodate that request,' said Knight, grinning horribly.

'Mr Andrada need not worry at all,' said Rachel, placing her arm on the adviser's shoulder. 'He is our most valued client.'

'That's excellent news,' said the adviser. 'Rest assured, too, Mr Andrada has found a suitable location for the new national park, and preparations have already begun. Providing he can count on your support, of course…'

'Of course…' Rachel replied.

Fowler appeared from the group, stepping to Joe's side. He looked worried.

'This is very bad business, Joe. I don't like this one bit.'

'The national park?'

'That's just a sweetener. It's what Andrada wants in return…'

'Mr Fowler,' said Knight, interrupting him. 'I hope you're not filling Joseph's head with horror stories.'

'I was just pointing out my objections…'

'There can be no objections, Mr Fowler. Schelldhardt has pledged to preserve our planet. Our good work is of paramount importance. You know that.'

'At what price, Martin?'

'Silence,' hissed Knight. 'This is not the time.'

'I will not be silenced,' shouted Fowler, his cheeks flushing. Andrada's advisers noticed the disturbance, and were wandering towards them. Knight acted quickly, moving between them as a barrier.

'Rachel, why don't you escort Mr Fowler to the bridge. He looks as though he should take the sea air to cool down.'

'Of course,' said Rachel.

'I'll go with you,' said Joe.

'Very well,' Knight smiled. As he turned to leave, Knight grabbed his arm, pulling closer to his ear. 'I expect you to do the right thing, Joseph. The time has come to prove yourself.'

They headed towards a passageway that led from the main deck to the bridge beyond it, with lifeboats suspended above the entrance. The crowd seemed rowdier than ever, jostling and dancing as they walked. Fowler was sandwiched between the two of them, walking silently, with his head bowed. Rachel peeled away to talk to a security guard, and he waited with Fowler beneath a lifeboat. Alone with Joe, his face was ashen, and he breathed heavily.

'Andrada wants weapons. The national park is located in disputed territory. He's going to start a civil war.'

'Schelldhardt can't supply weapons to him.'

'Don't be so sure. A corporation of this size can do anything, trust me.'

'But why? Surely it isn't worth the risk of ruining their reputation.'

'For the same reason as always, Joe. To grow, of course. It's all about Andrada's continued investment. He is pumping a fortune into the company, and there will also be lucrative carbon credit deals for Schelldhardt, not to mention the massive publicity they will receive around the national park. Everything else is completely secondary. For Andrada, it's just another land grab. The rainforest is a fraction of the area he stands to gain in the war, and he is happy to give it away. He wants complete control of the region for political reasons. The hostilities will never be linked to Schelldhardt in any way. We may be preserving a rainforest, but we will be enabling a genocide in the process.'

'Genocide is a strong word,' said Rachel, appearing behind them. 'It's little more than a neighbourhood dispute. Why don't we discuss this somewhere quieter?' she added, gesturing towards the passageway. As Joe glanced back, every face in the crowd was turned towards them, and for a split second they seemed to completely freeze, before the fair rumbled back into life.

The passageway was almost in darkness, and there were puddles of seawater beneath their feet. He could barely hear the sound of the carousel, drowned out by the roar of the ocean. Inky waves glittered on the horizon, where the moon was obscured by a veil of dark cloud.

Rachel stopped walking.

'I need to talk to Joe alone.'

'Very well,' replied Fowler. He splashed through the gloom to the far end of the passageway, where he waited, gazing blankly out to sea over the handrail.

'Something is wrong, Rachel. We need to get off this ship.'

'Joe, calm down,' she laughed. 'I think Fowler has spooked you.'

'No, it's not just Fowler. There are other things happening that I can't explain. I don't feel right,' he said, fighting to force the words out, 'and you seem... different, too.'

'You've been working too hard. A job like this takes a huge adjustment after university. I've found the same thing,' she smiled, taking his hands in hers, 'and I'm just the same as I always was. Relax.'

She looked beautiful in the moonlight. He dearly wanted to forget about everything else, but his fears were not so easily abated.

'Schelldhardt is not the company we thought it was.'

'It's so much more, Joe. We can finally change the world, just like we always said we would. We have our chance to make a difference.'

'This is not the difference we should be making...'

She only smiled, moving closer still to him, her arm clutching his waist. He could feel the silk of her dress against his skin and her breath on his neck. Waves thundered against the ship, the motion drawing them together.

'Difficult decisions have to be made to do our good work,' she said, embracing him. 'I need you to help me drive the Andrada deal through. He will be landing on the ship in a couple of days.'

'What about Fowler's concerns?'

'It's an exaggeration, Joe. He has his own agenda. But even if he was right, wouldn't a few hundred lives be worth the risk? There's a much bigger picture. Think of how our planet will be saved for generations to come. It would be a small price to pay.'

Listen to her, Joseph. There must be an acceptable level of human mortality to preserve our environment. We just need you to define it for us. We need you to tell us the precise number of lives that you would sacrifice to save the planet.

The voice seemed to be coming from directly behind him, but he spun around only to see the metal wall of the ship.

'You must have learnt your lesson from the Caribbean, Joe. Doing nothing can be more detrimental than anything else. We need Andrada's financial support.'

'Rachel, people will die.'

'The end will justify the means. Leaders have to be strong. Remember what we have been taught. Good is whatever is necessary to grow, and all of this is necessary.'

It was impossible to focus. He grasped at a chain dangling from a lifeboat, certain that he was going to fall again. The sea shimmered beyond, but it only made him dizzier as he tried to focus on the horizon. He couldn't do it.

'I can't help you. I'm sorry,' he said, easing away. 'You're wrong.'

As he pulled away from her, the music from the carousel abruptly stopped, and there was instant silence. People stood motionless on all sides of the deck, watching them in the distance. Even Fowler turned quietly towards them.

Rachel appeared shocked by his reaction. For a moment, she looked unsure what to do next, but then smiled. He tried to retreat, but she held him tighter, her lips moving from his neck to his ear.

'Do you remember the time when we walked home together after the Christmas party?' she whispered.

'Yes, of course,' he replied, wrong-footed by the change of topic. Her body was pressed against his, and he could feel the beat of her heart.

'That was the happiest time of my life,' she smiled, caressing his back. 'I always hoped that one day it might happen again if I waited long enough. Perhaps today...'

It was everything that he had ever wanted to hear, but these were not her words; every instinct told him that. However much he rationalised, he could not stop himself from believing her. He *wanted* to believe her.

'All of this is happening for a reason, and the reason is that we should be together,' she said, wiping a tear from his cheek. 'This is our destiny.'

Her lips met his, and all remaining reason was lost in her kiss. He immersed himself totally in the moment, and the fearful voices in his mind were finally silenced. The feeling was so perfect that he wanted his life to end right there, but even as he fought to sustain the sensation, she was gently pulling away from him.

'Do it for me, if not for Schelldhardt,' she said. 'I have made promises that have to be kept. If they are not, there will be consequences.'

'What promises? We can leave the ship together.'

'These are promises that are not easily broken. I'll understand if you want no part of this, but I have no other option,' she said, resting her head against his chest. When she looked up, there were tears in her eyes, and she looked scared. 'I'll face the consequences alone if I have to.'

'No,' he said. 'No, I won't let that happen.'

'Then swear to me that you will help with Andrada…'

The world was slipping in and out of focus. Fowler was still watching silently from the end of the passageway. It felt as if his mind was being torn apart. His longing to lose consciousness was overpowering, but Rachel sobbed again, before finally breaking down completely on his shoulder.

'Of course,' he said, holding her tightly. 'I'll do whatever you want.'

She smiled, and kissed him tenderly on the lips. He held on to her, afraid to let her go, but unable to shake the feeling that everything was about to get much worse.

In the distance, the carousel began to turn again.

Judgement

'You were so close to denying her. So very, very close, but you failed. It had nothing to do with the environment, or a genocide. It was just about your feelings for her again.'

'I was confused...'

'Do you really value this woman above right and wrong?' said the voice angrily. 'Is there nothing you wouldn't do for her?'

Joe didn't reply at first. He was exhausted from thinking about it. There were patterns in the darkness. Tiny, shimmering coloured lights. It was beautiful.

'I've had enough of your questions,' he said wearily. 'Just tell me what to do.'

'I'm afraid that I cannot do that.'

'I want it all to end. I just want peace.'

'There is no end for you here. What do you think this is?'

'I have no idea, but it isn't real. None of this is real.'

'That is why you fail! Why does it matter what this is? You are here and you have to make choices. That's all that there is — yourself and the decisions you make. There will never be a revelation. You will die without knowing for sure what this was — just like everybody else. You have to act. I need you to act.'

The mention of death sent his mind off at a tangent. The feeling of weightlessness. The darkness. It was too peaceful to be anywhere else.

'I think this is my judgement.'

'We are running out of time,' said the voice, breaking in frustration. 'It's too late in the day for you to discover faith now. You should not kill. You should not steal. How does that help you? These are simplistic instructions for a complex world. What if you need to steal to save a life? What if you need to kill to save your family or your fellow countrymen in a war? Who decides the relative value of principles in situations like these? That's why the world is in chaos. It's why cities are flattened in the name of democracy. It's why a school is blown to pieces in the name of God. That is exactly why all of this is necessary…'

'I think that I am being tested,' he interrupted.

'Is that so? Well, I am not God,' sighed the voice, 'and you are just trying to make sense of the misery of your existence. To think that you suffer for a reason justifies the suffering. It is comforting to believe that someone is keeping score, and there will be some reward at the end of it. You *want* this to be your judgement, but I'm afraid it isn't. Why would God test you anyway? It makes no sense.'

'To prove that I am worthy.'

'That is just ridiculous. We won't achieve our goals unless you start to think rationally. You believe that this is the God who created the earth and the sea and the stars, and yet created you, with all your imperfections, just so you could prove your worthiness? This is the same God that created the wings of a butterfly, and the beauty of a coral reef, yet created you as a kit in the hope that you would somehow put yourself together. It's complete nonsense. If God wants worthiness, worthiness would be created right from the start.'

Joe felt so utterly exhausted that he struggled to reply. He longed for everything to be over. If he could fast forward time to that final moment of peace, then he would do it without hesitation.

'I don't want to do this any more,' he said at last.

'I won't let you give up now. There might be another possibility you haven't considered. Maybe this particular God is looking to you for answers. Perhaps they have no better idea of what they should be doing than you. How could any God ever be *sure* of their decisions any more than you are — roaring fearful commands from an infinite heaven, and revelling in their perceived omnipotence, but eternally mindful that a curtain may slide away to reveal the laughing creator of the great creator, judging from the side-lines? Whatever we think, we cannot know. Uncertainty can be the only universal certainty, but we are all still forced to act. So why don't you show me what *you* think is right? There is still one more day before I hand you over. You must deny this girl.'

Chapter Twenty-Five
3rd January 2014

'So what exactly is the path of good response?' said Knight, tilting his head backwards as he spoke to the audience. He was pale and gangly, reminding Shendi of the wispy spiders that scrabbled around the rafters of his summerhouse. 'To explain, I would like you to close your eyes and imagine something for me.'

Shendi glanced around the lecture room, and saw most of the other attendees had followed the instruction. He reluctantly complied, unaccustomed to obeying the commands of others.

'I'd like you to imagine a grand concert hall. Inside that hall, an orchestra is about to play. The orchestra that you are each picturing will be different. Some of you may be imagining young people in your orchestra. Others may be imagining old. Some of you will be imagining men. Others will be imagining women, or a mixture of both. Maybe you can even see their faces, which, of course, will all be different, as will be the clothes that they are wearing. They are all going to play the same piece of music. Although your orchestras are different, they will strive to play this piece as perfectly as they can. A conductor approaches, and hands them each a sheet of music. The sheet of music is the path they must follow for this perfect performance, and the conductor is their guide.'

Knight paused, and Shendi wondered whether he should open his eyes. He erred on the side of caution, not wishing to be singled out for attention.

'With that mental image still in your minds, I'd like to explain where our work fits into this picture. Your orchestra is analogous with the human brain. Just as the age, sex and composition of your orchestras vary, so do our brains. The common piece of music they must play represents a decision to be made. Any decision. In the analogy, the sheet music is the ideal route through the brain to reach the perfect decision.

We call this the path of good response,' said Knight, walking across the stage.

Shendi finally dared to open his eyes. Knight was standing by an open laptop on the podium. He clicked onto the next slide of his presentation before stepping forward to face the audience once again.

'There is a famously misquoted line, attributed originally to George Santayana, which states that, "Those who fail to learn from history's mistakes are doomed to repeat them." What is true of history, is also true of ourselves. During the course of our lives we may develop addictions, compulsive disorders, and a whole variety of other behavioural problems that are negative to our well-being and to those around us. Our lives can quickly degenerate into a cyclical repetition of mistakes. What if there was a way to correct these errant pathways through the mind? Imagine if a drug addict could make decisions unencumbered by their chemical cravings. If a yo-yo dieter was able to resist unhealthy food. Perhaps even the psychopathic tendencies of a murderer could be curtailed from within. Our intention is to break these negative cycles, and liberate the minds of the sufferers.'

Knight paused, and clicked onto a new slide of the presentation, where a three-dimensional image of the brain was displayed, labelling the various different areas.

'The pathway for a decision in our mind is extremely complex, but by meticulously cross-referencing responses from millions of subjects using new generation MRI scanners, common patterns emerge, both errant and desirable. To assist the brain in following the desirable route, we introduce our product, the conductor. The conductor ensures that this route is followed as closely as possible. If the brain deviates towards an identifiable errant path, the conductor attempts to realign the thought process. Of course, this is a huge simplification, but hopefully you can see the principle.'

Shendi was intrigued. He had arrived at the university exhausted, feeling the effects of his whistle-stop itinerary, but from the moment he first heard about the research, he knew he had to come. He could easily have sent a representative in his place, but had long since learnt that the best way to get a true feel for a potential investment was to arrive unannounced and anonymous. Besides, his reasons for coming were entirely personal, and there was nobody he trusted enough to share them with.

This would help, he knew it. It had become just too painful to watch him make the same mistakes that he had made. Against all of his best business principles, he was desperate to invest. Shendi's many detractors often joked that he would exercise due diligence before ordering a coffee, but if they could see him now they would be amused. He was ready to sign a blank cheque in pure speculative hope, but there was a clarity and order to the process that he found irresistible.

Knight handed over to his colleagues, and they explained in more detail how the conductor worked. The presentation was highly technical, and largely passed over the heads of the assembly, including Shendi. He followed what he could, but preferred to keep Knight's simple analogy in mind when bombarded with names and facts.

The presentation ended with a question-and-answer session. Knight fielded what he could, referring to other members of the team for anything technically related. A woman in a suit held up her hand, and Knight's assistant passed her a microphone.

'Isn't this brainwashing?'

Knight took the microphone back. 'Isn't this brainwashing?' he repeated to the audience. 'Absolutely not. In fact, this process couldn't be further from it. We are already brainwashed, ladies and gentlemen, from the moment we first open our eyes. Brainwashed by our parents, brainwashed by our teachers, friends and colleagues. Brainwashed by the whole of the society around us. Just think about that for a moment. Think about your own religion and your own politics — even the sports teams that you support. How many of these opinions did you form for yourself without the influence of others? How much of this could you really claim is the fruit of your own free thought? We are products of our environment, and we call this conditioning our belief mask. It defines who we are, but also isolates us from others. You only have to look at any social media application to see polar opinions screaming from the page. We are all so certain that our own views are correct, but are blind to the belief masks right in front of our faces, colouring all of our conclusions. However good our intentions, we are unable to see the flaws in our own thinking objectively, because they become part of ourselves.

Our belief masks can even become mental prisons. We may declare that we are a capitalist, a socialist or a feminist, and then try to justify everything in the world around us to fit our masks. The conductor strips the belief mask away, allowing us to make decisions with the objectivity of a newborn baby.'

'How can you define this path of good response, as you call it? Surely that is subjective itself?' said another woman nearby.

'The path is defined by analysing the scans from millions of brains, from different cultures and races in response to key questions. By cross-referencing these results, we are able to establish consistent patterns, and identifiable errant reactions to different scenarios. Our sampling is so wide and varied that we can be confident that we are compiling an accurate and meaningful result.'

'Is this artificial intelligence?' asked another.

'There is nothing artificial about it. These decisions are ultimately made by the human brain. Please remember that the conductor is only initiated if a known errant thought pattern is identified, and it is completely configurable. This does not replace human judgement.'

The questions continued for another fifteen minutes, and Shendi began to feel anxious. Nobody had asked the one thing that he really wanted to know, and as he could sense that they were approaching the end of the presentation, he was forced to put his hand in the air.

'How far away are we from seeing your conductor, or anything like it in a human being?'

Knight smiled, somewhat patronisingly, before speaking into the microphone. 'We have achieved a great deal in a relatively short space of time, but there is significant development and research required, not to mention the ethical issues we would need to address before this kind of work is fully sanctioned. Testing this product alone could take many years. Imagine you are driving along a busy country road, and there is a car racing towards you in the opposite direction. If one of our clients is driving that car, we need to be one hundred percent certain that they see fit to stay on their own side of the road.'

The presentation came to an end, and the lecture room began to empty. Knight remained by the lectern, answering questions from the circle of people that surrounded him. Shendi slowly descended the stairs, hanging back until the last of them had left. Knight was packing his equipment away into boxes when he approached. He sensed that he was trying to ignore him, and seemed overtly focused on shutting down his laptop.

'A fascinating presentation.'

'Thank you,' said Knight, without looking up.

'What is that?' Shendi asked, pointing to some electronic equipment on a trolley. Knight glanced up, but continued to fiddle with the laptop.

'It's what we use to communicate with the conductor. Currently, it is little more than a computer circuit board, but once *in situ* we will be able to interface directly with our patients.'

'Interface?'

'Talk to them. It's how we intend to test the installation.'

'So you could ask the patient any question? Test any kind of scenario?'

'Theoretically, yes, but these are very early days. Look, I'm sorry, but I really need to leave.'

It was a moment of absolute epiphany. Shendi was too stunned by the implications of his reply to react at first. What had been an interesting idea had just transformed into a compelling new proposition altogether. This could help both of them...

'What would you require to implement this in a patient within two years?'

Knight laughed as he unplugged the power adaptor from the wall socket. 'As I said in the presentation, there are numerous factors that would make that impossible.'

'Even with an unlimited budget?'

'Although that would be very welcome, there would still be the ethical and sanctioning issues to deal with,' he said, closing the lid of the computer. He carefully wound the power cable around the adaptor. 'We simply wouldn't be able to achieve those things within that timescale.'

'What if there was a place with every facility you required, away from the public eye?'

Knight looked up for the first time as he put the computer into the case, smiling. 'I don't think there is such a place.'

Shendi leant towards him. 'There is, and you should be taking this conversation much more seriously.'

Chapter Twenty-Six

Bow-ties flummoxed him. Having struggled to master the shoelace, and then the regular necktie, it seemed unfair that life should introduce another clothing tripwire so late in the day. Rachel was a stickler for a real bow-tie, never allowing him to compromise with an elasticated substitute when attending their university balls. Joe always protested, but there was nothing he liked better than standing toe-to-toe with her while she helped him tie it. He loved the intimacy, and made a point of never perfecting it himself.

He had made a pretty good attempt at the knot himself tonight all the same. He ducked beneath a patch of condensation on the bathroom mirror to check his reflection, straightening his collar and pulling back the shoulders of his tuxedo. Schelldhardt would be proud; he looked quite the hungry young go-getter they wanted him to be.

He left his room just before eight, and arrived at the red lounge in time for pre-dinner cocktails in the reception area. He recognised the concierge from his first visit, which seemed almost another lifetime ago. The man smirked in a kind of restrained acknowledgement — at least that's how Joe interpreted it, reciprocating with a little nod of his own.

'Are you waiting for other guests, sir?'

'No, not tonight.'

'Can I get you a drink?'

'I'm fine, thank you,' he replied. He was about to pass through the oak-panelled door, when he noticed that the concierge was still watching him.

'I trust you know how to conduct yourself in the red lounge now, sir?'

'I know exactly, thank you,' he smiled, pushing his way inside.

It was obvious, even by Schelldhardt's standards, that the meeting was significant, not least because it was being held on a Sunday evening. Total Time, the new company initiative, was now in full force, with posters on every wall around the ship. The smiling young model in the picture looked delighted that she was now available every second of the week, all year round.

He was whisked away to a function room, where canapés and champagne were being served. A pianist was playing in the corner of the room, where pockets of guests were gathering. Knight hadn't arrived, but Joe could see Williams in his tuxedo talking to another director. The senior management were out in force. Joe grabbed a flute of champagne and a canapé, feeling awkward standing alone. It gave him something to do with his hands. He bit into the caviar blini, but squirted sour cream over the back of a nearby woman's dress in the process. She was oblivious to his accident, and he quickly swallowed the evidence.

Sexism was alive and well amongst the Schelldhardt hierarchy, and having agreed to support Rachel with Andrada's deal, they had insisted that he came to the meeting in her place. Andrada preferred to deal with men.

Knight arrived in the room. He had opted to wear a barong rather than a tuxedo, and he looked like a lanky ghost in the long, white embroidered shirt. It was obviously intended as a gesture of respect for their guest, Angelo Andrada, but he appeared to be satisfyingly uncomfortable in his attire. Andrada — their man in Manila, as Knight referred to him — was undoubtedly the sole focus of the proceedings. Whatever he wanted, Schelldhardt infallibly made sure that he got. His personal wealth ran into billions, and he was rumoured to own vast areas of south-east Asia. Possession of land and property was his obsession, having apparently grown up in the humblest of surroundings, and he continually endeavoured to expand his portfolio, playing a global game of Monopoly.

A waiter informed Joe that it was time to assemble in the main entertaining hall. As expected, Andrada insisted on entering the hall last, and everyone had to wait in position before he arrived. It was a venue Joe had visited before, but it had been utterly transformed: suspended from the ceiling was a colourful Filipino dragon, some thirty feet in length, with two sets of wings that spanned the entire width of the room. The fearsome head was illuminated with a red lamp within that glowed in the gloom. Beneath the dragon was a model of a city that had been constructed in incredible detail — magnificent beneath a series of spotlights, it formed the centrepiece of the room. Along the walls were racks of lighted red candles, from floor to ceiling, and everywhere Joe looked were sumptuous decorations of crimson and gold.

There was a hush, and then applause when Andrada entered the room. He was a short, slight man, with grey hair and a face that belied his years. His liquid brown eyes darted around the room, seemingly assessing if the level of adulation was adequate. He greeted Knight and Williams, before taking his seat at the head of a table adjacent to the model of the city.

Joe was unsure exactly what was expected of him. He lingered awkwardly at the periphery of the party, nursing a glass of champagne that was warming fast. He noticed that the other guests were not showing the same restraint, and they already mingled less self-consciously now. There was a brief presentation for Andrada. Schelldhardt had purchased some small islands off the coast of Scotland for his collection. The land was insignificant compared with the vast area he stood to gain if Fowler was right. Williams made a gushing speech, praising his special contribution to the company and the environment, and there was a warm round of applause. Thankfully, Andrada said only a few words to express his gratitude in return, and the party resumed immediately. It was hard to imagine much business taking place today.

The champagne flowed freely and, after an hour, the drugs arrived, as per the standard Schelldhardt timetable. The company was at least consistent in its decadence. Opium pipes replaced the regular trays of cocaine, lovingly tended by scantily dressed young men and women circulating through the crowd. One of them, a young woman with a beautiful smile, stopped when she reached Joe. She drew on the pipe, before blowing smoke into his face. He pretended to inhale out of politeness, but did not take the fumes into his lungs. This time he was determined to keep his wits about him.

Williams was deep in discussion with Andrada at the table. Joe wandered over to the model of the city, even more impressive close up. The ambitious construction project would house Schelldhardt's entire operations in the Philippines. As well as the geometrically challenging office blocks, there were schools, hospitals and parks. The sheer scale of the development was breath-taking.

'Impressive, isn't it?' Knight said, surprising him. He had an unpleasant habit of appearing when he was least wanted. For once, though, Joe found himself in agreement.

'Is this a similar size to Schelldhardt India?'

'Much bigger,' said Knight. 'It will have almost double the capacity of our operation there.'

'Why do Schelldhardt need so much extra capacity?' he said, running his hand over the textured landscape.

'We don't. This is a direct replacement for Schelldhardt India.'

Schelldhardt India was one of the company's flagship locations, promoted on almost every piece of corporate communication. Its significance had been rammed down his throat since he joined. Schelldhardt had been one of the first companies to outsource much of their operation, and the Indian headquarters had long been established as a centre of excellence. It was more than a company location: it was a living, breathing city. Closing it would have a catastrophic effect on the area.

'Don't look so surprised, Joseph. This won't be the last movement of our operations. We will engage the services of the remotest Amazon tribe if we can leverage the cost benefits. Schelldhardt is flattening the economic landscape. This gives everyone a fair playing field.'

'Fairness, of course,' Joe laughed. 'The company prides itself on that.'

'The priority is delaying Cloudburst,' Knight said, ignoring him. He reached for his pocket. 'Which reminds me, I need you to familiarise yourself with this,' he said, passing him a piece of paper.

'What is this?'

'It's a list of Andrada's requirements. I would like to remind you of our mutual friend's commitment to this project. You would be acting against her best interest if you refuse to co-operate,' he said, edging closer. 'You have made your bed, Joseph. Get yourself a drink and study the list carefully. I don't want to see you skulking around the room any more. You belong to us now.'

Joe couldn't look Knight in the eye. It was a relief when he finally wandered away, and he grabbed a glass of champagne from a passing waiter, scanning Knight's list. It wasn't just pistols and rifles that Andrada needed — the arsenal looked comprehensive enough to wage a small war. Fowler had been right.

The music was becoming louder. Knight joined Andrada, beckoning Joe towards them.

'I've heard good things about you,' said Andrada, smiling. He was quietly spoken, and it was difficult to hear what he was saying. 'Mr Knight told me you are going to assist with my new project.'

'Yes, I have seen your requirements.'

'Excellent,' said Andrada, resting a hand on his shoulder. 'Do you foresee any problems sourcing any of them?'

'Not at all,' he replied, watching Knight over his shoulder. 'We will ensure all of your needs are met. I will see to it personally.'

Andrada followed his eyes towards Knight and smiled. 'This is very welcome news,' he said, raising a glass towards him. Joe could feel Knight watching him, and forced a smile. Their glasses met. 'I agree, Mr Knight. This young man has great potential. He is definitely someone I can see us working with, just like you said. Let us drink to saving rainforests.'

'To saving rainforests…'

Joe felt physically sick by the time he left the table. The next time the girl with the opium pipe passed him, he didn't resist, taking a large draw of his own. He nearly choked, but managed to inhale some of the smoke. After a few more attempts, he found himself slumped in a chair, with no recollection of sitting there. Andrada had pulled up a seat next to him, and they were watching dancers in the middle of the floor. There were men and women wearing traditional Filipino costumes of blue, yellow and orange, dancing over long lengths of bamboo. Joe was mesmerised by the speed of their feet, and the vividness of the colours. The spectacle seemed almost more than three-dimensional, and the rhythmic tapping of the bamboo on the floor, coupled with the cries of the dancers, was hypnotic. He applauded enthusiastically when they finished, much to Andrada's amusement. The dancers were replaced by a group of children, who started to play some kind of game inside a circle they had drawn in chalk on the floor. Andrada tried to explain it to him, but he struggled to hear him. The dragon hanging from the ceiling was called Bakunawa. Bakunawa wanted to eat the moon. It was all so surreal that he wondered if everyone was high. The children were running around in a circle holding hands, while a child outside the ring tried to break inside to catch another. Their laughter was genuine and infectious, and it almost reduced him to tears.

After a few hours, most of the guests had left and he was still sitting with Andrada, who was going into great detail about the new Philippines office. Williams and Knight joined them, bringing a couple of bottles of champagne with them. They both looked a little unsteady on their feet.

'We expect great things from the new office, Mr Andrada,' slurred Williams, spilling most of the drinks as he poured them.

'I could tell you about our excellent infrastructure and the unrivalled professionalism of our management, but all you really need to know is that my staff will work for you until they bleed from their eyes, for a fraction of the cost,' Andrada smiled.

'Schelldhart India is dead. Long live Schelldhart Philippines!' laughed Williams, raising his glass. Andrada smiled, touching glasses. 'I propose a little more entertainment here, and then we reconvene in the gaming room in a couple of hours,' said Williams, signalling to a woman across the room. Andrada silently nodded.

'Remember that you will make everyone else uncomfortable if you don't participate,' whispered Knight. Joe immediately felt anxious, and his suspicions were confirmed when the pipe-tenders returned from the darkness at the end of the room. In the candlelight he could see that they were naked. The girl that had previously brought him his pipe approached him, standing with her hand extended.

'It would seem rude not to accept,' laughed Knight, to the amusement of Williams and Andrada, who were also watching him.

'We work hard and play hard,' smiled Joe, rising to his feet. He followed her across the room and through a door into an adjacent room, with their laughter ringing in his ears.

The room was small, but a bed had been prepared from a series of plump silk cushions. A citrus candle burned in the corner of the room, the only light within, but the scent was too overpowering for the confined space, and it turned his stomach. There was one small window where he could see back out into the hall — the dragon's fiery head still blazing in the gloom. The girl pulled a curtain across and it became just a faint glowing orb behind the fabric. He felt her hand brush across his cheek, and gently held it in place where it was.

'This isn't what you think it is. I'm not like them,' he said.

'Not like them?'

'I just want to stay in here a while,' he said, turning to face her. The smile that he had found so attractive disappeared instantly from her face.

'And you think that this pretence is better?'

He didn't know how to reply, and they stood watching each other in silence — two prostitutes in the darkness.

There was a noise outside the door that woke him later. He didn't know how long he had been sleeping, but the citrus candle had burned out, and only the faint light from the hall lit the room. As his eyes adjusted to the darkness, he could see that the girl had left, and he had been sleeping at the edge of the pile of cushions. He staggered to his feet, nearly tripping over his own shoes. When he looked at his watch in the faint light from the window, he could see that it was almost time for him to meet the others in the gaming room.

There was a sound again. It was a man's voice.

Slowly, he pulled back the edge of the curtain, taking care not to be seen. The dragon's head was no longer illuminated, and it was harder to see into the hall. He ducked when he sensed movement right by his window. When he looked up again, he saw Williams emerging from the room next to him. He was holding the hand of a young boy, and they disappeared together into the darkness.

Chapter Twenty-Seven

The gaming room was full to its capacity as their odd little group entered its smoky sanctuary. Joe was still slightly high, and he questioned whether he had imagined what he had seen from the window. He tried to convince himself that there was an innocent explanation, unwilling to acknowledge the unpalatable alternative. Rachel had to remain his focus.

Williams was deep in conversation with Andrada, and Knight drifted along behind them, ridiculous in his barong. The room was filled with laughter, accompanied by the sound of clinking glass, and the rattle of roulette chips — swept away from the tables in relentless waves of failure. It was reassuringly bustling after the silent intimacy of the girl's room.

Andreas didn't notice them enter at first. He was grasping the waist of a curvaceous brunette, who found the comment he whispered in her ear hilarious. His role seemed to involve snooping around the gaming room and flirting with the female customers, both of which had been achieved effortlessly in a single flurry of activity as Joe watched.

'Mr Knight,' he said, embracing him. 'You look wonderful!'

'We'd like some real corporate entertainment, Andreas. The annexe, please,' smiled Knight.

'Of course. All of you?' he replied, noticing Joe with distaste.

'All of us,' Knight said, gesturing towards the velvet green curtain.

The first thing Joe noticed was that the air was much cleaner and cooler in the annexe, and he breathed deeply, exorcising smoke from his lungs. He was standing in a brightly lit reception area, which was starkly decorated, with a dozen wooden chairs assembled back to back in the centre, and a single desk at the rear where a grey-haired woman in glasses sat. It appeared as though he had stepped out of the red lounge, and off the ship altogether. The room might have been a doctors' surgery. The woman smiled when she saw Knight, and then carried on working.

'Perhaps the jungle first, gentlemen?' Williams said, gesturing towards one of the doors. Andrada looked uncertain. 'There will be plenty of time for the rest later,' he reassured him.

When Williams pushed the door open, the stench hit them almost immediately. It was pungent and overpowering, emanating from somewhere ahead in the darkness. Even after his eyes adjusted, Joe could see no more than vague outlines in the blackness. There were loud noises echoing from the same direction, which sounded like cheering and something else that he couldn't place. As he stepped forward, he blundered straight into a sheet of heavy rubber, smacking him full in the face. Knight pushed it aside, and his senses were momentarily overwhelmed; there was a circular pit in the centre of the dingy room, filled with bloodstained sawdust. Two cages faced each other, and within each was a growling pit bull terrier, primed to tear the other apart. The dogs snarled with their teeth bared, and their squat muscular bodies thrashed violently from side to side, rattling the cages in their eagerness to destroy each other. There were circular wooden benches, staggered at different heights around the ring, where the audience sat. Joe recognised a few of them from the steering committee meeting, impeccably turned out in their dinner jackets and dresses. He gagged at the smell, and turned to leave the room, only to walk straight into Knight.

'I'd think very carefully before leaving, Joseph. Remember our discussion earlier.'

Joe nodded, and rejoined the others. As he stood with his hand over his mouth, a man approached, passing them each a makeshift programme. It was a list of other animals that had appeared, or were soon to appear in the pit.

'No bears,' said Andrada, disappointed.

'I'm afraid not tonight,' said Williams. 'There are alternatives…'

'Let's go,' he interrupted, scowling.

Their visit was thankfully over before it had started, and it was a relief to fumble their way back towards the entrance in the darkness.

The reception area seemed bizarrely tranquil again by comparison, with only a few feet separating it from the unpleasantness he had just witnessed. The receptionist was sitting alone, silently working through her paperwork. He wondered if she even knew what was in there.

Andrada was still complaining to Williams. He waved his hands around a great deal to emphasise his point, and Williams appeared to be doing his best to pacify him. As Joe watched them, he was aware of Knight sidling beside him.

'Winning money means little to men like Andrada. They require other kinds of stimulation,' Knight said. Joe wasn't sure if this was an explanation or some kind of apology, but he just nodded. Andrada flatly declined the invitation to the second room as they passed it, pointing straight to the third door in the corner of the reception area. He clearly wasn't prepared to compromise any further.

The brass plaque on the door read, "Top Table Betting", which certainly sounded more inviting than the jungle. The room within was also a far cry from the animal pit. A white carpet covered the floor, and the walls were painted in a pastel shade of green, with intricate plasterwork cherubs cavorting along the length of the room. There was a circular table, covered in green baize, standing in the centre of the room, with four oak chairs positioned around it like sentries. A red hue to the light within persisted, and he wondered if there was something seriously wrong with his eyesight. The waiter who greeted them was immaculately dressed in a white tuxedo. He set four crystal glasses on the table, and poured large shots of whisky into each one.

'Please join me, gentlemen,' said Andrada, moving to the furthest edge of the table. Joe settled directly opposite him, with Knight to his left and Williams to his right. The room was completely silent, and Andrada watched him with his fingers folded beneath his chin. He was noticeably more animated since they had arrived.

'The famous annexe of the red lounge, Joseph,' Andrada smiled, gesturing around the room. 'But the name barely does it justice. It is a place where dreams come true. Perhaps yours tonight.'

'I doubt that very much,' Joe replied, more abruptly than he had intended. He sensed Knight flustering beside him, but Andrada appeared more amused than offended by the remark.

'That depends on you. The more that you are willing to bring to this table, the more there is to be gained,' he said, with a slight American lilt that Joe hadn't noticed before. 'Are you a courageous man?'

'That's difficult for me to answer.'

'Then I shall be your judge,' he smiled, raising his glass to his lips. His hand shook slightly as he held it there, watching him. 'This isn't just a gaming table. Before I am prepared to trust anyone in my business dealings, I need to know them. A man's dreams soon become transparent here.'

'As you wish, Mr Andrada, but there is nothing particular to know about me.'

'We shall see,' said Andrada, sipping his drink. 'There is something very important that you should know. There are no limits at this table. We are, of course, talking about far more than just money, Joseph.'

'I understand,' he replied. After everything else that had happened, he expected little else, and was still too high to worry as much as he knew that he should do. Knight and Williams were silent beside him.

'I truly hope you do,' smiled Andrada.

They continued to drink at the table. Williams and Andrada talked business, but he had little interest in their discussions. The national park wasn't even mentioned in passing, and their real interest was overtly financial, as Fowler had warned. He felt numb, unable to contemplate what he had agreed to. They spoke so flippantly about clearing villages — it was as if they were discussing their weekly trash removal. An hour into the discussion, and he was struggling to sit there any longer. Andrada noticed that he was distracted, and interrupted their conversation.

'Less talking shop. I think it's time that we got to know each other properly,' he said, beckoning towards a second man in a tuxedo. The man carried a small black box to the table, setting it down on the green baize in front of them. 'Open it, Joseph,' said Andrada. Joe reached for the box, and lifted the lid to find a single coin within. 'It's a 1943 copper penny. Extremely rare and collectable now, but I wouldn't part with it for the world,' he said, taking the coin in his closed fist. 'There is a story behind it. The man who gave it to me said that it is a lucky coin, and I finally came to agree with him.'

'Who was that?' said Joe, taking a sip of whisky. Andrada just smiled, eventually setting the coin down on the table.

'I grew up in a poor family, Joseph. I shared a tiny bedroom with my three sisters in a very modest home. There was barely enough food for us all to eat. My father was a hard-working man, but he didn't own the land that he farmed. An American leased it to him. He wore the most magnificent boots that I had ever seen. Tough, brown leather boots, studded with metal, and fastened with thick brass buckles. They were nothing like my father's simple sandals, and I was in awe of him. I always heard him coming to our home in those boots, long before I saw him,' he said, his eyes glazing over. 'Unfortunately, he didn't just come for money. It was a very familiar ritual. When he arrived at the house, he would send my father out to farm for him. No sooner had my father reached the second sugarcane field, than he would take my mother's hand and lead her to the bedroom. It was all horribly predictable. The walls were so thin that my sisters could hear everything that was happening in that room. Sadly, so could I. He wasn't a... sensitive man.'

'That can't have been easy for you,' said Joe, quickly taking another gulp of whisky.

'I despised him for it. Not the American, but my father for letting it happen. He knew what that man was doing, but let him persist. I understood his reasons, but I would rather have starved than endure that humiliation. We all should have starved. This went on for month after month, year after year. It was unbearable,' he said, shaking his head. 'In the end, I could stand it no longer. It was my eleventh birthday. There were no gifts from my parents, of course, so I decided that I would provide my own present. That afternoon, I saw those boots by the fire, and took my father's axe from the barn, waiting for the man to leave the bedroom,' he said, his voice trailing away. 'But I was small, and he was much too strong for me. I was crying when he took the axe from my hands. I thought he would kill me for sure, but he knelt in front of me and pulled this coin from his pocket. He said that it was a lucky coin, and asked if I was a courageous man. If Lincoln showed his face in a toss, then he would give the land to my father and never return. If the coin landed the other side up, then he would take my mother away with him forever. It was a terrible decision to make, but I agreed. I could bear the situation no longer. He looked me straight in the eyes as he tossed that coin. I'll never forget his stare.'

'So you won?'

'No, I never saw my mother again,' he laughed, leaning back in his chair. He smirked at Williams, before fixing his eyes back on Joe. 'So why is this a lucky coin, you might be wondering? The American left my father the land when he took my mother away. My father was heartbroken and died two years later. I took over the farm at thirteen years of age. By my eighteenth birthday, I owned every farm in the district. It made me strong,' said Andrada, straightening in his chair with pride. 'I always bring this coin with me to the annexe. I give everyone the same chance to fulfil their dreams as the American gave me that day. Mr Williams wanted control of the board at Schelldhardt. I asked him to prove his commitment to the company by wagering the opportunity against one of his own kidneys on the toss of this coin.'

'So it was lucky for him,' said Joe, glancing at Williams.

'Oh no, Joseph, not this time either. I'm afraid he lost too,' laughed Andrada. 'Show him, Mr Williams.' Williams reluctantly stood and removed his tuxedo. He turned his back towards them, pulling up his shirt to reveal a large scar down the left side of his back. 'But what really impressed me about Mr Williams was that he came back to the annexe three months later, and wagered his other kidney for the same stake. Then I knew that I was dealing with a man who would give everything for Schelldhardt. Once again, it proved lucky in the end.'

They were all laughing now. He was certain that they were insane. His thoughts were still scrambled by the opium he had taken earlier. Even as he sat motionless at the table, it felt as if it was turning like a rotisserie, and he continually fought to re-establish his balance. It was only a matter of time before their attention was drawn back to him, and he needed to compose himself. Seemingly on cue, Andrada turned towards him.

'So tell me, Joseph. What is your dream? Do you desire money, or power?'

'Not really.'

'Perhaps you would like to do something good in this world? I hear that you are a noble young man.'

'I would,' he said, hesitating, 'but there is something else.'

'Go on,' said Andrada, leaning towards him eagerly.

'There is a colleague of mine. I would like Schelldhardt to release her. She should be free to walk away from the company, and be suitably recompensed.'

'I see,' said Andrada, leaning back again. There was disappointment in his voice. He twirled the glass in his hand, watching the light play on the ridges of the crystal. 'That doesn't sound like much of a dream. Are you sure that is all?'

He nodded quietly, already regretting that he had mentioned Rachel at all. It wasn't just Andrada he feared. How would the others react to the request?

'Suppose that I was able to fulfil your wish. What would you be prepared to stake in return?'

'Anything,' he replied without hesitation.

'Anything?' Andrada scoffed. 'That's a dangerous thing to say at this table.' Williams shifted uncomfortably.

'Anything. I want her to be released as soon as possible.'

Andrada's expression hardened, and it was clear that Joe had insulted him in some way. He glanced from Joe to Knight, and set his glass down on the table. His muted deliberation seemed to last forever, and he appeared agitated. Finally, he breathed deeply, measuring his words.

'I don't think you are giving this table the full respect that it deserves. Perhaps it is time to demonstrate the gravity of your choices here,' he said, gesturing to one of the waiters. The man nodded, and appeared to understand the request, manoeuvring beside Joe. He was breathing heavily. Reaching inside his tuxedo, the man pulled a small revolver from within. Joe froze as he felt the cold muzzle pressed against the side of his head.

'You see, Joseph, when you say that you are prepared to wager anything, I have to take you at your word. Are you sure this is what you want?'

Williams and Knight watched him silently. Despite the danger, he felt strangely calm. It seemed that he had finally run out of options. If he couldn't persuade Rachel that she was in danger, then perhaps this was all he could really do to help her. He knew that they would not stop. Andrada looked on expectantly, awaiting his reply.

'Yes, it is, but on one condition,' he said, swallowing the last of his whisky. 'I want her to be released, whether I win or lose.'

'Is this completely necessary, Mr Andrada?' interrupted Knight. 'Joseph is a very valuable member of…'

Andrada raised his hand to silence him. 'Very well,' said Andrada, picking up the coin. 'Either way, she will walk free, you have my word. It is time to prove that you are a courageous man, Joseph. If Lincoln shows his face, you may yet share the pleasure of her release. Look me in the eye.'

Andrada hesitated as he prepared to toss the coin. His unblinking stare was both penetrating and disturbing in equal measure. In response, Joe could only look back, defeated. He no longer had the energy to resist them. The gun was pressed harder against his head, as if trying to force some final reaction from him, but he only swallowed hard and mentally prepared for the worst. It looked as though Andrada was about to toss the coin, but suddenly lowered his hand.

'Wait,' said Andrada angrily. 'I see nothing in his eyes. You have brought a broken horse to this table, Mr Williams. This is no fair wager!'

'Mr Andrada, please,' whined Williams.

'He offers himself too willingly,' shouted Andrada. He slammed the coin back on the table. 'This is not in the spirit of the annexe!'

Williams and Andrada argued angrily, and Williams guided him away from the table, where they continued to bicker in private. As their discussion reached a heated crescendo, Knight shouted to get their attention. At first, they didn't hear him, but when he stood and shouted louder a second time, they slowly began to calm.

'May I suggest an alternative?' smiled Knight.

Fowler was on his knees, with his arms bound behind his back. Two burly security guards had bundled him through the door, marching him to the head of the table, where they kicked his feet from beneath him. He was still wearing the same suit from the fair. There were scruffy grey whiskers poking from his chin, and his normally immaculately parted hair bounced wildly at angles from his head.

'No coins. No stories,' said Knight. 'Mr Fowler would betray everything that Schelldhardt stands for. I propose an alternative proof of Joseph's commitment. If he shoots this man, the girl goes free. If he does not, she stays with us. A simple choice.'

Andrada looked from Fowler to Williams, still uncertain.

'It would solve a secondary problem for us,' insisted Williams. 'Mr

211

Fowler has become… difficult.'

Silence. The atmosphere was suffocating.

Knight fidgeted awkwardly beside Williams. When it seemed that there would be no compromise, Andrada finally nodded.

'Very well. Give him your gun,' he commanded to the waiter, who pushed the revolver into Joe's hand. At first, Joe did not respond, but the waiter shoved him so hard that he almost fell from his chair. Knight nodded encouragement, and Joe's arm trembled as he raised the gun towards Fowler's head, who winced as it levelled with his eyes.

'Please, Joe,' Fowler whimpered.

'Shoot him,' Andrada commanded. 'Shoot him right now, and she will be released.'

'No, Joe!' Fowler cried, before the waiter slapped him around the face.

Silence again.

Joe looked from Fowler's helpless figure to the expectant faces of Andrada and Knight. If there was another solution, he could not think of it. It was Rachel's only way out.

'It's time to decide, Joseph,' said Knight. 'Shoot him to save her. You have our word that she will be freed.'

The pain in Joe's temple was excruciating. The gun wavered wildly in his hand, and Fowler cowered away every time the nozzle pointed at his face. Joe closed his eyes, unable to look at him, but he could still hear his whimpering.

'Do it!' said Knight.

Joe's finger tightened on the trigger. Barely conscious now, he screwed his eyes tightly together, picturing Rachel the day they had driven to Portsmouth together. She was holding her bank statement, smiling in the rain. A different world. He had to pull the trigger. He had to save her.

But Fowler was innocent…

'Now, Joseph!' commanded Andrada.

Something was happening to Joe. As quickly as the image of Rachel had formed, so it began to fade, and an odd calmness washed over him. It seemed to percolate through his mind, restoring clarity where there had been confusion. His trigger finger relaxed, and he lowered the gun. As he fought to regain his breath, he pictured the photograph of his father that he had kept beneath his pillow all those years ago. The expression on his father's face, for so long enigmatic, now made perfect sense: this was too much, even for Rachel...

'I won't,' he said, stumbling away from the table.

Stunned silence.

For a moment nobody moved. Knight eventually scrambled to his feet, but Joe pushed him aside, and charged for the door.

As he ran from the room, he was certain that he could hear their applause ringing out behind him.

The park was in darkness. Joe stumbled across the grass, confused. He had awoken on his bed, still wearing his tuxedo. He must have collapsed there after running from the red lounge. Images of the previous evening still haunted him, and he knew that he had to find Rachel quickly. He had betrayed her.

The crèche door had been unlocked, and he felt his way blindly along the corridors to the park. Now inside, he followed the glow of the windows, eerily blue, towards the centre of the terrace where he had stood before. It was much calmer tonight. It gave him a fighting chance.

There was a noise right in front of him, and he nearly fell backwards in fright. It was a fish splashing in the pond. He had almost walked straight into the water. Changing direction, he held his arms out before him, feeling his way through the darkness in silence. It was possible that the security staff patrolled the park, and he didn't want to give them any extra help in finding him.

His hand found the ratchet at the centre of the terrace window, and he began to turn the mechanism as quietly as he could. He felt the sea air rushing in, and could hear the roar of the waves hitting the ship below. It was noisier than he had anticipated on such a calm night, and he checked over his shoulder to see if he had disturbed anyone. The park was still.

He continued to turn the ratchet, every click painfully magnified in the silence, until the window was fully open. The wind blew freely in, but thankfully with only a fraction of its previous force. The gap that now appeared was much narrower than he recalled, and it was also less accessible than he remembered. To climb out, he would be in a precarious position, balanced on just a single sheet of glass. He tried to hoist himself up, but it was too high to get a foothold. He needed something to climb on.

He wrestled a bench from its fixing in the grass, pivoting it into position just below the window. There were voices in the distance, but it was impossible to place them in the darkness. As quietly as he could, he stepped onto the wooden slats of the seat, and then scrambled up onto the backrest, grasping the sides of the window for support.

It was an unstable position, and he was mindful of his silhouette against the blue-lit glass. If there was anyone nearby, they would see him now. That thought gave him the impetus to launch himself upwards on the glass, which he hit with an unnerving shudder. He immediately began to slide down the window until he extended his arms and legs, bracing his body to a halt.

The voices were getting closer.

What next? He twisted onto his back, and then edged fraction by fraction up the glass into the roaring darkness, until he could see the white side of the ship towering above him. It was flat and unyielding, like the wall of a skyscraper, and swayed backwards and forwards against the purple sky. It was impossible to hear anything above the rumbling of the sea and the wind that howled around him. His jacket whipped open and closed, as he held onto the glass with all his strength.

He lay there blinking, frozen with fear.

There was little to grasp hold of, apart from a narrow ledge a few feet above him. All the other windows were closed, but if he could just climb higher there might be some other way inside on the next floor. He twisted sideways, looking for anything that might aid his progress, and as he did, he saw the waves foaming angrily below. The sound was deafening. If the glass broke now, he would fall to his death for sure.

The only option was to try to climb higher.

With a burst of determination, he reached for the ledge above him, his fingers barely gripping the wet expanse of metal. He levered his body away from the surface of the window, but just as he managed to position himself vertically, his shoes lost purchase, scrabbling against the surface of the glass, before losing contact completely.

He was left clinging to the side of the ship, unable to move either up or down.

The waves were crashing below. His fingers were already burning with pain and he knew that he wouldn't be able to hold on for long.

He felt a tug at his ankle that made him yell in surprise.

A second yank broke his grip on the ledge, and he fell backwards, twisting in the air until he landed face-down on the glass of the window with an echoing thud. He lay there, gasping, as he registered that he had stopped falling. The relief was short-lived. There was another tug from below, like the jaws of a shark, trying to drag him into the blackness beneath. He fought to cling to the window, but a second hand grabbed his other leg from below, and as he thrashed to free it, he immediately began to slide down the window back inside the ship.

'What are you doing?' he shouted, kicking out as he slid down into the gloom. There were several figures below, that grabbed him from both sides, bundling him to the ground as he wriggled to escape. He could only make out their vague shapes. 'Let go of me!' he shouted, until they held him in position so that he couldn't move.

'That was stupid, Joseph. You could have been killed,' said Knight somewhere in the darkness. 'You give me no option but to do this,' he added, moving closer.

Joe tensed his body in fear, and he felt someone undoing the cuff of his shirt. A torch was switched on, illuminating his arm. Another figure rolled up his sleeve, and he saw the needle of a syringe slide into his arm as they restrained him.

He slipped away.

Chapter Twenty-Eight

Arnold Shendi hated to fail, particularly when it came to technology. His own empire was built upon it, and he refused to call Carla from the bedroom just to operate a simple laptop. He squinted at the screen once again. Even with his glasses on, the writing was too small to read, and he switched on the lamp beside the couch in frustration. When his face was just inches from the surface, he finally managed to locate the icon to connect to the system.

The video call bleeped for several seconds — the speaker echoing in the silent hotel suite.

'Mr Shendi,' said Knight, appearing on the screen. 'I've been trying to call you.'

'I know. I've been away on business for a few days. Do you have an update for me?'

'Yes, I have some good news.'

Shendi glanced up. Carla was standing awkwardly in the doorway. She pulled the belt of her silk dressing gown tighter.

'Can you hold for a moment?' he said, muting the line.

'I'm sorry… I heard voices,' she said.

'It's fine; you can go back to bed,' he said, staring back at the screen again. She turned to walk away, and he had a sudden change of heart. 'No, actually, wait. Do you remember the document I showed you in Kensington?' She nodded. 'Things have developed. Come and see.'

Carla crept into the room, perching next to him on the couch.

'Who's that?' said Knight, when he saw her face.

'It's nobody,' he replied. 'So what about my update?'

'The second phase of quality assurance is complete. We should be ready very soon.'

'The second phase? You told me this would be ready last week. I don't have much time.'

'This is not a straightforward process,' said Knight, rubbing his eyes.

216

'Sandbox taught us an awful lot, and we can't afford to make the same mistakes again. There is a fine line between testing to the limit, and exceeding it. We could expedite the process if you would let us overlap our testing with another patient.'

'No, it has to be Anteros. Sandbox's situation is unfortunate, but Anteros must be your absolute focus now. You promised me this would be beneficial.'

'Absolutely. We are seeing clear signs of improvement in him, but we have to be sure.'

'I thought you were already sure.'

'We have complete confidence in the conductor. However, we were seeing unacceptable variances in testing. Ironically, we believe that it was our method of testing that was causing the problem. In a real-world scenario, we are certain that this wouldn't have happened. It was a Catch-22 situation where we could not prove that the conductor worked without the testing, but it was the nature of the testing itself that was causing the problem.'

'Are these issues now resolved?'

'Completely. The biggest problem we encountered with Sandbox was his failure to accept the reality of our interface. We began to see the same signs with Anteros. Our first phase of quality assurance was just too abstract, and he wouldn't accept what was happening to him. The conductor simply wasn't engaging the necessary regions of his brain. It was a valuable lesson learnt, and in the second phase we tried to establish a consistent environment for the process. We are finally seeing vastly improved results.'

'So why can't we move on now? The board meeting is next Wednesday, and I want to make the announcement then.'

'That doesn't give us enough time.'

'You knew the deadline. I've given you everything you needed, and you promised me that you would deliver.'

'We're trying our very best, but phase three is uncharted territory. This is a big step up again. Changing a belief mask completely has many risks associated with it, and we could experience all kinds of problems. We need some contingency.'

'I'm not interested in problems, Mr Knight. I only want solutions. I have made the necessary arrangements for Anteros to join the board meeting, as agreed. My test scripts have been independently audited for authenticity. I just need *you* to fulfil your promises to bring this all together.'

'An extra week would be very helpful…'

'There are no more weeks!'

'I see,' Knight said, looking flustered. 'Have you tried your access yet?'

'Yes, my user name and password were accepted. I saw the landing page.'

'Very well, we will push on immediately. I'll send you details of the schedule later today.'

Shendi smiled at Carla after the call. The room seemed much calmer without Knight's anxious twittering, and he folded his arms behind his head and relaxed. He didn't know why he wanted to share the experience with her, but she was the closest thing he had to a companion now — even if he paid for the pleasure.

'Sometimes you have to push hard to get what you want,' he said.

'So it actually works?'

'Yes, it's incredibly exciting,' he said, closing down the laptop. 'My dreams are about to become a reality, quite literally.'

'Why are you so keen that it should be this… Anteros?'

'We are kindred spirits,' he smiled, 'and besides, there is a great deal of history between us. In a week's time, this young man is going to join the Schelldhardt board meeting. There will be global publicity surrounding the event when the company announces the technology that is installed in his mind. This young man, whose decisions will be scientifically proven to be untainted by prejudice, will also declare his public support for me, reuniting the board.'

'How will that clear your name from… the accusations?' she said, awkwardly.

'That's why I like you, Carla,' he smiled. 'This young man will express his complete confidence that I had nothing to do with the death of my business partner, Philip.'

'I don't understand. Why would he say that?'

'Because, by the end of next week, he will know the truth. I have given Knight precise details of what happened. They have used their machines to prove that I have told the truth, and the results have been independently audited. This alone would be enough to clear my name, but once he sees it for himself, there will be absolutely no doubt in his mind.'

'How will he see it?'

'He will experience the events, exactly as I did. He will understand the decisions I made by making them himself,' he said, feeling a rush of excitement, 'and I am going to witness the whole thing. What will make this declaration so compelling is who he is. There can be no better way of clearing my name of Philip's murder than the testimony of his own son.'

Arnold Shendi: Script One

'You are about to experience something different,' said the voice in the darkness.

'Where am I?' asked Joe, unable to see anything around him.

'This is going to feel a little odd. I want you to relax.'

There was a strange sensation at the top of Joe's head, as if his skull was filling with a cold liquid.

'Stop!' he shouted, but the feeling persisted until the icy numbness reached his eyes and ears. He lashed out his arms and legs, but hit nothing. When he tried to shout again, there wasn't a sound. At the point when the sensation became unbearable, a warm calmness gradually began to replace it. He submitted, letting his limbs dangle freely from his body.

'You are Arnold Shendi. Who are you?'

'I'm Arnold Shendi,' Joe said.

'That's good, Arnold. I want you to focus carefully on my words. You are standing in your father's office. It's a hot summer's day...'

13th July 1985

His father was sitting behind his familiar walnut desk. The window was open, but the air gusting in felt warmer than that inside. It was blowing from the Sahara, a friend had told him; London would be hotter than Madrid that day — one of those rare victories for the British weather each year. Phew, what a scorcher, the tabloids declared! The cars in the village had been covered in a fine layer of dust all week, and some enterprising neighbourhood children were knocking from door to door with a bucket and sponge. Despite the heat, his father was still wearing a suit and tie, engrossed in his ledger. Surely, he had noticed him entering the room?

Shendi coughed, and he looked up, seemingly puzzled at first. His appearance was worse than his mother had warned. He looked frail, and seemed to have aged years in the few weeks since he had last seen him. His hair was thinner, and the patches of grey now predominated the black. Could he really have deteriorated that quickly, or had he simply not paid enough attention before?

'Arnold,' he smiled, clicking his ballpoint pen, 'it's great to see you.'

For a moment, he looked like he might stand, but then appeared to think better of it. He wasn't a demonstrative man, and even a pat on the shoulder was emotionally challenging for him. 'You've been away, I hear? I didn't even know you had plans.'

'Yes, to the Lake District. It was a last-minute arrangement,' he said, feeling his cheeks flush in the heat. 'I only got back yesterday. I'm heading out again today.'

'Today?'

'Yes, I'm seeing the Live Aid concert in London.'

'Oh, the charity event. I read about that in the newspaper,' he said, smiling into space for a moment. He appeared to be lost in thought.

'Mother said that you wanted to see me?'

'Yes, yes, sit down,' he said, gesturing to the chair across the desk. 'There is no easy way to say this, so I'll come straight to the point. I need your help, son.'

'My help?'

'As you know, business isn't good. In fact, the last two years have been plain awful. That damned new road...'

'Yes, Mother said that trading has been difficult.'

'It's worse than your mother knows,' he said, rubbing his face. He was shaking, and the wedding ring slid on his finger as his hands moved across his cheeks. How much weight had he lost?

'What exactly is wrong?'

'I have substantial debts,' he said, screwing his eyes tightly together. When he opened them, they were slightly bloodshot.

'You mean the company has debts?'

'I mean both. I have remortgaged our home to pay the store's wage bill this month.' He said the words so calmly that it took a few moments for them to register.

'Are you crazy? Insolvent trading is illegal!'

'We aren't insolvent. It's just a cashflow problem. We have plenty

221

of unpaid accounts that will more than cover the deficit.'

'But your home,' he said, still unable to comprehend what he had heard. Even by his father's standards, this was ridiculous. His attempts to save the store had long since ceased to be a source of inspiration to him. It was like watching a punch-drunk prizefighter who was just too stupid to lay down. 'This is beyond anything I can do…'

'I just need help in the office. We are understaffed, and there's more paperwork than I can deal with. Your mother helps when she can, but she doesn't have much of a head for figures, and…'

'You can't let her know the truth,' Shendi said, looking towards the window. The room felt hotter than ever, and he wanted to yell in frustration.

'It would only be until after Christmas. I'm sure things will have picked up enough to hire some help by then.'

Shendi shook his head, sadly. His father always looked to Christmas for the store's salvation, but was oblivious to reality. The very people he was trying to help deserted the town in December, favouring the new shopping centres. The store's grand Christmas revival was as elusive as Santa Claus himself. It was a false hope. Although it was the worst possible time, he had to speak now.

'This is awkward,' he said, grimacing. 'I was going to tell you when I had the chance, but the opportunity just hasn't arisen. I'm planning to move away.'

'Away?'

'I'm going to rent a flat with an old friend from university, Philip. I'm not sure if you remember him?'

'Yes, I think I do. Quiet chap.'

'We're planning to start our own technology company.'

Shendi felt terrible, springing the news on him like this, particularly in the circumstances. As his only child, he knew there had always been an unspoken assumption that he would one day take his place at the head of the company. Ever since he was small, his father had led him around the creaking old building, introducing the colourful characters on each floor, and explaining each new sales line at length. He had sown the seeds for his future career right from the very start. Even Shendi's university years he viewed as a whimsy to be indulged, and nothing to be taken too seriously. His education was irrelevant in the grand scheme of things, after all.

'There's a lot of work involved with starting a new venture,' his father said, trying to force a smile. 'I mean, how would you even finance such a thing?'

'We have some money saved. We hope to borrow the rest.'

'Borrow! You think the banks will lend to a couple of young upstarts? There are businesses failing every day, Arnold.' Even as he said the words, Shendi was sure he was unaware of their irony. He didn't see reality, even now.

'If we are successful, then I really would be able to help you. Perhaps you could even diversify. Technology is the future.'

'This is pie-in-the-sky nonsense! You would be better served staying here and running a real business.'

'This place? Just look around you — it's a mess. The paperwork is chaotic,' he said, grabbing a pile of loose letters from the desk. 'These are important documents, just lying around waiting to be lost! I couldn't work in here. I just couldn't.'

'This is a real business. It's our family business.'

'This is a charity! The store is haemorrhaging money, and there's nothing you can do to stop it. It's over, don't you understand?'

'The people of this town need the store. What would they do without it?'

'That's not your responsibility! You have to let it go.'

'What about their jobs?'

'You can't pay their wages with your own home forever!'

'Just a few months, Arnold. We can get through this, like we always have. You could postpone your business plans. I may even have the money to help you by then. Please, I need you...'

The room felt unbearably muggy, and he was beginning to feel dizzy. His father was a proud man, respected throughout the town, and it broke his heart to see him begging like this. The situation was impossible. His father believed that hard work and determination could see him through anything, but the world was changing. The time of their department store was over, and even superhuman effort could not prevent that. Shendi couldn't help him in this office. The only chance was to succeed in his own right and return later.

'Arnold, are you okay?'

'I'm fine,' he said, rubbing the top of his head. It felt as though he was developing a migraine. He needed to leave.

'Do you want some water?'

'I'm sorry, but I really can't do this,' he said, clambering to his feet. He could barely look at his father's defeated face. 'I have to go.'

Arnold Shendi: Script Nine

'You are Arnold Shendi. Who are you?'

'I'm Arnold Shendi,' Joe said.

'Thank you, Arnold. You are standing by a window. It's a hot summer's day…'

20th June 1993

Shendi could not recall a more beautiful sunset. He watched as the sun finally slipped behind the chalk hills, drenching the meadows with its dying crimson light. A breeze blew through the open window, sending the tiny metal telephones of the windchime into a noisy dance.

How long had he been standing there with the mobile phone in his hand? His legs were aching, and it was hard to keep his eyes open. It must be after nine o'clock, and it was obvious that there would be no more calls from Philip today. It was so infuriating… He had done everything in his power to keep him safe. If Philip only knew how difficult it was to deal with someone like Hayward! Shendi valued order and control above everything, and it maddened him that he had allowed himself to become trapped in this ridiculous situation.

He wandered back towards his desk, sliding open the bottom drawer. There was still half a bottle of port left. Not enough to forget, but enough to ease his mind. He no longer bothered to decant it, pouring a large measure straight into the crystal glass, still sticky with the residue of his last drink. The photograph of Sonic's christening refused to be ignored. The smiling faces felt strangely different, in a way that he couldn't define. It made him anxious as he stared at it, finally pushing the frame face-down so that he could see it no longer.

If he didn't call the mobile phone number, Philip would involve his solicitor and the business may well come crashing down around his ears. If that happened, there would be huge personal repercussions; Hayward did not strike him as a forgiving character. If he did call the mobile number, Hayward's people would deal with Philip in their own inimitable fashion, and the business would be safe, along with his own sorry skin.

It was impossible to decide! He swept the folders off the desk in frustration, banging his head against the wooden surface. If only Philip would accept a few years in prison. The man was an idiot. It was by far the best solution for everyone, but he just couldn't see it. He wouldn't see it. Shendi swallowed his drink, and immediately poured another one.

Hayward had seemed charming on that train journey when they first met. He exuded confidence, and his enthusiasm for their business was infectious. Shendi was at a low ebb, and wanted to believe everything that Hayward had said to him. Their concept was visionary. It was the best business plan he had ever seen, in all his years of working in the City. The right kind of investors would fall over themselves for the opportunity to be involved, and high street banks were only good for loaning to hairdressing salons... He had lapped up every word.

Shendi had inherited a stubborn streak from his father, and he refused to let his own fledgling business die. The combination of these factors had led him straight into Hayward's clutches, and he had been groomed by a very clever man, meeting by meeting. Hayward was probably in his late forties now, a good fifteen years older than himself, and in truth, he had been a little in awe of him. His demands were reasonable at the outset, but as their finances became murkier, he became more demanding. It seemed that almost nothing would satisfy him now, and he didn't know why he persisted in pushing harder and harder.

Shendi filled his glass, almost emptying the bottle in the process. Leaving the last drain made him feel better about himself. Was there some kind of curse over his family? Were they doomed to build their business empires, only to watch them collapse? His head ached as he mulled his options over and over again.

How could he betray Philip and his young family? The more he thought about it now, the more he realised what a mistake it would be to play any further into Hayward's hands. The man's demands would never end. If he had control over him now, how much worse would it be if he followed his instructions? The mobile phone was supposedly untraceable, but what if it wasn't? He may as well have handed him a loaded gun. This could all be part of a ploy to seize control of the company altogether.

It was a moment of clarity amidst the madness.

He reached for his own telephone instead. He would call Hayward now and let him know what he had decided. He twirled the cable tight around his thumb while he waited for an answer, the tip of it turning white. Perhaps he had dialled the wrong number? He called again, this time turning the circular dial more carefully. It rang again for an age, and he was just about to hang up when he heard the click of someone lifting the receiver.

'Peter, it's Arnold Shendi.'

'I know who it is,' said Hayward, his tone arrogant and unfriendly. 'Why are you calling me here?'

'I wanted you to know that I'm not going to do it.'

'You're not going to do what?'

'I'm not going to call your friend in Paris.'

'I see,' Hayward said. He was silent on the line for a moment, and Shendi felt his stomach churning. 'You're making a mistake,' he said at last.

'I can't go through with it. I'm willing to accept the consequences.'

'Have you been drinking again, Arnold?'

Shendi had only slurred his words slightly, but Hayward seemed to pick up on every nuance in his voice.

'Not enough to influence my decision.'

'Perhaps you should sleep on it?'

'No, I've made up my mind. This is my final answer.'

'It isn't a wise one.'

'Perhaps, but I couldn't live with myself any other way.'

'It's too late to discover your conscience now, Arnold. I would have expected this to be easy for you.'

'What do you mean by that?'

'Let's just call it our little secret for now, but I know how good you are at covering your tracks. I'll be in London next Wednesday, and we really should meet to discuss the future.'

He hung up, leaving Shendi staring into the gloom of the darkening office. Was he making the biggest mistake of his life?

227

Chapter Twenty-Nine

Carla had an incredible physique. Shendi continued to admire her in silence, curled like a cat beside him in the bed. It never ceased to amaze him what money could buy, and just how different human beings were to other animals. The law of the jungle had long since been superseded by the law of the dollar. Even the most inadequate of men could find themselves some company with a little cash. He always noticed the whispers and barely disguised gossiping when he entered a restaurant with her, but what was the harm? Both parties were getting what they wanted. Love was a transient state of mind that he no longer pursued, and it had led him to the darkest regions of his soul. The thought made him shudder.

He ran his knuckle up and down Carla's spine as she sat upright in the bed next to him. She turned her head and smiled. It was a genuine smile, and sometimes he even fooled himself that she liked him. Perhaps he would call down to reception for a bottle of champagne.

'Do we have another show today?' she asked.

'I'm afraid not. The scripts are all complete.'

'That's a pity. I was almost beginning to warm to you,' she laughed.

'That's why I like you, Carla,' he said, smiling.

He felt so relieved. Joseph had now seen with his own eyes that he had nothing to do with his father's death. It was surely a formality now that he would speak out on his behalf at the board meeting. They had stayed in the hotel for a week now, each night sitting propped up in bed with his laptop on the covers in front of them. The system had worked even better than he could have possibly imagined, and it was like stepping back in time as they watched the events of his life unfold before them on the screen. Night by night, they had sat discussing the decisions he had made once the transmission was complete. It was like being the star of his own soap opera, complete with expert commentary.

His enforced gardening leave prevented him from attending the board meeting in person, but he was confident that Joseph would provide the testimony he needed to unify the board, and finally bring him back in from the cold. How could he not, after seeing what had really happened to his father, and understanding the decisions he had made? The additional bonus was that he would now be able to establish a relationship with him, and help financially as he had promised Jane all of those years ago. Perhaps even his estranged wife, Catherine, would see him in a better light. It was the first time he had felt truly happy in years.

'It would be interesting to watch the board meeting through Joseph's eyes, wouldn't it?' he said, staring at the ceiling. Carla rolled towards him, running her fingers through the hairs of his chest.

'Could they do that?'

'Why don't I find out?' he said, climbing out of bed. He puffed out his chest as he passed the mirror, before pulling the robe onto his back, and padding out of the bedroom. He returned with his laptop moments later, plugging it in beside the bed.

The video call took a while to connect, but when it did, there was the unexpected face of a young man on the screen, who cleared his throat nervously.

'Is Mr Knight there?' Shendi asked, plumping up the pillow behind his back.

'I'm afraid he isn't, sir.'

'How about Mr Brace?'

'He isn't here, either. I can try to find out where they are for you.'

'Don't worry, it isn't important.'

'It's no bother. I can look in their calendars?'

He was trying so hard to please, that Shendi didn't have the heart to stop him. Carla whispered in his ear and giggled. Her breasts were exposed, and the young man was trying not to look at her as he tapped at the keyboard, flustered.

'I can call back later?'

'I'm nearly there,' he said, glancing up again. 'Mr Knight's calendar is just loading.' As he waited for the computer to respond, he tried to look everywhere except at the screen. Shendi pulled the covers away from Carla, so her entire naked body could be seen. She giggled in his ear again.

'Any news?'

'According to his calendar, he is testing the Anteros system with Mr Brace now.'

'I'm sorry,' said Shendi, moving closer to the screen. Carla immediately covered herself up when she saw his reaction. 'Did you say Anteros?'

'Yes, they are running the last script. There's a note right here.'

'There must be some mistake. They have already run the last script. Number nine.'

'I'll check the note,' he said, his fingers flicking around the keyboard. His face was a picture of concentration as he studied his computer. 'It says here that they are running Appendix A.'

'There is no Appendix A.'

'I'm sorry, sir, I don't really know too much about this.'

'I see,' said Shendi, rubbing his chin. Perhaps there could be a simple explanation. He knew ultimately that his relationship with Knight was one of salesman and customer, and there might be details he was withholding. There was no reason to be too alarmed after the success they had already enjoyed. It could just be a final test for Knight's own satisfaction. 'Is there any indication of where Mr Knight might be testing so you can contact him?'

'I can't see anything here. There is a reference to an item of mail. I can check in Mr Knight's tray if you like? There might be some more information.'

'Yes, please.'

The young man disappeared out of view of the camera, and Shendi could hear the shuffling of paper. He was beginning to feel impatient. He was sure there was nothing to worry about, but he just wanted to know what was happening. The man returned with a large envelope.

'This is what the script arrived in. There's a sticker on the front with Mr Knight's writing on it. It's a reminder to email you. Did you receive any emails?'

'Let me take a look,' Shendi said, tapping at his keyboard. He hadn't checked his messages that day because he believed that the testing was complete.

There was indeed something from Knight. It was the schedule for the testing of Appendix A. When he scanned further down the message, he froze. Knight claimed to have received the script from one of Shendi's business associates, yet nobody else knew anything about the testing. 'You have to find Mr Knight and tell him to stop the test right now. I think this is some kind of sabotage. I'll log on to the system and see what is happening,' said Shendi, feeling light-headed.

'Yes, sir,' said the young man, turning to leave.

'No, wait. Is there anything else in that envelope?'

'I don't think so,' said the man, peering inside. He reached in with his fingers, ferreting inside. 'Wait, yes, there is something. It's just a compliments slip.'

'What does it say?' said Shendi, feeling his heart racing.

'It's from a Mr Peter Hayward...'

The mere mention of the name was enough for him to freeze. How could Hayward be interfering now! He had been so careful.

'What does the compliments slip say?' he shouted, beside himself with rage.

'There's just one sentence. "Everything that you have been told is entirely true, but the entire truth has not been told."'

Arnold Shendi: Appendix A
Summer 1985

She could not be controlled or organised like the rest of his world, and that's why Shendi loved her more than any of it. He first met Elena in March, during his third year of university. He had started Sussex later than most of his peers, already twenty-three when he studied for his finals. Those years of extra maturity empowered him to approach her at a record fair that he was visiting with his friends. She was older than him, nearly thirty, and he believed that he could pass for similar. He had never looked young, wearing glasses from the age of five, and his hair was thinning prematurely. He also had a stocky physique that was obviously doomed to expansion in later life. As unglamorous as he was, he realised that this was his prime, and the knowledge encouraged him to be bold. Elena later said that it was this confidence that attracted her. Perhaps it was the only compliment she could really pay him, but he accepted it all the same.

He saw her flicking through the imported Japanese vinyl section at the fair, browsing the sleeves of artists that he had never heard of. It was the artwork that was important to her. She literally judged a record by its cover, drawing a linkage between the imagery and the music. She said that she would try anything. By speaking to him that day, she only reinforced the point.

Elena was of Spanish descent, with beautiful golden skin and green eyes. There could rarely have been a more mismatched couple strolling the streets of Brighton, and he could not believe his luck. The differences didn't end with their appearances; while he studied business, she read poetry. He planned and organised, while she dreamed and fantasised; but somehow it worked between them. When he was with her, he wondered why he had ever worried about anything in his life, and their chemistry was electric. He hadn't understood kissing until they met — never quite sure what his tongue was doing in another's mouth. When he kissed

Elena, the world stopped around him, and they even kissed in public. How his parents would have disapproved! Ignore them, Arnold, his father would say, glancing over his newspaper when they ate lunch in the park. Young people in love were something to be mistrusted; but now he was one of them. They had morning sex, lunchtime sex, evening sex, outdoor sex and even sex with another couple. She encouraged him to do things he would never have dared to do before.

Every personal taboo was broken one by one in those glorious months that followed. He missed a deadline for an essay submission at the most crucial time, spending the entire day in bed with Elena instead. He would have been horrified just to be marked below a first before, but to miss it altogether... The savings account that he had scrupulously nurtured through his teens was ravaged with complete abandon. His bank statements were littered with cash withdrawals at odd times of the night, and even, God forbid, penalty fees. He got drunk. Actually drunk, relinquishing all control of his actions, and nothing seemed sacred any more. He even stopped wearing his socks to bed at night.

Shendi continued to rent the same flat after university finished, and when his three flatmates moved out, so Elena moved in for a few months. It was the happiest time of his life. With her at his side, Brighton was transformed into an exotic and wonderful place. They went to the beach, a place that he had always shied away from — huddled together in the sand, listening to the sea. They had picnics. They walked hand in hand along the promenade, something he had never imagined himself doing. They listened to her radio in the park as a German teenager won Wimbledon on a scorching summer's day — drinking Riesling wine from plastic beakers. It was an intoxicating daydream of happiness that he hoped would never end.

But there was a problem: another man shared his love for her.

His love rival was married. Elena had embarked on an affair with him a few years before she met Shendi, and she hadn't seen fit to tell him that they were still seeing each other — assuming that he somehow must have realised. He hadn't, and the revelation shook his world, even tarnishing the memories of the time he had spent with her.

The married man could only meet her every Tuesday, leaving his family home for the night under the pretence of business. Shendi grew to hate the day, initially begging her not to see him at all, but Elena refused to give him up. Why did it matter? When they were together, they were together. She always came back to him the next day, didn't she?

He knew that she wasn't cruel. Her liberal nature went against the very grain of his being, but that was the whole point. She wanted him to realise that the reason he felt so deeply for her, was because of it. He needed to control her, but loved her because he couldn't. This maddening paradox tormented him, but she made no attempt to placate him. Instead, she tried to teach him to appreciate the beautiful agony of his emotions in their own right.

Is he handsome? Very! Is he rich? Extremely. Doesn't that make you feel all the better that I'm here now? It should do.

It was impossible to argue with her, because he knew that she was right.

But that was when she was there. He cried himself to sleep like a baby on those Tuesday nights when she wasn't, sometimes waking in such a fearful panic that he didn't know what to do. He just couldn't bear to think about where she was, and struggled to breathe — to the point that he thought that he would die in his bed. The feeling ate away at him, and he already began to dread the following Tuesday's arrival on a Wednesday morning. He could not tell Elena for fear of pushing her away altogether, knowing it was a fault in his character that he had to address somehow.

A temporary reprieve presented itself by chance. He noticed a card in the local newsagent's window advertising a cottage for hire in the Lake District. It would be an ideal opportunity to spend a week together entirely alone, without telegraphing his underlying intention. The cost of the rental was a great deal of money to him, but he was truly desperate by this point, and decided to break into his savings accounts again just to preserve his sanity. A week could be enough to regain his bearings. With another rush of blood, he bought a second-hand Ford to drive her in. It was reckless expenditure, but the spending spree wasn't over yet, and a chance conversation with the newsagent resulted in the purchase of two tickets for the forthcoming Live Aid concert. It was more money than he had spent in his life, but it would be a perfect holiday.

Elena was delighted, and they packed their suitcases into the old

Fiesta on a muggy Saturday morning in early June. He had paid for them both to be insured on the car, and they split the driving on the seven-hour journey, lapsing between laughter and contented silence the whole way. The cottage could not have been more inviting, and even the notorious Cumbrian rain was merciful. They took long country walks, made love on the hilltops overlooking the lakes, and spent the evenings drinking wine and watching the sun setting. Everything was exactly as it had been, and Shendi was blissfully happy again. When Tuesday came, he revelled in their isolation, and it was the best day of the holiday so far. He brought Elena breakfast in bed, and they stayed there most of the morning. In the afternoon, they took a long walk to Scafell Pike. The meadows of the Langdale valley were carpeted in wildflowers, and they ambled through the daisies and buttercups, stopping to admire each new perspective of the cloud-shrouded hills around them.

By the time they returned late afternoon, pink-faced and contented, Shendi was exhausted. Elena ran a bath, and he crashed on their bed, feeling his cheeks and neck stinging from the sun. Elena emerged from the bathroom with a towel around her, which she dropped right in front of him, and he could only lay there admiring her body. He watched as she dressed, stepping into silk lingerie, and applying her lipstick in the small dresser mirror beside the window.

He soaked in the bath after her, feeling the knots of tension in his shoulders release in the warm water. The holiday was exactly the tonic he needed, and he wished that they never had to leave. Pulling on his best shirt, he joined her downstairs, where she poured them each a glass of Chianti from a bottle they had opened the night before. They drank it in the kitchen together, laughing at sheep spooking one another on the hillside. Elena had never looked more beautiful.

When they stepped out of the cottage into the warm evening air, the light was already beginning to fade. He assumed that they would be eating at The White Lion, a hostelry three miles along the road, but he didn't care where. Elena stopped on the path in front of him to watch the last rays of light disappearing over the hill, and they kissed.

It was a kiss that he would remember forever, even if he didn't understand what it meant at the time.

To his delight, Elena made straight for the driving seat, and he didn't argue, stepping through the damp, long grass towards the passenger side. It would be nice to have a few drinks without worrying, especially tonight of all nights. When he had his hand on the door handle, she looked over the roof towards him.

'Where are you going?' she asked. He laughed, thinking that she expected him to drive after all, but her expression didn't change. 'It's Tuesday.'

She stared at him without smiling. The words barely made sense at first, but when he realised what she meant, he struggled to breathe. In the angry exchange of words that followed, she revealed that her married man had booked a luxury hotel in town for the night, taking an express train from London that day. She would be back late the following morning. Despite his initial, petulant attempts to prevent her from using his car, he finally resigned himself to his fate, watching her pull away from the drive; all his obstinancy could amount to was a delay in her return. He stood in the doorway of the cottage, in total shock, as the car disappeared over the hill in the distance.

That night was the most agonising he had ever experienced, and he finally snapped.

When she returned the next day, he had not slept or washed, and every bottle of wine left in the house had been drunk. She sailed through the door, bright as the morning sunshine, and put her arms around him as if she had just returned from a shopping trip.

'It was a wonderful hotel,' she said, kissing his lips, 'but not as homely as the cottage.'

She had misjudged his mood, or perhaps she hadn't — deciding that this friendly flippancy was her best approach. Either way, it was a mistake.

'That's good,' he said, pulling her body closer to his. He remembered the silk lingerie beneath her clothes — never intended for him at all — and tears formed in his eyes. She didn't notice, her face too close to his own, and he pressed his mouth against hers, kissing her passionately.

'You have missed me,' she said.

'Yes,' he said, kissing her again. He began to play with the hair loose around her shoulders, twirling it between his fingers, and she ran her hand over his back. He pushed his mouth harder against hers, the tears now rolling down his cheeks. He wanted to keep her. He wanted her to stay here and never leave him again, but it was an impossible dream. He had never felt so impotent. Every kiss meant nothing at all.

'Are you okay?' she asked, sensing something was wrong, but he didn't speak, still holding her against his body so that she couldn't see his face.

'I can't,' he said.

'You can't what?'

He shook his head silently, beside himself with absolute misery. His shaking hands were around her slender neck before she knew it, and there was nothing he could do to control himself any longer. He had to possess her, but she would never allow it.

'Stop,' she gasped, but he only squeezed tighter, sobbing loudly as he pushed her against the wall so she could not escape. She scratched at his face, and kicked with her legs, but he persisted, manoeuvring himself around her until she was helpless. He wailed in despair as he held her pinned against the wall, squeezing the life out of her body.

'Stop!' shouted a voice again, but this time it wasn't hers, and he knew for certain that he was losing his mind. There was the ghostly image of a young man in a suit standing beside him. He was looking straight through him. 'Stop the test right now.'

His terrible rage was unabated, his fingers cramping with the effort of maintaining their grip on her throat. As she slackened in his arms, he finally dared to look into her face, but it wasn't Elena who stared back at him. The face of the young woman, wide-eyed with fear, was familiar, but he didn't understand how. He knew her somehow, but he didn't. This was madness, and he now accepted it.

The walls of the cottage crumbled away around him, and he was sure that it was the end of the world. In truth, he no longer cared. The floor opened into a void beneath his feet, and the ceiling darkened into night above him. Before everything disappeared into total blackness, he remembered something.

Her name was Rachel.

Chapter Thirty

Joe awoke, choking. He tried to sit up, but it felt as though he had left half of his head on the pillow, and slumped back down again, coughing. There were tears streaming down his cheeks. His dreams had been so vivid. Rachel had been there, he was sure of it. He could see her face clearly in his mind, and she was terrified. There was something else that he couldn't quite recall, but the feeling haunted him. He was shivering uncontrollably.

A drip was hanging from a stand next to his bed. The tube trailed away to the floor, which was emptying into a puddle of clear liquid on the carpet beside the bed. Drops of blood had crusted on his forearm where he must have pulled the needle free in his sleep. It felt as if he had been lying there for an eternity. He could smell sweat on the bedclothes, and his mouth was so parched that his tongue had cracked in the middle. It was painfully sore.

He swung his legs to the side of the bed. After composing himself for a few seconds, he rose to his feet like a new-born giraffe. Swaying there, nothing made sense. He was in his bedroom, but he had no recollection of how he had got there. The room drifted in and out of focus, and he found it hard to concentrate on even the simplest of actions like stepping forward. It felt as if he was still drugged.

He noticed for the first time that he was dressed in a green surgical gown. Someone from the medical centre must have taken him there, but there was no sign of them now. He stumbled across the bedroom, nearly falling twice, before he finally reached the kitchen to get some water. The first few mouthfuls were like swallowing broken glass, but he drank faster all the same, mostly missing his mouth. He tried to focus on his surroundings, but it felt as though the room was perpetually turning on its side. The more he stared out into the lounge, the less he understood the scene before his eyes. There were plates of partially eaten sandwiches on the coffee table next to the couch. Standing next to the table was a trolley with some kind of electrical equipment on it that he didn't recognise.

Someone else had been in his room.

He wanted to investigate, but there was a daunting expanse of carpet between himself and the trolley. He hunched onto his hands and knees, and crawled across the floor, stopping twice to regain his bearings, before finally hoisting himself up onto the couch.

Not only were there sandwiches on the table in front of him, but there was also a half-eaten apple, browning where it had been bitten, and a glass of milk. Whoever had been sitting there had left halfway through their meal. The sight and smell of the food made him gag, and he pushed it out of view. The trolley next to the table was intriguing. A large monitor was propped on top of a rectangular computer base. There was no mouse or keyboard, and just a headset lay beside it. The screen was blank, but there was a blue light glowing in the corner of the frame. On a shelf beneath the computer, there was a clipboard and pen with a series of handwritten notes. Adjacent to this was what looked like a mobile phone, only slightly larger.

His head throbbed and he only wanted to move once. He opted for the mobile phone. The screen of the handset lit up when he touched one of the buttons, simultaneously awakening the computer screen, which duplicated the display. He wasn't holding a phone at all: it was some kind of remote control. There were several options on an initial menu, and he scrolled down aimlessly, unable to make sense of what he was seeing. He was about to put it down again, when a single word caught his attention: Sandbox.

Intrigued, he touched the word on the controller screen, and a whole sub-menu appeared below it with a series of dated entries. He selected one at random, and then, after a few seconds delay, a picture formed on the screen. The video ran for fifteen minutes, and it took him most of the time to digest what he was seeing. He remembered the occasion well. It was when Sandbox had met him in the cinema. But who had filmed the footage? The video was shot entirely from Sandbox's perspective, as if he were wearing a camera, but surely, Joe would have seen it. And why film this anyway? There was something else at the periphery of the screen: a separate window of controls displayed a series of colourful graphs. He couldn't understand the values they were measuring, but as he selected the area of the screen on the touchpad, they overlaid one another into a single graph. Through the middle was a thicker jagged line, and the other values were plotted around it, either above or below. The line was labelled, "PoGR".

'Call upon this in your hour of need,' said Sandbox on the video, as he passed Joe the new-age spiritualist book. The disdain on Joe's face was obvious, and he wished he hadn't been so rude, seeing the moment replayed back to him like this. He had forgotten all about the book, but re-living the meeting now, he noticed an intensity in his voice that he had missed before. Sandbox really wanted him to have it.

He vaguely remembered seeing the book when he had packed his case, choosing not to take it with him to save space. It was probably on the bedroom floor. The thought of moving again was unpleasant, but he had been sitting there long enough for the drug to lose some of its potency, and his head was starting to clear. He left the video playing and went to fetch it.

The book had been kicked under the bed when he had packed his things, and it took him a while to find it. There didn't appear to be anything exceptional about it. No codes written on any of the pages, nor passages highlighted. He fanned through the pages, disappointed, and was about to put it down when he came across a handwritten note on the inside of the back cover.

"Anteros, the answer to your problem lies within. Regards, Sandbox."

It was such an odd thing to write at the back of a book.

He sat on the corner of the bed, trying to fathom out why he had taken the time to write it, and why he had gone to such lengths to get the book to him. He stared at the page, baffled, and as he did, he noticed something. Holding the book up to the light, he could see that the message wasn't written directly on the inside of the cover, but rather on a sticker carefully positioned on top of it. As he peeled the corner back, he could feel that there was something beneath it, within the cover itself. When he pulled the contents out, everything became clearer. This was how Sandbox had moved around the ship so easily. It was a security pass.

He changed quickly, swapping the surgical gown for a pair of jeans and a shirt. He had no idea where he would find Rachel, but he needed to try immediately. Something was very wrong, and she needed his help. Anything could have happened to her since he had been bedridden in his room.

When he returned to the lounge, much steadier on his feet now, he saw that the computer monitor was still playing. He picked up the control, and was about to switch it off when he noticed something else. There was a cross-reference linking the video that had finished with another menu: Anteros. Red group new member. Anteros was the word written on the piece of plastic that Sandbox had given him. His mind drifted back to the interviews at Marryfield House. He had been allocated a red badge.

He sat back onto the couch, holding his mouth in disbelief as he scrolled through the entries under the Anteros menu. It wasn't possible. He selected one of the options, and it revealed a video of himself sitting at the restaurant table in the red lounge, the night he had collapsed. The whole video was taken from his own perspective, as if he was holding the camera in front of his face. He could hear his own voice as he spoke to the other diners. How could this footage have been taken?

He stopped the video, and scrolled through some of the other entries. There was something very unnerving about the names of the items he found there — the memories of dreams that had seemed all too real at the time, but he had somehow blanked from his mind.

The most recent entries were simply labelled "Shendi", and as he fast-forwarded through the video, his skin began to crawl. He recognised the name, of course. Shendi was Schelldhardt's deposed CEO, so he was always in the press — particularly since suppressed allegations had been made against him — but there was something else that his mind refused to accept. The video footage was somehow familiar, in a way that he couldn't understand. He knew exactly what each person was going to say on the screen before they said it, but the memory was much more than that. He understood Shendi's feelings in a way that did not seem possible. He thought of his mother, and her anger whenever Shendi appeared on the television screen. It had always struck him as odd.

Shendi had been his father's business partner.

The recollection hit him hard, almost taking his breath away. His mother had always kept it from him, and it explained her reluctance for him to join the Schelldhardt scheme. She was still trying to keep them apart all these years later, blaming him for his father's death, but she had no idea that he was innocent. However, there was something else that she didn't know about...

When he flicked to the last entry on the video, he remembered the horror of what he had seen before he awoke. He could recall the exact sensation of the woman's neck between his hands. The anger. The hopelessness. The recollection made him dizzy again.

It was a video of his thoughts. Sandbox had said that they knew what he was thinking. As impossible as it seemed, it was true. Ever since he had been on the ship, he had experienced a sensation that something wasn't quite right. Knight had always been one step ahead of him, and this explained how.

He sat motionless in shock. They could be watching him right now. There was a status indicator next to the name Anteros, and when he hovered over the entry on the controller, a message appeared.

"Anteros monitoring disabled due to essential maintenance."

He scrolled back to the Sandbox menu. The status read "Sandbox monitoring enabled". This is what Sandbox had been trying to tell him. Anteros was his system name. They had been watching both of them. Joe picked up the controller and pass, stuffing them both in the pocket of his jeans, and slid as quietly out of his cabin as he could.

The corridor outside his room was empty. As he crept towards the lift, he heard a man's voice from the cabin next to his own. Sandbox's old room. Silently, he pulled the pass from his pocket, sliding it into the receptacle of the door lock. A green light appeared, with a bleep that was worryingly loud.

The man inside stopped speaking, and Joe froze, terrified that he had been heard.

The man continued his conversation after a few seconds, and Joe slowly pushed down the handle, opening the door just a fraction.

He could see directly into the lounge. A man was sitting in a leather armchair with his back to the door. He was talking into a headset, watching a monitor mounted on a trolley that looked identical to the system in his own room. Joe hesitated, then pushed the door open just wide enough to squeeze inside. He froze again, waiting for a reaction. When there was none, he turned left towards the bedroom.

Sandbox was alone in the room. He was lying in the bed, with a drip attached to his arm. His scarred face, emaciated and yellow, twitched incessantly as he slept. The bedpan beside the wardrobe had not been emptied.

Joe wanted to do something to help him, but wasn't sure what. The voice was silent in the lounge next to him again, and Sandbox's features regained some normality. The moment the man began speaking again, so the muscles began contorting in his face. Quickly, Joe pulled the drip from Sandbox's arm. Hopefully, he would regain consciousness without it, just like he had. He would come back for him later.

Joe peered out of the bedroom and the man was fiddling with the screen controller, still wearing the headset. Joe edged out past the lounge and into the corridor.

He needed to find Rachel quickly.

Deck six was a disappointment after the weeks of anticipation.

He was thankful that Sandbox's pass had worked, but he wasn't sure which way to turn from the lift, opting for right on instinct. The corridor snaked to a central open-plan office space, with dozens of smaller glass cubicles at the periphery. It was much noisier than the compliance deck, with a backdrop of ringing phones, whirring photocopiers and chattering voices. He wandered around the office, unsure where he was going. People milled past him, going about their business as normal.

'Can I help you?' said a tired-looking woman in glasses, calling across from her cubicle. He wandered towards her, turning the pass around his neck backwards.

'I'm looking for Rachel Harding.'

'Are you new?'

'Yes. I've been seconded to this department.'

'Welcome,' she smiled. 'Second office on the left.'

As he approached the glass-partitioned room, a security guard emerged from a cubicle further along the office. Joe ducked, pretending to tie his shoelace. They may not be monitoring him on their systems, but if he was found on the wrong deck it would be equally detrimental. The woman who had directed him was watching him suspiciously, and he turned away from her as he stood again.

Rachel didn't see him at first, too engrossed at her computer screen. When she did, she opened the door of the office, smiling warmly.

'Joe…'

'You're okay,' he said, his voice trembling.

'Of course I am. What are you doing here? The ship isn't docking until tomorrow,' she laughed. 'Don't you listen to *any* announcements!'

'I thought you might be in trouble…'

'Why, what kind of trouble? You look awful.'

'The Andrada deal. Fowler was right. We should have listened to him, Rachel.'

'Joe, calm down. I've no idea what you're talking about. Do you need some water? You look pale.'

'I don't remember leaving the red lounge after the fair.'

'What on earth is the red lounge? You're starting to worry me,' she said, the smile leaving her face. 'Why are you shaking so much?'

'I'm fine,' he said, his legs almost giving way beneath him. Either he truly was insane, or the final piece of the puzzle was slowly falling into place.

'You're not fine. I'm going to get some help.'

'No,' he shouted, pulling the door of the cubicle closed behind them. The security guard was moving in their direction and he felt hopelessly exposed behind the transparent glass pane. 'I don't have much time. Something is happening that I can't fully explain. I have a favour to ask of you. A huge favour. I know you have spent your entire life helping me in one way or another, but if you do this one thing, I'll never ask anything of you again.'

'What is it?'

'I need you to get off this ship tomorrow.'

'And go where?'

'Anywhere else. It sounds crazy, I know, but I don't have time to explain everything now,' he said, nervously looking through the door. The guard was no more than three cubicles away. 'I won't be able to come back here again. We'll have to meet outside the ship when it docks.'

'Joe, I can't just walk off the ship.'

'You must, Rachel. You have to trust me. I wouldn't ask you unless I was certain it was important.'

She stared at him in pity, or fear, he wasn't sure which. The security guard shared a joke with the man in the adjacent cubicle, and he could see that he had his hand on the door handle through the glass. He was ready to leave.

'I have to go right now,' he said. 'Please don't let me down.'

Chapter Thirty-One

Joe stared in disbelief at the storage room where the red lounge had stood in his dreams. Lit by a single fluorescent strip, the dusty alcove, normally locked in the daytime, reeked of polish, and was packed full of cleaning equipment. Brooms, mops and tubs of detergent were stacked in the exact place where the grand oak-panelled reception area should have been. His own twisted Narnia had never actually existed beyond this door. Knight had even hinted as much, no doubt enjoying the risk of revealing the truth just to humiliate him further.

No, Joseph. What happens in the red lounge doesn't happen at all.

He thought about the annexe, and of Fowler's terrified face. None of it had been real. Resting his head against the door frame, he finally accepted reality.

The controller bleeped in his pocket, and when he took it out, there was a message on the screen saying that Anteros monitoring would be resuming in ten minutes. Knight would shortly discover that he wasn't lying drugged in his bed. He would also know exactly what he was thinking, making any attempt to escape impossible. Every effort to deceive would be transparent, every surprise known, and every move anticipated. It was hopeless.

There was a noise further along the corridor, and he pulled the door of the cupboard towards him, squashing behind it. The shuffling figure that passed him was not the security guard that he expected, and he stepped out to greet him.

'Anteros,' said Sandbox, startled. 'What are you doing in there?' The surgical gown was hanging loosely off his skeletal frame, and he looked as though he barely had the strength to walk.

'I understand now, Sandbox,' he said, embracing him. 'I understand all of it.'

'I knew you would do it, sir. I knew if anyone could find it, you would.'

Despite his appalling condition, he managed to smile. His face was so gaunt that his teeth appeared too big for his jaw, and his scarred skin was pulled taut over his cheekbones. Joe knew that he had to help him, too. He glanced down at the controller in his hand. Sandbox interface monitoring was also currently inactive. They were both off the grid. There was still time if he acted quickly...

'We are going to escape together.'

'But how?'

'We have to distract the security team. I need you to operate their equipment for me.'

The Escape

'Anteros interface monitoring is reactivating,' said Brace, sitting at the screen in Knight's office. Knight only nodded, massaging his temples. It was still unclear what impact the unscheduled Shendi testing would have. He needed to be cautious. There was too much money at stake, and when he jumped, he had to be sure that it was in the right direction. Shendi and Williams were both political heavyweights, and he had worked far too hard to throw everything away now. 'We have a problem,' said Brace, leaning towards him across the desk.

'What kind of problem?'

'He's on the move.'

'That can't be,' replied Knight, leaping from his chair. 'I was in his room a few hours ago. He was out cold.'

'See for yourself,' said Brace.

Joe entered his pass into the lift control, looking over his shoulder for the third time. It seemed like the longest wait of his life until the door slid open, and an even longer one for it to close behind him once inside. He punched the button for the top deck of the ship, and the lift slid upwards towards the surface. Sandbox's pass had served him well again.

It was raining heavily when he jogged out on to the deck, the raindrops firing back off the slippery surface. His jeans and T-shirt were plastered to his skin by the time he reached the lifeboat station, where he waited to see if he had been followed.

The deck was deserted.

Oppressive, grey clouds smothered the ship, which wrestled in the waves to break free. The wind howled through the lifeboats overhead, making it impossible to hear if there was anyone in pursuit.

He activated the emergency lifeboat mechanism. It made little difference whether the point of activation was identified now. He would be off the ship by the time they reached him. The mechanical arms whined into life above his head, lowering the lifeboat to deck level, where it could be loaded. With one last look behind him, he slipped beneath the heavy, white tarpaulin covering the vessel, and waited to be lowered into the ocean.

'He's in the lifeboat,' said Brace, studying the screen.

'Get all available security staff onto the deck now,' shouted Knight to the guard waiting in the corner of the office. 'He must not leave this ship.'

'I understand,' said the guard, turning to leave the room.

'Where is he now, Mr Brace?'

'I can't see anything. He's beneath the cover of the lifeboat. Everything is white.'

'That's good. It will take a few minutes for the craft to launch,' said Knight, rubbing his chin thoughtfully. 'They'll reach him before he is lowered into the sea.'

Even as he was speaking, something bothered him. At first, he could not pinpoint his exact concern, but then the realisation dawned on him...

'Did you say that everything is white?'

'Yes, why?'

'Look out of the window, and tell me what you see,' said Knight, pursing his lips.

'What do you mean? It's difficult to see anything because of the rain.'

'What colour are the lifeboat covers, Mr Brace?'

Brace clambered from his chair, craning to look up at the decks above through the rectangular porthole.

'They're orange,' said Brace, looking confused. Knight didn't respond at first, smiling into space.

'Clever boy, Joseph. Very nearly,' he muttered to himself, before turning back to Brace. 'Call security back immediately. He isn't in that lifeboat at all. I want a thorough search of the compliance deck. You will find him sedated in a bed somewhere. Also, check all other monitored systems. Somebody else must be suggesting this to him.'

Chapter Thirty-Two

'This is an interesting situation,' said Knight, inviting Joe to sit. 'Ordinarily, I would say what a surprise it is to see you, but, as you know, it isn't.'

He was still groggy. Sandbox's attempts to sedate him had only been partially successful, and his arm was covered in a patchwork of purple and yellow bruises from the failed attempts. Sandbox had tried to move him to the kitchen area unconscious. They had been unable to discuss the hiding place in advance, so Joe would remain unaware of where he was concealed. Both sedated, they planned to stay hidden long enough for the ship to dock, but they were found behind a stack of vegetables in the pantry. He had no idea of what had happened to Sandbox.

It had been a while since he had visited Knight's office. The colourful print of a brain scan dominated the wall, but his attention was drawn to the second man sitting in the corner of the room. He recognised his white-bearded face from Marryfield House — one that he had found quite reassuring at the time. There was a familiar trolley of electrical equipment in front of him, and Knight smiled when he saw him looking at it.

'I'm sure you remember Mr Brace from your interview. He has been studiously tracing your steps since we regained contact. Under the circumstances, we didn't feel the need to keep this hidden from you any longer.'

Joe smiled, but didn't respond.

'Would you like a cup of tea?'

'No, thank you.'

'Oh, you're more of a coffee man,' Knight smiled. 'Americano, one sugar. You tried it in that little café in Oxford for the first time. What a lovely day that was,' he added, folding his arms. He luxuriated in the silence, obviously enjoying the moment. 'Learning about you has been like learning about life itself. It's the little things that make us happiest,

250

you know. And it's choice that really kills us.'

'Why am I here?'

'We have ourselves a situation, Joseph. Our plans have gone a little awry.'

'What exactly are your plans?'

'Straight to the point, and why not? I'm sure it must be baffling you.' Knight smiled, fishing the teabag from his cup. 'Please take the Anteros interface offline, Mr Brace.'

'I'm sorry?'

'You heard me correctly. And when it is done, would you leave us, please?' It clearly wasn't a question, and Brace hesitated, before punching at the controller in his hand. He looked reluctant to move. 'Are we offline, Mr Brace?'

'Yes,' Brace snapped, realising that it was his final cue to go.

Joe heard a faint beep from the controller, still in his jean's pocket, at the same moment. Brace bundled all of his equipment onto the trolley, and then rattled across the office with it. He glanced over his shoulder indignantly, before leaving. The trolley was clattered by the closing door as he backed out of the office. Knight winced.

'Firstly, I'd like to congratulate you on your excellent escape attempt, Joseph. It was very creative, but I'm afraid that the devil is in the detail with these matters. I know that better than anyone now,' he grinned. The sound of the departing trolley diminished, eventually leaving the room profoundly silent. 'You may think it's reckless that we're left alone, but I know you even better than you know yourself. Did you notice the pot of sharpened pencils right in front of you? I put them there especially. Just before coming into this room, you toyed with the notion of finding something sharp on my desk, and pushing it into my face. It was an amusing little sequence of thoughts — running through the ship to rescue the girl, with alarms ringing in your ears. Quite a superhero moment you were having, in fact. Only we both know you aren't capable of that. If it was Sandbox sitting there, I'd insist on a cage around him, of course, but not you.'

'You did that to him.'

'Oh, Joseph, even now you still see the world as black and white. Have you learnt nothing from any of this? I'm the bad guy, and you're

251

the good guy, correct? If only it were that simple! Sometimes the truth *is* black. Sometimes the truth is white, but nearly always it lies in the infinite shades of grey between the two. That is what all of this is really about,' smiled Knight, picking up his cup and saucer. 'We are actually trying to help Sandbox.'

'Help?' Joe laughed. 'You forget that I've seen him.'

'Granted, he does have some very worrying underlying issues, as I know you've discovered — running around the ship without his clothes on. He even found his way into this office at one point, rooting through our testing schedules, and helping himself to things that weren't his,' said Knight, his expression changing. 'But if you are referring to his physical injuries — those terrible scars on his face — they were inflicted many years ago, by a small child in the playground with a rock in his hand.'

Joe could barely meet his eyes, swallowing hard.

'That isn't true…'

'A nasty shock, I'm sure, but I think you'll agree that it proves my point,' he said, sipping his tea. 'It's not just Sandbox who needed help. You were broken. You just couldn't see it.'

It was impossible to reply. At some level, he had always known the truth, but had never been able to acknowledge the thought.

'Oh, cheer up, Joseph. We can't change the past, but we can change the future. You have been very fortunate to have someone like Mr Shendi fighting your corner all of your life. He brought this together especially for you. Sadly, his situation has changed, and I need to make sure that we stay on the same page.'

'What do you want?'

'It's not what I want,' said Knight, leaning back in his chair. 'You have become an expensive piece in a game of boardroom chess. Whether you turn out to be a pawn or a king entirely depends on you, but in order to win the game, you first have to understand the players.'

'What if I just want to leave the company?'

'That isn't an option for you. There is too much at stake, I'm afraid. Plus, you have some rather expensive hardware inside your skull. That's how all of this works, of course.'

'You actually operated on me?' he said, flabbergasted. Knight was unmoved by his reaction, sipping his tea.

'Relax, it was a very minor procedure, and easily reversed. We installed the conductor after you were drugged at the welcoming party. Marie was most accommodating to begin with, but she lost her appetite for the task in hand after a while.'

'She was scared.'

'Quite rightly so. This is a very precarious situation. Money does strange things to people, and there is a lot of money involved. You need to understand that.'

'That has nothing to do with me. I didn't give my consent for any of this.'

'Your consent?' Knight laughed. 'I'm afraid you've never had a choice. Shendi wouldn't have had this any other way. He has bankrolled the entire project to date. Did you ever wonder why you received the invitation to Marryfield House with an academic record like yours? I knew that you would only come with the girl. That's why I extended the invite to your friends. None of you would have made the cut any other way, I'm sorry to say,' he said, folding his arms behind his head. 'But we digress. Let's talk about how you fit into all of this and what happens next...'

Knight explained the path of good response, describing in detail about Arnold Shendi, and his relationship with his father. Much of it Joe had already worked out for himself, but the boardroom manoeuvring made sense of the gaps.

'So, Shendi wanted to help me?'

'Yes. We didn't fully understand his motives to begin with, but they have become much clearer in the light of recent revelations. He obviously saw the same... issues in you that he saw in himself, and wanted to intervene. He has been watching your progress very carefully. I suspect that it wasn't entirely selfless, though, as you have seen. Much of it was fuelled by remorse over your father's death, and he also saw the potential to save his own skin. What happens next, after recent developments, is less certain.'

'You said that there were other players in this game?'

'Indeed, there are. Your friend, Mr Williams, represents the interests of other members of the board who have an alternative agenda. Shendi is a rich and powerful man, and is still the CEO of the company, but they believe they can remove him with your help.'

'Why do they want to do that?'

'To grow, of course, Joseph. Don't forget your training. Growth drives everything that Williams and Schelldhardt do. You are not just a rich man's plaything, but the proof of concept for a much bigger initiative. Let's just say that there are artistic differences between them: Williams wants to exploit the true potential of the conductor for Schelldhardt's gain. Every worthwhile invention in history has been either monetised or weaponised, and this will be no exception, if he has his way. I view Shendi as more of a purist, fighting his own guilt-driven moral crusade. He has unfortunately become a roadblock. When we initially began work on the conductor, the intention was merely to correct spurious behaviour. Shendi was totally sold on the idea of helping people, starting with you. Williams saw much more potential in the product. Just like many great experiments of the past, he realised that the residue left in the test tube was more interesting than the product itself.'

'What do you mean by that?'

'By removing all erroneous thought patterns from the process, what you are left with is a perfect choice. This was how he sold it to the investor community at least. He called it the next logical step forward for humanity. It is a fact that the world is becoming more fragmented in its views than ever, and as a result, we are all drifting apart. When you think about it, might has always determined what is right, throughout human history. The most powerful nations have always dictated the global morality. Their empires rise and fall, along with the ideals that they promote, but they are always underwritten by military strength. As weapons become more unilaterally devastating, it is much more difficult to exercise that military strength. A new kind of dominance is required. Financial muscle has replaced missiles, and Schelldhardt wants to set a new global agenda that aligns with their business model. Williams preached to our investors that true human progression can only be driven from within the mind itself to solve the world's problems. Without consensus of thought, there will never be consensus of action, and we will remain trapped in an eternal struggle for power. In reality, he only cares about delaying Cloudburst, and removing as much uncertainty from the landscape as he can. Discord really is quite detrimental to company growth. However, he was horrified by your approach to business in the red lounge. If you could have seen his real face...'

'Why is that amusing?'

'I'm sorry. In his own way, Williams is equally ridiculous. He didn't consider for one second that your decisions would not align with his own principles. He is the consummate company man, and is so blinded by his belief mask that it was inconceivable to him that you would see things differently. While he loves the *idea* of your integrity and fully intends to exploit it, he also needs your actions to align with his own agenda. He wants you to do the right thing, but only if it's what he wants himself. He was furious watching your exploits in the red lounge.'

'But the red lounge wasn't real?'

'The red lounge was a conceptual location for our quality assurance process. He could see exactly what you intended, and knew that it was very real to you. In fact, you became unable to distinguish between the red lounge and reality. We had to physically drag you down from that window in the park. The path of good response is the ideal reaction to a given situation. We needed to know the exact point that you would compromise a particular principle. Precisely where you drew the boundaries between different ideals to see how closely you followed the expected reaction. We knew that the girl was your particular weakness. It was simply a case of finding what it took for you to deny her. Then we knew that we had succeeded, and the conductor had done its job.'

'You went too far.'

'We went to your limits, as we had to.'

They sat in silence for a moment as Joe reflected on what he had been told. Knight was watching him with his hands clasped together, his face a picture of arrogance, as it always was.

'So, what now?'

'Good question. What now indeed? We await Mr Shendi's next move, now that he has witnessed the latest script. It didn't put him in the best light.'

'He saw that?'

'Yes, and I'd imagine it made very uncomfortable viewing. He expected you to attend the forthcoming board meeting, but I'd imagine that is very much in jeopardy now.'

Shendi had been watching him the entire time. He had access to their systems. It explained why Knight had asked Brace to switch off the interface while they were talking. He didn't want Shendi to witness their conversation. It took Joe a moment to absorb the significance of the situation, but as Knight continued to waffle, he wondered if there could still be a second opportunity to escape...

As slowly as he could, Joe slid his hand into the pocket of his jeans, feeling for the buttons of the controller. Knight was unaware that he had it. He coughed, covering the bleep, as he switched the Anteros interface back online.

'So, where do you fit into all of this?' said Joe.

'Me? I'm just the project manager. I find the politics and squabbling tiresome, but it goes with the territory.'

'Then why don't you stop the project? Surely you can't just sit back and watch all of this fall apart.'

'Stop the project! Please tell me you're not as naive as you sound,' he laughed. 'Let me spell it out for you. Fifteen years ago, I was the head of a programme developing a drug to treat advanced forms of skin cancer. The slight inconvenience was that our patients continued to deteriorate in the trial. I thought that we would be allowed time to resolve our issues, but the programme was closed in its infancy because of budgetary constraints. The point I am trying to make is that if you are developing a drug to fight a disease, it is painfully obvious if you fail. There is no way to put a positive spin on dead people. It has been a long, hard climb to get myself back in a position like this, and I am enjoying the perks of my success.'

'But surely your results are equally transparent here?'

'Do you really think so? This is a dream project, Joseph, with an unlimited budget and an ambiguous goal. The only measure is a line on a graph plotting the value of a decision. How could our investors ever dispute the results?'

'Someone must be monitoring your work.'

Knight just laughed again. 'There is no sanctioning body here. Anyway, how do you think these people made their money in the first place? I lie to their faces and then sleep like a baby, because I know they are no better than me. Especially Shendi. The man's a murderer! He's finished. I suggest you look to Williams like I intend to. It's all about being on the winning side at this point, and we need you to jump the right way with us.'

'I see,' said Joe, standing. He slowly made his way to Knight's side of the desk, approaching the image of the brain scan on the wall.

'What are you doing?' asked Knight, backing away in his chair. Joe smiled when he saw his hand reaching for the telephone. He wasn't quite so confident about Joe's reaction, after all.

'I love this picture on your wall. What is it?'

'It's an image of my brain.'

'There's an awful lot of red. Do you have anger management issues?'

'Sit down now, please, Joseph.'

'There was something else I noticed about this picture while I was sitting there,' said Joe, adjusting his position in front of the frame. It had nothing to do with the image itself, but the frame that surrounded it. The glass cover was completely reflective, and he moved closer until he could see his face perfectly within it, like a mirror, imagining how Shendi would see his face on the screen. He only hoped he was still watching.

'We don't have all day,' said Knight. Joe ignored him, still standing in front of the picture.

'All my life I have felt as though somebody was watching over me. I always believed it to be my father, but now I know it was you. You were there in the street when I broke the car window. It was you watching when I received the offer to join this company. You have probably heard enough to know that this isn't all you hoped it would be. I know this must come as a great disappointment to you. I also know how you have suffered, and I understand why you wanted this. I have felt what it is to be you,' said Joe, staring into his own eyes in the reflection.

'What are you talking about, Joseph? Sit down.'

'I know that you cared for my father and had no part in his death. I also know what it is to love a woman you cannot have, and how you tried to stop me making the same mistakes as you did. If you truly want to help me now, like you promised my mother all those years ago, then this is your chance. You are still the CEO of this company, and, more importantly, the biggest shareholder. If there is one thing I know about

Schelldhardt, it is that they listen to money above everything else. I want to walk off this ship tomorrow and carry on with my life. I think this is what you need as much as I do.'

Joe turned away from the picture, to see the colour draining from Knight's face. He was holding the phone to his ear.

'Whatever you think you've done is irrelevant. Security will be coming,' Knight whined, as he sat back in his chair.

'I know,' said Joe, smiling at him. 'But will they be coming for me?'

Chapter Thirty-Three

Arnold Shendi was dwarfed by the voluminous pillow, his glasses reflecting the laptop glowing in the darkness. He sat motionless, still in shock at what he had seen. Carla was beside him in the bed, but neither of them spoke, and the only sound was the rain hitting the window.

He was trembling — still shocked by the unexpected final transmission. Everything he had planned and hoped for was now in ruin. Joseph looked more like Jane than his father, but there was something so familiar about his mannerisms that it was almost as if Philip was still alive. Seeing him eye to eye on the screen had finally brought home both the reality and enormity of what he had done.

'What are you going to do?' said Carla at last.

'I have no idea,' he said, shaking slightly. 'I still don't understand how any of this happened.'

'I might be able to help you with some of it.'

'You?' he said, turning towards her. She was sitting in the half-light watching him, her eyes pools of darkness in the shadows.

'You're not my only client, but you are the most trusting,' she said, moving closer to him. 'That's why I like you, Arnold.'

'What are you saying?'

'I'm saying that Peter Hayward is one of my oldest friends. He arranged our introduction so that I could watch over you for him. He wanted me to read your diaries and find out everything I could about your past.'

'You're working for Hayward...' he said in disbelief. Hayward hadn't contacted him since his last desperate blackmail attempts after Philip's death. The stories linking him to the accident were leaked to the press much later, at the time of the Schelldhardt takeover. He had always suspected that Hayward was behind the trouble, but he no longer understood his motive. Their financial past was buried now, and he believed there was no way he could know about the rest of what had happened, until the last script had been sent to Knight.

'This makes no sense. How did Hayward get the information for the last test?'

'He found an ally in Williams. Their ultimate aims were different, but they had a common interest in undermining you. Williams wanted to oust you from the company, and when I told Hayward about this project, he saw a way to help both of them. While you were sedated under their machines to verify the other scripts, Williams took the opportunity to question you alone. Hayward told him exactly what to ask you.'

'How could Hayward know?'

'Poor Arnold, you still don't understand even now, do you? That was no chance meeting with Hayward on the train all those years ago. He has been planning revenge for a very long time. It was never about money, or your business. This isn't the first time you have shared a woman with him...'

'Elena,' he said, with a shiver of realisation. Hayward was her married man.

For a moment, he couldn't breathe. He felt himself regressing to the awkward young man he had been in his twenties, unable to prevent Hayward from destroying his world yet again. If he had despised the man then, he despised him all the more now.

He slammed the laptop onto the floor in fury, and Carla scrambled out of the bed, pulling on a robe. She looked on, terrified, as he pounded the mattress with his fist, moaning in frustration.

'You should know that Hayward's people are outside if...'

'I trusted you!' he shouted.

'The truth must be told, Arnold.'

As he looked into her frightened eyes, he remembered the expression on Elena's face in the cottage, and he forced himself to breathe slowly. He would never allow that to happen again, for her sake. Instead, he began to cry. At first, he fought back the tears, but soon his shoulders heaved uncontrollably as he sobbed.

'I loved her.'

'In your own way, yes,' Carla said, pulling on a coat over her nightclothes. 'It was just the wrong way.'

'Everything is ruined.'

She hesitated by the door, with perhaps the only genuine expression of emotion he had ever seen from her. She looked sorry.

'My part in this is over. Hayward has his revenge, but you can still help Joseph, even if you can't save yourself.'

He was unable to speak, and gasped for air between the relentless spasms of misery. He sat there for several minutes, as the tears flowed down his cheeks.

'What can I do?' he said at last, sniffing.

'Call them now. You still control the company. Get Joe off that ship before Williams knows anything about it.'

He looked away towards the window, where the rain shook the glass, and his breathing began to calm. Strangely, at the time when everything was lost and there was no hope, he felt his strongest connection with the people that had passed through his life: Elena, his mother and father, his wife, and his friend Philip. The thought raised goose bumps on his skin, and he began to feel a sense of peace.

'Am I a good man?' he said at last, but the question wasn't intended for Carla this time, and she opened the door to leave. He didn't notice. His thoughts were much further afield, aboard a vast ship somewhere at sea, where the son of his best friend needed far more help than just the money he had promised him.

The Kiss
3rd December 2011

The canal path glistened ahead of them in the street light. Their footsteps were all that could be heard, crunching in the ice, as they covered the frozen ground in tandem. The sound echoed from the canopy of branches twisting above their heads, leading them further into the flickering orange shadows. It was freezing and late, but he didn't care. They had barely stopped laughing since they had left the party, linked arm in arm. Their steps were in unison, and her body was pressed against his. He wished that they could be fused together forever. It was a night that he simply didn't want to end.

They startled a sleeping moorhen as they passed. It slipped between the reeds into the darkness of the water, gliding across the surface until it disappeared under a fallen branch into the blackness. It was beginning to snow again. As he looked skyward, it seemed that everything was moving in slow motion. The snowflakes tumbled around them, swirling in idle funnels over the water. The reeds danced in accompaniment, swaying one way and then the next in lazy unison. They had slipped out of time altogether.

The Santa hat fell from his head, and he stooped to get it. Rachel laughed as he fumbled to retrieve it, spilling the open bottle of beer dangling from his coat pocket in the process. It fizzed angrily in the ice. When he stood again, he found himself toe to toe with her. She was wearing an identical hat, and he pulled it down over her eyes. She laughed again. As she repositioned it, he felt an uncontrollable impulse to do something he had always wanted to do, but had never dared. Giddy with happiness, he leant forward and kissed her.

Only it wasn't a kiss.

It was a meeting of mouths.

It was an invasion of privacy.

It was a mistake.

They froze. This was meant to be the awakening of his princess, but as her eyes met his, he saw everything in those fleeting seconds — first the confusion, and then the shock. Finally, worst of all, nothing.

Silence again, eye to eye, calculating. As they took stock of what had happened, he saw that protective, almost maternal reaction to any mistake he made, springing instinctively to life in her again, and she placed her arm on his shoulder. She wanted to reassure him that everything was okay — that this was just another one of his misjudgements that she had already forgiven, but none of that mattered to him. He tried to speak, but couldn't form a word. Rooted to the ground, he wanted to disappear altogether. She hesitated as she watched him struggle, but then turned away and carried on walking.

He tried to think of what he should do next, but nothing seemed appropriate. He was helpless. When she sensed that he still hadn't moved, she turned back, looping her arm inside his, and dragged him with her. It was as if nothing had happened, and that was the way she wanted it to remain. He stumbled beside her, overwhelmed with absolute emptiness. Not a word was spoken.

When he looked back on that day, he would always be conflicted: the happiest moments of his life were immediately followed by the saddest and most hopeless. She gave him the answer to every question he had ever wanted to ask in those few seconds of silence, but he didn't want to hear a single one of them.

Chapter Thirty-Four

There was no sign of Rachel.

The brightness was blinding as Joe stepped from the gangway onto the dock. The sun glared off the pristine sides of *Ananke*, as he dragged his bulging case along the jetty. Across the glittering water, he could see a walled city built into the hillside, crammed with white-walled buildings roofed with terracotta. He had no idea where he was, or where he was going.

He trundled along the tarmac, shielding his eyes, and not knowing which direction to take. His dark suit trapped the heat, and his shirt was already sticking to his back. The sun smarted his skin, and he stopped beside some fishing boats for shade. A ruddy-faced old man was emptying a net full of sardines into large baskets. They reeked in the heat. He toyed with the idea of asking him for help, but the man seemed too engrossed in his work.

'I see you dressed for the weather,' said a voice behind him. Rachel was sitting on a whitewashed wall beneath a prickly pear tree, sipping a carton of orange juice. She was wearing shorts and a T-shirt, with dark sunglasses propped on her head.

'You had the advantage of knowing where we were landing.'

'Don't you listen to *any* announcements?' she laughed, hopping down from the wall. He approached her, and she kissed him lightly on the cheek.

'I didn't think you were here,' he said.

'Five more minutes and I wouldn't have been.'

'I'm sorry, I had a bit of trouble getting away.'

'It would have been a fantastic prank.'

'Yes, I should have done it,' he smiled, wiping the sweat from his brow. 'I owe you a huge explanation.'

'Tell me later. It's too hot to think about it here.'

They wandered along the jetty towards the town, stopping to feel the breeze blowing across the horseshoe bay that bordered the harbour. There were people on the beach, no more than dots of colour in the wide expanse of white sand. It looked idyllic, but Joe was happy exactly where he was.

'Do you think our buggy will be coming soon?' she said.

'I suspect that was a one-way trip.'

'I feel part tourist and part bag lady with this luggage.'

'You're all bag lady,' he grinned.

They walked further, side by side, dragging their luggage behind them, until they reached a wooden Customs office at the end of the quay. Despite there being no one else for miles, the moustached officer tried his best to look bored when he checked their passports, silently handing them back as if they had dirtied his hands. He turned the volume up on his radio without a farewell. Joe still didn't know which country they had entered, and Rachel refused to tell him.

'Why does it matter?' she laughed.

'I like to try to speak the language. It's polite.'

'Which languages do you speak?'

'A little French.'

'Save your breath, then.'

The quay led to a promenade, where a handful of cafés were serving lunch. He could smell fish and garlic, wafting from the tables laid on the pavement. Two men shared a plate of seafood, breaking open the shells with their fingers.

'Are you hungry?' Rachel asked.

'Not really, but I could do with a drink.'

'I'll get them,' she smiled. 'You can take the cases.'

He dragged their bags around a square glass table, forming a wagon circle of luggage. An olive tree provided shade, and he positioned their chairs so they looked out over the harbour, where the sun blazed through the masts of the moored yachts. The lull of the conversations around him was broken only by the cry of a seagull, and the distant sound of a moped.

Rachel returned, carrying a bottle of chilled white wine and two glasses. When he tried to turn the label towards him, she pulled the bottle away, laughing.

'No spoilers!'

'You're right, it doesn't matter where we are. We're free,' he said.

'Yes, that's exactly how I feel — liberated.'

'Liberated and poor. I'll drink to that.'

They raised their glasses, glinting in the sunlight, and the wine tasted better than all the champagne he had drunk on board. Or probably hadn't.

A contented silence followed, and the world went about its business, as they gazed out over the waterfront. After a while, Joe turned towards Rachel. Her cheeks had reddened in the sun, but it only accentuated the deep blueness of her eyes. She noticed him watching, and smiled.

'So what is this secret reason that we had to escape?'

'What if I told you that, in order to leave, I had to promise never to discuss it? Would you trust me?'

She watched him, looking for any sign that he was joking — he was unflinching. He was desperate to tell her everything, but couldn't. Eventually, she smiled.

'I'd think you really didn't like photocopying.'

'I wasn't a natural,' he laughed.

'What if I told you that I was still undecided whether to leave the ship until a couple of hours ago? I was toying with the idea of calling you a doctor when I received a phone call myself.'

'From who?'

'He didn't tell me his name, but he said that he had made "attractive" arrangements for me to leave the ship. Like you, I am sworn to secrecy about the details, but he told me it came from the very top.' Joe only smiled. It was Shendi, of course. Rachel reached for his hand across the table, her touch still thrilling him. 'Is everything okay now?' she asked.

'I think so, but I don't know if I'll ever be sure.'

It was true, but whatever was to come, he was here now. Sitting back in his chair, the dappled sunshine played on his face, and he savoured the simple joy of being outside. It was possible that he was still lying in a bed somewhere, being monitored under their machines. How would he ever know for certain? He was beginning to recall conversations with an unknown voice in the darkness, which he now assumed to be Knight's. Some of those words stayed with him; he could never know the true nature of his world, but he was beginning to agree that it didn't matter. It was a world that he could not escape. There was just him and the decisions that he made. He must go about his life, with just an ancient half-written rule book that he barely believed in as a guide. Just like most people. There was no choice but to make choices.

He had no idea if Williams would persist with the programme. The path of good response was a seductive idea, and if taken to its logical conclusion, he could see the beauty of what it could bring. A world where all human thought was pure — free from prejudice and bias. Where mankind was able to move on towards a universal right, liberated from conflict and division, and following a single, perfect path. Ironically, it had been Williams's own distorted beliefs that had corrupted it, and Joe had little faith that this would not always be the case.

He was light-headed from drinking on an empty stomach, and his mind wandered to Shendi, and all the things that had happened in his life. Instead of seeing the differences between them, he now saw the similarities, and they bothered him. He knew what a man could be capable of. He knew what *he* had been capable of as a child. Perhaps romantic love could only ever be called as such if it was reciprocated. If not, it would always be something else altogether, sitting at some point between the innocence of longing and the darkness of obsession. It was only a question of degree, just as Knight had insisted about most things. He was not alone, he knew that much. From every adolescent crush, to the millions of lonely people loving another in faint hope, he was part of a huge family, but it was time for him to leave them all.

'Do you remember that Christmas when I kissed you? We never spoke about it,' he said.

'Do we have to now?'

As he looked at her at that moment, he saw the same ten-year-old girl who had tried to protect him all those years ago. The same woman who had tried to protect him ever since. In that instant, he knew with absolute certainty that he would always love her, but she would never feel the same way about him. A life without her would be no life at all; for so long, this had been central to his thinking, but shamefully he had never stopped to consider the reverse. A life *with* him would be no life at all for her. He had simply been too blinded by his own desperation to think of anything else, even her. Now he knew that his selfish pursuit, through school, through university and into the workplace, had to end.

After all, he was Anteros, god of requited love, avenger of unrequited love, and if he would not spare her, then who could?

'I just wanted to say that it was a mistake. I hope you didn't read anything into it. I've always meant to apologise.'

She watched him in silence from across the table, and he knew that she understood. His eyes were stinging and he had to turn away, but she gently turned his face back towards her, and smiled. The most beautiful smile he had ever seen.

'There's no need,' she said.

'To friends,' he said, raising his glass.

'Friends forever,' she replied, her glass meeting his.

The breeze from the sea had become stronger, lifting the tablecloths at their edges. Other diners were paying their bills, and the waitresses were packing the tables away. It was time for them to leave.

He savoured the last few moments sitting alone with her there. It felt as if he had burned his entire life to the ground, but he sensed that beneath it all there was still something left. Something unexpected. It was the faintest trace of a new sense of purpose. When he could bring himself to look at her again, Rachel was smiling. She turned the wine bottle towards him, finally revealing the label.

'Ah, as I always suspected,' he said. 'I may need some help to get home from here.'

'I'll try my best,' she said, squeezing his hand. 'As long as you aren't driving.'

Epilogue

Arnold Shendi's notoriety in Swanton was not as evident as he had suspected. He needn't have dirtied his brogues taking the back route into town for all the attention he received when he skulked into the market square. In fact, complete indifference greeted the smartly dressed gentleman hiding beneath the camel fedora hat. He hesitated beside the Christmas tree, listening to the enthusiastically off-key strains of the school choir.

Most of the refurbishments were already complete, but he wanted to witness the finishing touches for himself. He crossed the cobbled pavement, treacherously slippery from the recent rain, and pressed his fingers against the wire perimeter fence of the building site. A workman in a fluorescent jacket glanced up, before continuing to shovel sand into a rattling concrete mixer.

The department store already looked impressive, with the five turrets and white-faced clock restored to their previous glory, and an eye-catching sign blazing the name "Elliots" into the darkening sky. There were new features as well: beneath the clock face was a huge statue of his father, pen in hand, seated at his desk.

As Shendi stared at the lifeless bronze face, he was filled with both regret for the past and optimism for the future. Like Joseph, he couldn't change what had happened, but he could influence what happened next. The shop was his father's legacy, and he was determined to preserve it.

He heard movement at his side, and turned to see an old woman struggling with her hands full of shopping bags. She stopped, lowering the bags to the ground, and patted her chest to emphasise what an effort it was to carry them.

'I used to work here,' she said, as if he wouldn't believe her.

'Did you like it?'

'I did. He was a lovely man,' she said, nodding towards his father's statue. 'A real gentleman.'

Shendi swelled with pride. 'Do you like the other new statue?' he said, pointing to the roof of the building, where his grandfather stood, shaking a huge fist skywards.

'My eyes aren't very good, but it looks very nice from here,' she replied, looking in completely the wrong direction. Shendi felt a sudden warmth towards her, and wanted to do something to help.

'Do you need a lift home with all of those bags?'

'I'll be fine,' she said, hoisting her shopping from the ground again. She stood breathing deeply in preparation for her next few steps, but before she moved, she turned in his direction again. 'I'll tell you one thing, though. That place never made no money then, and it won't make no money this time neither.'

She appeared confused when he laughed.

'I'm sorry,' he smiled, not wishing to offend her. 'I'm sure you're right.'

He laboured up the hillside in the fading light, stopping occasionally to look back at the town, twinkling below. It was dark by the time he reached the very top, just as it had been over thirty years before. There, in the gloom, was the bench bearing the plaque, "The spirit of the meadow". The place where it had all begun.

He never did see the Live Aid concert. On that wonderful summer's day in 1985, the world united with a common aim, and it seemed that no child would ever starve again — a promise that everyone somehow forgot. Careers, families, financial survival. There always had been, and always would be, a million conflicting reasons why the right thing didn't happen. Randomly colliding politics and personalities, for ever nudging each other away from the correct path. That was all Shendi had ever wanted to change at Schelldhardt.

On the same humid night in July, he buried the woman he loved right there, in the ground owned by his family for generations. Hayward must have always suspected, but never knew quite enough, probably bamboozled by Elena's gloriously flighty nature as much as he was.

It was so much colder tonight. He sat on the bench — a private memorial he had later erected to mark her grave beneath — and took his phone from his pocket, looking up into the starlit sky as it rang.

'Hello. My name is Arnold Shendi. I have some new information regarding a crime committed over thirty years ago.'

When the call was over, he lowered himself onto his knees, pressing his forehead against the cold earth, and told her he was sorry. Even now, more than anything, he wanted to be with her. Joseph had seen it: the real yearning that he had kept hidden from himself was for absolution. His quest for self-justification had always been a deception, because no matter how much he had tried to rationalise, deny and disbelieve, his mask had never sat comfortably on his face.